SHOOT TO KILL

STEVE COLE

DOUBLEDAY

YOUNG BOND: SHOOT TO KILL
A DOUBLEDAY BOOK
HARDBACK: 978 0 857 53373 9
TRADE PAPERBACK: 978 0 85753374 6

Published in Great Britain by Doubleday,
an imprint of Random House Children's Publishers
A Random House Group Company

 Penguin
Random House
UK

This edition published 2014

1 3 5 7 9 10 8 6 4 2

Penguin Random House is committed to a sustainable future for our business,
our readers and our planet. This book is made from Forest Stewardship Council® certified paper.

MIX
Paper from
responsible sources
FSC® C016897

Set in Bembo Schoolbook 13pt/17pt

RANDOM HOUSE CHILDREN'S PUBLISHERS
61–63 Uxbridge Road, London W5 5SA

www.**randomhouse**.co.uk
www.**kids**at**randomhouse**.co.uk
www.**totallyrandombooks**.co.uk

Addresses for companies within The Random House Group Limited
can be found at: www.randomhouse.co.uk/offices.htm

THE RANDOM HOUSE GROUP Limited Reg. No. 954009

A CIP catalogue record for this book is available from the British Library.

Printed and bound by Clays Ltd, St Ives plc

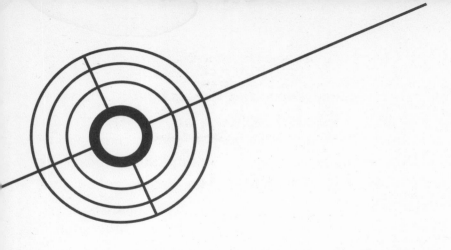

You Asked for It

Someone's messed up, now someone's gonna pay.

S   It stood to reason. That was why Mac Reagan was hunched down on the asphalt roof of the Timberfoot Packing Company on Fifth Street.

He wished he'd brought a drink along with the tools of his trade – or a coat, at least. It was lousy weather for May; a big storm was blowing in off the Pacific, and no one knew how hard it would hit. The bulked-up clouds looked set to fall on downtown Los Angeles and its maze of tenements and warehouses. Night was stepping up fast.

And with it, the kill.

Mac's nerves amplified the noise of the city: the dejected rattle of the Venice Line streetcars heading south along Hill Street; the roar of traffic and clatter of road repairs ripping up the peace outside the swanky Biltmore Hotel; striking workers in Pershing Square chanting amid bamboo and banana trees. The darkening sky lent strength to the neon hoardings as they hummed awake.

Mac looked down at the machine he cradled in his hands. He wiped a grimy thumb over the hard plastic magazine; it was loaded. His finger curled around the trigger without him even thinking.

Mac shuddered, remembering other rooftops, other jobs.

He was ready to start shooting.

'So. You made it.'

Mac jumped at the voice behind him. It was the Kid – and right behind him, some older guy Mac didn't recognize, big and broad. They had crept up onto the roof behind him without a sound. But the Kid didn't normally show in person . . .

He knows. Mac stiffened. *He's here because he knows what I did.*

'You seem nervous, Mac,' the Kid went on quietly.

'No, sir.' The words crumbled from Mac's dry mouth. *Stay cool*, he told himself. 'Sure, I made it. Like always.' He took his finger off the trigger of his Parvo movie camera and double-checked the 135-millimetre lens was in place. 'Here I am, all set to shoot the action up close.'

The Kid nodded, but the big guy just stared, eyes like stones wedged into his craggy face, hands holding something behind his back.

'You're the hitman,' Mac murmured, 'right?'

The guy's face barely twitched. 'I'm a whole lot of things.'

Mac pulled a Lucky Strike from a crumpled pack in his pocket, lit up and looked across to the three-storey block opposite. A young woman was at the wide-open window, staring out. He peered at her through the Parvo's fold-out eyepiece: her face was flawless ivory, and looked just as hard.

2

Long blonde hair hung down to the fake pearls around her neck.

Mac checked the focus. 'Is she the target?'

'No. The target is the man who's coming to see her.' The Kid tutted quietly. 'I know her kind. Another starry-eyed sob story who dreamed she could cut it in movies. I hate girls like that. Don't you hate girls like that, Mac?'

Mac grunted, shivering as the wind began to build. He'd filmed plenty of girls like her when he'd worked for the movie studios, even dated a couple . . . Funny how fast the last one had walked when the studio closed and the money dried up.

The memories crackled like the smoke in his lungs. No job, no cash, Mac had washed up with some bad-news characters from the LA underworld. They'd put his talents with a camera to new uses. Plenty of rich people were being naughty in the City of Angels, and if Mac caught them on film, well . . . They would hand the mob a whole lot of cash to get hold of that footage. Mac took two per cent of the payout, and the film was filed under 'Forgotten' . . . at least until the next time. It was easy work.

Only when a new gang from the Midwest breezed in and took charge did things turn sour; only this last year, when the Kid showed up.

From that point, the stuff Mac was paid to shoot had moved beyond simple blackmail. Stuff that could turn the hardest guts. How many times had Mac had been forced to relive the violence frame by frame at the print lab downtown, making movie prints from the negatives . . .

Through the viewfinder, Mac watched the girl turn to greet a man who'd just walked up behind her – and felt a rush of nausea. The cigarette fell from his slack lips.

'That's Louie.' He turned to the Kid and the big guy, who was holding a rifle now, a Browning automatic. 'Louie Weiss. He's a good buddy of mine—'

'I know,' said the Kid, smiling now. 'Such a good buddy, you let him work your shift in the print lab two days ago. The bad news is, the day he does, a whole lot of film reels go missing.'

'I don't know a thing about—'

'Shut up.' The Kid pointed to the camera. 'Get shooting.'

'But—'

'*Now.*'

Mac's heart smacked a sick beat against his ribs as his fingers curled around the leather handle of the Parvo. The magazine rattled and whirled as he turned the crank handle, feeding out the film at sixteen frames per second. Louie stood square in the camera's eyepiece, pin-sharp at the window beside his new girl; he'd told Mac he was seeing someone new, sounded real up about it . . .

'All right, I asked Louie to cover me.' Mac's grip on the camera was tight and sweaty. 'I was sick, see? I was sick real bad.' He was willing Louie to look up and see the Browning's barrel zeroing in, to get the hell away. 'Please . . .'

Louie *did* look up, right at Mac with his camera. The frown on his face froze as a gunshot cracked out. A hole blew open in Louie's lined forehead and he jerked backwards, lost from sight. The girl opened her mouth to shriek – as a second blast from the Browning tore through flesh and fake pearls. The girl was blown sideways, clutching her gory neck as she fell.

Numb as he gazed on through the eyepiece, Mac realized at last that he was still filming. He slammed the Parvo down on the rooftop, turned angrily towards the Kid.

Straight into the swing of a baseball bat.

With a sickening smack, Mac's nose broke open. The world spun. In a blink Mac was laid out on the roof, choking on his own blood. The big guy loomed over him, the rifle in one hand, Mac's camera clamped in the other. Then the Kid stepped forward.

'There was a whole pile of movies due to be printed and sent out that day.' The Kid was still wielding the bat; something else he must've snuck up here. 'Guess what, Mac? The wrong film cans went to the wrong addresses. And one extra-sensitive reel of film is nowhere to be found.'

'Sensitive?' His head splitting, Mac struggled to his feet, dabbed uselessly at his pouring nose. 'You mean, the one that was s'posed to go to the private mailbox?'

'What happened to it?'

'I . . . I don't know.'

'Did you and Louie think you could blackmail us?'

'No! I swear it. Look, Louie doesn't read so well – maybe he . . .' Still grappling with the sickening rush of events, Mac turned back to the gloomy apartment across the street and the grisly figures sprawled inside. 'I guess Louie messed up.'

'I guess you both did.' The big guy was holding the movie camera in both hands now, ready to start rolling. 'I think Mac is telling us the truth, Kid. Which means that little movie could've been sent out to any one of God knows how many addresses . . .'

'Let me go,' Mac pleaded. 'Come on, I won't squeal.'

'You won't squeal, huh, Mac?' The Kid raised his baseball bat, motioned to the big guy, and the camera's whirr rose again into the night. 'But maybe you'll scream . . .?'

Mac turned but had nowhere to run. He heard the hard whistle of the bat as it swung into his ribs, felt the snapping deep inside. He couldn't breathe – so he couldn't even shout out as a further blow pulverized his left kneecap. Reeling, Mac teetered on the roof edge. For a second he caught sight of the Kid's smiling face, and the neon gleam on the Parvo's lens.

Then he was flying from the third storey. Straight down.

When Mac opened his eyes he'd hit the sidewalk. Paralysed, broken in a spreading puddle of blood, he heard sirens wail like the city's last salute.

Should've brought a coat, Mac thought again as the first specks of rain bounced off his eyeballs. *Should've brought the drink. Such lousy goddamn weather for May.*

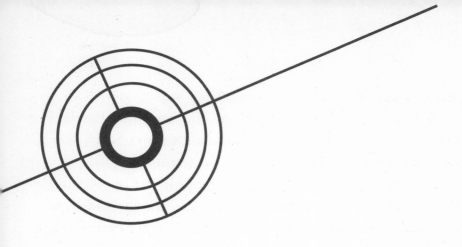

1

Do as You're Told

'Are you James Bond?' The girl in the trouser suit ran across the old courtyard, flushed and smiling. 'The new starter, just arrived from Paddington?'

'Afraid so.' Taken aback, James looked into her dark, striking eyes. She was about his age, and almost as tall, with bobbed black hair. 'Yes, I'm Bond. And you?'

'My name's Beatrice Judge. I've been waiting for you to arrive. Welcome to Dartington Hall.'

With a grunt of anger, she punched him in the stomach.

Caught unprepared, James staggered back. A ragtag of girls and boys descended and grabbed his arms. They slammed him up against an ivy-clad wall and stood in a tight semi-circle, blocking his way.

James didn't struggle, more bemused than concerned. Dartington Hall was supposed to be a progressive school – a no-uniforms, co-ed, anything-goes kind of place. But he supposed it would have its traditions, just like anywhere else, and maybe ragging the new boy was one of them.

The girl pushed through the little scrum, her handsome face hardened, trying to intimidate, James supposed.

'Listen, Beatrice.' He smiled briefly and coldly. 'The train to Totnes took hours, the cab from the station broke down on the way, and now I'm supposed to have an entrance interview in the school office. Whatever joke you're playing—'

He broke off as she pulled a knife from her jacket pocket and waved it in his face – once a table knife, it had been filed to a murderous point. 'Does this look like a joke, Bond?'

James nodded past her. 'Perhaps you should try asking that teacher?'

The lie was hardly inspired, but it was enough to distract. As his attackers glanced behind, James knocked Beatrice's arm aside and shoved her backwards. She fell against her friends, while James turned to the wall and grabbed thick handfuls of ivy. He scaled the brickwork in seconds; the old, gnarled branches gave excellent footholds and the vines would've held his weight twice over.

Or three times, it seemed, as Beatrice Judge and two of the burlier boys from her rabble were climbing after him.

What was their problem with him being here?

It couldn't be greater than my own, he reflected.

It was the third week of June, and James was due to start the next school year at Fettes College in Edinburgh in September. Fettes sounded a lot like Eton, his last boarding school, and held for him neither fear nor a good deal of interest. In James's book, school was somewhere you did well enough to get by until you were old enough to get the hell out. Now he'd been slung out of Eton, forced to start over. And after all he had been through, James had hoped to have the whole summer to relax before making for Scotland. But Aunt Charmian, his guardian, had business in Mexico and had arranged for him to board here at Dartington in the meantime. She knew someone high up at the school, and hinted heavily that a deal had been struck of which James would approve.

Much as he loved Aunt Charmian, right now he wasn't holding his breath.

James hauled himself onto the roof and crossed the rain-slicked slates, working out his next move. On the far side of the building the wall was clear of ivy, but a drainpipe offered a quick route to the ground.

He waited, taking in the wider view. The school comprised a large quadrangle set amid acres of rolling Devon country-side. The entrance tower was smart and whitewashed, but many of the buildings on the grounds were as mouldering and creeper-clad as any stately home. Clearly 'progressive' here did not mean modern.

A scuffling at the rooftop edge alerted James to the arrival of Beatrice and her backup. He straightened, turned to face them. 'Care to tell me what this is about?'

'Care about this, you Eton reject.' Flanked by her friends, Beatrice advanced steadily. 'I'm not going to let you just waltz in here and take my place.'

'Your place?' James held his ground. 'I'm only here for a fortnight. I don't know what you're talking about.'

'Of course you don't.'

James didn't resist as the two boys gripped his arms, biding his time. They were strong, but he could sense their unease.

'I was down as one of the four,' Beatrice went on. 'I don't board here like the rest of them, see? Different class — I live local, in Totnes. That's what marked me out. Then we're told you're coming here and suddenly I'm dropped. The chance of a lifetime and it goes to you. Like the good stuff *always* goes to people like you.'

At that, James almost laughed out loud.

'So . . . I want you to tell the school you won't go.'

James raised an eyebrow, felt it brush against the curl of dark hair that hung down as always over his forehead. 'Go where?'

Beatrice nodded to the boys, who started dragging James back to the edge of the roof. 'If you refuse to take the trip, I'll be back in.'

'In your nice padded cell, you mean?' James shook his head. 'I think you should know, I don't like being told what to do.'

'Be reasonable, Bond.' Beatrice followed him to the precipice. 'A fall from here won't kill you, but it'll break plenty. You won't be fit to travel, and I'll be back on the trip.'

'What trip, for heaven's sake?' The crowd had dispersed; James was staring down at bare flagstones twenty feet below. 'You think the school will let you do anything after you've tried to cripple me?'

'It's your word against ours.' The knife was back in Beatrice's hand. 'We'll say you were showing off up here to impress us, and you slipped.'

'Well, it *is* slippery up here . . .' Suddenly James jerked his right shoulder forward, pivoting on his left foot as he tore his arms free. The rapid turn caused both boys to lose their foot-ing. James booted one up the backside and sent him sprawling into the other; the pair collapsed perilously close to the roof edge. Beatrice swiped at him with the knife but James dodged and kicked her feet from under her. As she went down, he turned and sprinted for the other side of the roof. He had no idea what Beatrice was talking about, but he wasn't about to humour her a moment longer.

'How's this for showing off?' James swung himself over the ledge, caught hold of the drainpipe and shinned down it, dropping the last six feet. He landed lightly with a crunch of gravel, then ran for the cover of the nearest building, more engaged than afraid: challenge, fight and flight, and he had barely been in this stupid school five minutes! A mystery too, just to add some unexpected spice. What was this trip Beatrice was so concerned with?

Curious, James peered out from behind the wall. No sign of Beatrice and friends still on the roof. Were they waiting for him to sidle back for his entrance interview at the office?

Perhaps a tour of the grounds first, James decided.

As he walked the length of the building, he saw that it con-tained a number of classrooms. The pupils inside were dressed casually, and James thought briefly of the miserable starched collars and top hat he'd had to wear at Eton. He paused at the end of the block, peering in; there were at least four teachers working with different groups, though James's attention was fixed mainly on the girls. To see so many here was a strange and arresting sight after years of boys-only boarding. A blonde was looking at him now with some interest. She was cool, with haughty good looks and long hair, a little older than him – maybe sixteen.

She gave him a smile. James didn't return it. For all he knew, every girl in the school was out to break his limbs on the flimsiest of excuses.

'There he is!' Beatrice and the boys were back.

James gave a cheery wave he hoped was infuriating and ran across a yard towards a cluster of old buildings. The largest bragged a portico, an open-fronted gallery supported by columns on the outer wall.

'Shall we see if you have more luck pushing me from this roof?' he called recklessly. As he gripped the nearest column and shinned up onto the portico, he wondered if the blonde girl in the classroom was still watching him.

'Who cares?' he muttered.

Without a backward glance, James scrambled across onto the flat roof of the neighbouring building; it smelled of horses. He ran lightly across the old planking – then gasped as rotten wood splintered underfoot and he plunged through it into darkness.

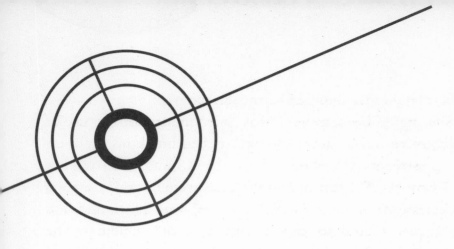

2

Chance of a Lifetime

James knew that a drop from this height would make Beatrice's dreams come true; he flailed about for anything that could break his fall. His fingers chanced on a roof beam. There was a painful lurch through his upper body as he gripped on hard, dangling high above the hay-strewn ground.

Ridiculously, given his predicament, and not for the first time, James found himself wondering why he felt this endless compulsion to take risks. There had to be some other, kinder way to bring colour to life . . .

'Good God!' The cry carried over the restless shift of startled horses. 'Where'd you drop in from?'

James, clinging still to the rafters, peered into the gloom. A figure was sitting outside one of the stalls, looking up from a large book he'd been reading by torchlight.

'Sorry to interrupt,' said James. 'I don't suppose you could move some of those haybales to soften my landing?'

The figure dropped the book indignantly. 'Do I look as though I'm built for hard labour?'

James realized the boy had not been sitting after all, but was standing. He was a dwarf, his body wide and compact, his hair a dark, unruly thatch.

James raised his eyebrows in surprise. 'You're . . .'

'Hugo Grande – by name, if not by nature.' With sudden, obliging urgency Hugo set about constructing a haystack below James. 'Wherever did you blow in from? Wouldn't be Eton by any chance, would it?'

James let go of the beam, landed safely in the hay and rolled over onto the dirty ground. 'Seems like everyone here has me at a disadvantage.'

'So *you're* the fabled James Bond.' Eyes bright with interest below his thick brows, Hugo held out a hand to help James up. 'Parents sent you here as a last resort, eh?'

'Aunt, actually.'

'Ah. Orphan, then?' Hugo spoke bluntly with no trace of awkwardness. 'That's rough, James. Well, I'm sure your aunt's decent.'

'She is. As a rule.' James rubbed the tender leg he'd put through the roof. 'I'm glad you were here to help, but shouldn't you be in lessons?'

'Bunking off,' Hugo said cheerfully. 'Cosy here in the stables. And no one cares if you skip classes.'

'There's no punishment?'

'For demonstrating one's independence? Naturally not! No rules and regs at Dartington Hall. To the progressive mind they're Tyrannous and Restrictive.' Hugo lowered his voice confidentially. 'Although, James, I'm afraid there's one girl who may be keen to give you a whipping.'

'Beatrice Judge? She's already tried.' James flexed his leg and glanced towards the door.

'Steer clear of that one – brutish little psycho. Well, I say "little" . . .'

'What's it all about, Hugo?'

Hugo looked surprised. 'Why, you're taking her place on the Great Expedition, of course. Your aunt's thick with Gillian, they sorted it out between them.' He held out his arms expansively. 'You, my dear James, are going on the adventure of a—'

'*Shhh.*' James had heard a noise at the stable doors. 'Someone's coming.'

'Could be Beatrice! Hide!' Hugo immediately hurled himself at the haystack and tried to burrow inside. But James held his ground and curled his fingers into fists as the door creaked loudly open and—

'James Bond?' The words had an American drawl. A petite woman with strong features stepped into the stable. She wore cream trousers with wide legs pleated at the top, a multi-coloured blouse, and several bead necklaces. Her long red hair was only partly tamed by the floral headscarf she wore. 'I'm Gillian de Vries, the Director of Education here at Dartington Hall.'

James relaxed and inclined his head. 'How do you do, Miss . . . ?'

'Just Gillian, please.' She looked past him to where two legs were protruding from the hay. 'Have you lost something . . . er, Hugo?'

'Only my dignity!' Hugo burst out and dusted himself down. 'Sorry, Gillian – we thought you were Beatrice Judge.'

'Ah! No. I just intercepted her and her friends; a witness with a weak stomach came and told me what was happening. I've sent them to the Head for . . . further discussion. James, you must give your side of the story, of course.' Gillian suddenly seemed to notice his dishevelled state. 'You're hurt?'

'Not by Beatrice.' James glanced ruefully at the hole in the roof.

'I see.' Gillian nodded. 'There were once sheets of corrugated iron protecting that old wood. But some of the children used them for rafting on the River Dart and never put them back.' She smiled brightly. 'Nothing broken?'

James shook his head.

'Shame! That would be a lesson learned, wouldn't it?' Her laugh was an earthy chuckle. 'Not to worry.'

'The poor fellow *does* worry,' Hugo piped up, 'as to why a local girl would attack him the moment he—'

'All right, I'll take things from here, Hugo. Off you go.'

Hugo looked aghast. 'To lessons?'

'It's a big ask, I know. But perhaps you could give it a try.' As Hugo left, shaking his head, Gillian turned to James. 'So. Your entrance interview.' She sat down, neatly and cross-legged, in the straw, and gestured to a rickety old chair in the corner. 'Save ourselves a walk, shall we?'

James couldn't hide his surprise. 'If you like . . . Gillian,' he said, pulling up the chair and sitting down.

'I suppose that after the rigidity of Eton, the way we do things at Dartington Hall will be something of a culture-shock for you. If you feel uncomfortable, I hope you'll say so.'

Gillian's appraising gaze searched out James's face; he saw her eyes linger on the scar on his cheek. 'Why were you expelled, James?'

For a moment, James longed to let it all out; to talk of the plots, their course and filthy currents, that had dragged him down close to death . . . of the maid at Eton who'd proved to be so much more . . . Then he took a hold of himself. He wasn't about to rake over those embers any time soon.

'I can't really talk about it. Forbidden.' James tapped his nose. 'Official Secrets Act.'

'Ah! I see.' Gillian smiled. Clearly, she thought James was joking. 'Well, I hope in time that we'll pry out some details of your time at Eton. It's your background that offers such an intriguing contrast to our other three subjects . . .'

'Subjects?' James frowned. 'Is this something to do with the trip Beatrice mentioned?'

'Poor Bea got wind of the trip prematurely – she was only ever an outside possibility.' A shadow passed over Gillian's face. 'I'm afraid there's no convincing her that you didn't conspire from afar to steal her place.'

'Her place where? What *is* this trip?'

'Aha! Well, we're all rather excited here, James.' Gillian had brightened again. 'The Head has sanctioned a rather special school expedition. Five of us will be visiting Dr Tobias Leaver, the great American philanthropist and experimental educationalist. Perhaps you've heard of him?'

'No.'

'I was a student of his in San Francisco, long before I came to England. He's been a huge inspiration to me over the years . . .' She smiled self-consciously. 'In any case, Dr Leaver currently runs a progressive academy in Los Angeles under the patronage of Mr Anton Kostler. Through his partnership with Kostler's Allworld company, he's already founded academies with a reputation for excellence in Kenya and Australia, and he's planning others . . .'

Kostler, Allworld . . . The names chimed in James's head. 'You mean, Anton Kostler the Hollywood producer?'

'That's right. Executive-in-Chief of Allworld Studios.' Gillian knelt up in the straw, her smile growing wider. 'A fully fledged "movie mogul", and a passionate supporter of progressive education to boot. He's looking to build more academies across the world, and Dr Leaver hopes to persuade him to invest in Dartington Hall – subject to some research into our current methods and pupils.'

'Why doesn't Dr Leaver just come here to see us?' James wondered.

'Because Mr Kostler has the final say in all his enterprises, and feels he can't possibly spare the time to make a trip to England.' Gillian rolled her eyes and smiled. 'Happily, he allows us lesser mortals to make a pilgrimage to him. And more happily still, the timing is propitious for the ride of a lifetime . . .'

James was starting to see where she was headed. 'This trip Beatrice mentioned . . . ?'

'We leave in under a fortnight – hitching a transatlantic lift to Los Angeles aboard Mr Kostler's personal zeppelin, as it passes through on studio business.' Gillian smiled and extended her hand. 'That is, if you're willing to travel with us . . . ?'

Travel to America, in an *airship*? James felt the familiar

flicker of excitement as his lips stretched into the first genuine smile he'd given in an age. *Fair enough, Aunt Charmian*, he thought. *You were right after all. Thank you.*

'I'm willing, Gillian.' James rose from his chair and shook her hand. 'Willing the next two weeks away already.'

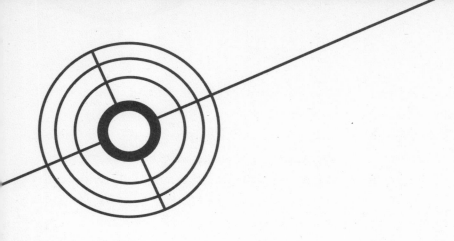

3

Sunlight and Darkness

Later, looking back, James would remember Dartington Hall as chiefly a sunlit place. His brief spell there – barely twelve days in all – felt such an escape from the strict expectations of Eton.

There was no sense of oppressive authority; the teachers were as soft as wool and endlessly encouraging. Pupils were viewed as individuals pursuing their own ends within the community, largely governing themselves. James was astounded to find there was no fagging, no rushing to obey when an older boy bellowed for service. The only running James had done was round the grounds before lessons each morning for his own enjoyment.

Like seniors of both sexes, he was billeted in a large, modern, quadrangular building called Foxhole, all smart red brick and gleaming grey roof-tiles. His study-bedroom was small, with cheap, modern furniture; there was no sense of history trying to smother you with its musty blanket of tradition here. And while it felt strange to have girls around, as both neighbours and classmates, the novelty was enjoyable – particularly since Beatrice Judge now gave him a very wide berth. After their run-in and her subsequent talk with the Head, she'd been acting the model pupil. *Well, good luck to her*, thought James – just so long as she left him alone.

That went for everyone else too. Because his stay was so short, James saw no need to make any new relationships. He'd stayed cordial with classmates, and found Hugo agreeable company, but had no real desire to make new friends. Friendship meant trust, and trust could be betrayed. It was a lesson James had already learned the hard way.

Never again.

For James, Dartington Hall was perhaps the closest he'd ever come to freedom. He'd been entered for Eton at birth by his father; how differently his life might have gone if he'd been sent here! But Eton was all about tradition and old values. Stability had been what his parents wanted for their son, and James felt sure they would never have endorsed a school that encouraged dissent and questioning.

Whatever, his days at Dartington remained golden in James's mind.

Almost up until their very end.

On the afternoon before the Great Expedition began, James lay on his stomach alone in the fresh-cut grass watching the other pupils about their business. He liked to take the details all around him and compile a profile of the living moment: a game of roller-hockey in play on the roof of the gymnasium . . . some boys nearby, scuffling in a feebly plotted fight . . . a group of girls by the pond, laughing and gossiping around a gramophone, enjoying the sunshine.

'Now' was the only time that truly mattered, James reflected. The past was a cold and bloody place; why linger there? History only mattered in as much as it shaped you as a person: the person who must face up to whatever fate – and a well-meaning aunt – was going to throw at you . . .

'So – ready to go, new boy?'

The low female voice brought him sharply from his thoughts. James rolled over to find a barefoot girl looking down at him; the girl he'd noticed in the classroom on his first day. He'd seen her around a lot since. Her blonde hair was centre-parted, with deep waves, and pulled back into clusters of smaller curls at the base of her neck. A simple, custard-yellow dress accentuated her slender form, the hem brushing around her calves. There were smears of black around the hips where she'd obviously wiped dirt from her still-grubby hands.

'Ready to go?' James crossed his arms behind his head and gazed up at her. 'I've been ready to go since I got here.'

'Well.' A half-smile pulled at her lips. 'Just thought I'd make the effort to introduce myself before we fly off into the blue tomorrow. I'm Boudicca. Boudicca Pryce.'

'Boudicca? I thought it was Boadicea?'

She sighed, looking weary. 'If we're talking about the first-century warrior queen of the Iceni, take it from me – Boadicea is a medieval misprint of her real name, which happens to be Boudicca. My parents are language scholars, you see.'

'Right.' James nodded, thought back to dull hours at Eton

spent wrestling with Roman histories. 'Doesn't the name mean "Victorious"?'

'It means my parents smile smugly every time they're told they spelled it wrong.' Boudicca shrugged. 'I let my friends call me Boody; it's easier and annoys the hell out of my father.' She held out a black-smeared hand. 'And you, so rumour has it, are . . .'

'James. James Bond.' He took her hand and shook it, noting the smuts and broken fingernails. 'I'm guessing you didn't get those studying languages.'

'I prefer workshops to libraries.' She sat down beside him. 'How have you found Dartington Hall?'

James shrugged. 'I've hardly been here long enough to notice.'

'Oh?' She looked at him, and he saw the blue eyes held flecks of hazel. 'I've seen you about, new boy. You stay quiet. Keep in the background. But you're always watching. It's as if . . . you're expecting trouble.'

Old habits die hard, thought James, with a pang of unease at her scrutiny. 'Perhaps if I'd watched more closely, I'd have noticed you spying.'

'I wasn't.' Red prickled on her cheeks as she looked away. 'I just use my eyes.'

James nodded and pointed to her oil-stained palms. 'And your hands?'

'I'm interested in machines,' she explained, rubbing at an especially black smudge. 'So much power and precision. I like to know how they work. Zeppelins, for example . . .' She grinned. 'Do you remember the *Graf Zeppelin* landing at Hanworth in '32 for the twenty-four-hour round-Britain flight?'

James smiled. 'I went to see it arrive.'

'Me too!' Boudicca laughed. 'I longed to be on board, but at forty pounds a ticket, my killjoy parents wouldn't allow it.'

'Well, now your chance has come!' James shook his head, wonderingly. 'Imagine, we'll clear the Atlantic in just two and a half days.'

'Top air-speed of eighty miles per hour.' Boudicca smiled. 'Of course, if my mother drove us in her Sunbeam, we'd probably make it in twenty-four hours straight!'

'What's she got?'

'Six-cylinder, four-seater coupé. In racing red.'

'Nice.' James knew the type. 'I've acquired a Bentley Mark IV. It's with a friend right now. But it goes like a dream.'

Boudicca snorted. 'You're too young to drive!'

'Perhaps I have a maturity beyond my years.'

'Perhaps.' She looked at him thoughtfully. 'Mother won't let me out on the road until my seventeenth, next year. Still, she thinks I'll pass that wretched driving test without too much fuss.' She closed her eyes and tutted. 'When you're clever at passing tests, parents come to expect it.'

'Do they?'

The words came out harder than James had meant, and Boudicca noticed. 'That sounded vain, didn't it? Sorry. False modesty is more becoming.'

'Perhaps. But honesty's more refreshing.' James saw that her eyes had lost a little of their glacial tint. 'Is that why you were chosen for our trip – all those tests you've passed? Or because if the engines break down we can let you loose with a spanner?'

'I suppose it's unusual for a girl to be interested in

engineering,' she considered. 'It was the ethos here at Dartington that encouraged me along that path. Plus – just to add to that refreshing honesty – academically I'm in the top two per cent here. So's Hugo – only I have to work like hell at it, and he doesn't.' She smiled fondly. 'Dr Leaver is interested in the effects of his dwarfism on his education. Hugo says his parents only sent him here so he can join a better class of circus when he leaves.'

'Sounds like Hugo,' James agreed, 'putting himself down before others try.'

Boudicca looked at him. 'And so to you. Why are you on board, new boy – background more than brains?'

'Gillian says that Dr Leaver wants to measure my Eton education against your unconventional schooling. Though my aunt knows the old boy, so I don't know how many strings she's pulled or how hard.' He stretched out on the grass. 'Still, there it is, and I'm not going to turn down a trip like this for the likes of Beatrice Judge and her foot-stamping.'

'You had a close call. She's dangerous.'

'I've known worse.'

'Well, anyway, you're not the only one coming along because of who he knows.' Boudicca smiled wryly. 'Daniel Sloman represents a "typical" Dartington Hall pupil. But by "wild coincidence", his uncle is Stuart Sloman – soon to be one of Anton Kostler's screenwriters at Allworld Studios.'

'Well, fancy that,' said James. 'What's Danny-boy like?'

'He's all right. A bit full of himself. Wants to be an actor. Or rather, he wants to be a star.'

'Is he any good?'

'Yes,' she said simply. 'Dan's put on lots of shows and

founded a film club here. Leading-man looks too.'

James smiled wanly. 'I hate him already.'

'You should love him, new boy,' Boudicca teased. 'See, Kostler sent the zeppelin to transport movie bigwigs from all over Europe for some grand event he's throwing. He wants his new screenwriter in Hollywood as soon as possible, and since there's just about space on board, we're allowed to tag along.'

James was impressed. 'So our fellow travellers are all in the movie business? Our trip is sounding more glamorous by the moment. What's Stuart Sloman written?'

'Oh, nothing I've heard of. Stage plays and low-budget film stuff. He's been writing for years, working in Dan's father's chain of cinemas to pay the rent. This is a dream break for him.'

'And for us, Boudicca!' James declared.

'Mmm.' She paused, studying her palms again. 'The girls all talk about you, you know. Boys too. There you stand: tall, dark, tantalizingly aloof, with a mysterious past . . . I was starting to wonder if you weren't simply pretty-but-dull, someone to avoid on this trip wherever possible.'

'So that's why you came over – to see?' James searched out those cool blue eyes. 'And the verdict?'

'You can call me Boody, new boy.' Abruptly, she rose and brushed loose grass from her dress with brief, precise gestures. 'Now, I must finish packing.'

'I suppose I should start.' James had been reminded by Gillian that all suitcases would be collected at six tonight to be weighed and loaded aboard the zeppelin – hand luggage only was permitted on boarding tomorrow.

He got to his feet. Boody looked at him. 'When you're through, you should come to Dan's film club tonight.'

'Film club?'

'It's held down in the basement beneath the common room. When his dad's cinemas made the switch to sound movies, Dan inherited a silent projector and a lot of old silent shorts to play on it. And tonight . . .' Boody's smile held secrets. 'Dan's invited Hugo and me to a special screening after hours. I'm sure he won't mind you joining us, since we're all to travel together. I mean, I don't know what Dan's got hold of, but it's sure to be fun.'

It was a friendly offer, James reflected.

Friendship meant trust. Trust could be betrayed.

'Thanks,' he told Boody. 'But I think I'll skip it.'

Then James turned and went back to his room without another word.

He packed his bags, which were duly collected for couriering to the air base at Cardington, then ate heartily of pie, cold meats and salad in the noisy dining room.

He then listened to the BBC on the wireless set in his room. The crackle and whoops of interference were like a sound-track to his nerves at the thought of taking off for America by airship. He pictured the zeppelin, moored in a vast hangar, being readied for the off tomorrow morning. Taking them away.

Around ten-thirty, guilt pushed him to write a letter to Perry. He'd not been in touch since his old friend had lent him fifty pounds to help him flee the country. James felt he owed him at least some kind of update before he fled England again . . . to share a little of what he'd been through.

He struggled with it for a while, then, like the many similar notes he'd started, it went straight in the bin.

A hefty banging on the door made him start.

'James?' It sounded like Hugo. 'James, are you still up?'

James checked his watch: it was now after eleven. Puzzled, he opened the door to find Hugo red-faced and breathless. 'What is it – can't sleep for excitement?'

'Boody sent me to fetch you. Oh my God, James! You've got to come with me, see what we've seen. We need you, James. You've got to—'

'Slow down,' James protested. 'What's happened?'

'Come on!' Hugo was hurrying away along the landing. 'You have to see this for yourself.'

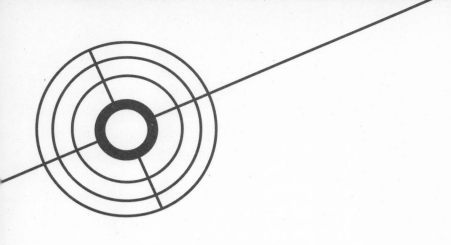

4

Silver Screen Scarlet

'D an had a treat in store for we elite few tonight,' Hugo began as he and James hurried across the quad towards the wing opposite containing the common room. 'You know the Alhambra Picture House at Totnes?'

'No,' said James.

'Flagship of Dan's father's chain of cinemas,' Hugo explained. 'A projectionist there has contacts in the world of film collecting; now and then he gets hold of really juicy clips! All the strong bits the film censors don't want you to see, cut from the movie prints, spliced together for your private viewing pleasure . . .'

'If you're prepared to pay through the nose or know the right people,' James concluded.

'Right.'

James pushed through the white double doors into the hallway of the block. The place seemed deserted, silent save for a grandfather clock clunking out the seconds. Hugo lowered his voice as they made for the staircase leading down to the common room. 'In the past Dan's got hold of the full harem scenes in *Son of the Sheik* and several fine views of Mae West. But tonight—'

'Wait.' James stopped Hugo at the top of the stairs. A tall, slim boy was lurking on the steps outside the door to the common room. He looked pale and preoccupied.

'James Bond,' said Hugo, 'this is Daniel Sloman.'

James hadn't seen Daniel up-close before. The boy had neat features, with a strong jaw and light brown hair styled immaculately, as if he'd bailed from a movie set somewhere.

'Boody says we can trust you,' Daniel said abruptly. 'Can we?'

'I've seen James in a crisis, Dan,' Hugo broke in. 'Cool and clear-headed, and a talent for trouble. He's all right.'

James raised an eyebrow, mildly touched by Hugo's commendation and thoroughly intrigued.

'Very well.' Daniel cast a fairly evil eye over James. 'Come in. See the show.'

The common room was a large rectangular space painted deep blue, its ragbag furniture shabby but comfortable. Boody didn't look up as James walked in; she was standing, hugging herself, facing the wall. There was a projector on a table at the back of the room, pointed at a bed sheet pinned to the wall – more a dirty white screen than silver.

'Those poor people,' Boody said quietly. 'So much violence . . .'

Hugo looked down at his feet. 'It *could* be special effects.

32

Trick shots and dummies. You know, filmed just to test them out.'

Daniel shook his head. 'No way were those scenes staged.'

'Well, if they're scenes removed by the censor, they're bound to be pretty strong,' James reminded them.

'*If*,' Daniel agreed. 'Take a look.' He set the projector rattling into life.

James watched as a countdown of numbers flickered across the makeshift screen until a bald, portly man in a suit appeared, filmed wonkily from some way off. A clearer picture followed as the same man was seen playing with small children in a garden. Then he was adjusting his tie and going into a large white building. There was no soundtrack; this was a silent movie.

'I'm certain that's Alexander Roberts, the film producer.' Daniel sighed heavily. 'Saw him at one of Father's gala openings – owns Associated British Features.'

'He's British?' James noted the wide pavements and palms in the background of the scene. 'Looks like he's abroad some-where. Is this newsreel footage?'

Boody shook her head, turning her back to the images. 'It's too amateurish for that.'

The images flickered on. Alexander Roberts was suddenly in an office, his shirt in tatters, held in his chair by two burly men. Roberts looked into the camera, sweating, terrified as a third figure advanced on him with a knife. The man stopped to glance back at the camera, white smile cutting through dark birthmarks over his cheek and neck. He held up the blade as if making sure the audience got a good look.

Hugo shuddered. 'I wish I'd never seen this. James shouldn't have to.'

'We need his opinion,' Boody insisted. 'If it really *is* all faked, we needn't worry.'

'Why would it be? Roberts isn't an actor, he's one of the biggest film producers in the country.' Daniel glanced at James. 'But Hugo's right. This is really not for the faint of heart.'

James stared on, his muscles tensed. Roberts was writhing in the grip of the two men, babbling in silence, face desperate. The man with the birthmark edged the blade closer to Roberts' forearm. The camera zoomed in on the knife as it pressed against the flesh and then bit. Blood welled, and with a jerk the camera jumped up to catch Roberts' terrified face – eyes wild, mouth wide and foaming in a frantic, disbelieving scream.

With the clunk of a big lever, Dan fast-forwarded the film; the torture continued at twice the actual speed, grotesquely comic and somehow still more unsettling. James looked away. He noticed Hugo, ashen-faced, wiping his eyes.

The next scene showed an angry, bearded man in what looked like an underground car park; his wrists were tied behind his back with rope. Hoods in suits and fedoras stood in a circle around him, pushing him from one to the other. The bearded man tried to kick one of them, and received a vicious blow to the kidneys in return. The focus blurred as he staggered to his knees, only to be hauled up and struck again, this time in the stomach. There was a thick puddle of oil on the floor and the bearded man fell in it; his face turned black as he tried to roll clear. But now the hoods had started kicking and stamping on their victim, all over his body. The man couldn't hold up his hands to protect himself, helpless as the beating went on.

Abruptly the projector snapped off into silence and the screen went dark as Dan flicked off the bulb. 'There's two more like that, then someone's strung up. With . . .'

'With a sack over his head,' Boody said softly.

'Could've been a dummy,' Hugo insisted.

'Or it might not have been.' Daniel cautiously ran the film back onto the original reel as if afraid it would bite. 'I don't remember reading that anything terrible had happened to Alexander Roberts. I suppose it can't be him. Even so, *someone* . . .'

He trailed off, staring into space. James could see how affected they all were. He was shaken too; he'd seen violence and death up close, for real, but it was no prettier on screen.

'Well,' James said heavily. 'If you want my opinion, I'd say what I saw was real.'

Boody winced at his judgement. 'But why? Why take the risk of recording crimes like this and putting them all on a single reel.'

'Two possible reasons,' said James quietly. At once, all attention in the room was riveted on him. 'Either it's a demonstration of strength with which to intimidate an enemy, or . . . someone just likes to watch.' He turned to Daniel. 'What's someone in Totnes doing with this reel?'

'This came from one of the under-projectionists. Idiot called Crispin. Hobnobs with film collectors—'

'Hugo told me.'

'Well, last weekend I was watching a film in the Box –

sorry, the projectionist's suite – and I overheard friend Crispin on the telephone in the next room. He was taking delivery of a "special film" and swearing on his life he'd keep it secret and safe.' Daniel put the film back in its canister and held it up. 'Well, it sounded like the film would be an absolute belter . . . and the man's an ass and I know all his hiding spots. So I pinched his blessed film can when I dropped in on the Alhambra on Wednesday.' He looked mournful. 'Reckoned it would give us a rich send-off.'

'When were you planning to give the reel back?' James wondered.

'When we get back. Only three weeks. Let him stew, I thought.'

'We should give it to the police,' Boody argued. 'James, you said you can drive. If we get hold of a car, you could take it to the police station in Totnes.'

James raised his eyebrows. 'So *this* is why you sent for me?'

'No way, Boody.' Daniel jumped in. 'I *stole* that film, remember? From my own father's cinema! Found it taped inside a drawer in the cold room, where the prints are stored. It's kept locked at all times, so it'll come out that I copied Father's keys. There'll be stink and scandal, Father will slaughter me, and I'll most likely be thrown out of school!'

Boody's eyes narrowed. 'You can't just pretend we never saw that film!'

'The point is,' Hugo broke in, 'the motorbus is coming at six in the morning to take us to the station. If James does take the reel to the police – they'll want us all in for questioning or a statement or something. Or, what if they tell us not to leave the country? That zeppelin's not likely to wait around with so many bigwigs on board, is it?'

'Leave the film in the manager's office at the Alhambra with an anonymous note telling him to watch it,' said James. 'That way no one will know it ever left the cinema. The manager will alert the authorities—'

'And it's like we were never involved!' Hugo reached up and slapped James on the back. 'Bravo, James. Wish I'd thought of that. Danny has keys to the place, but since it's the middle of the night and the buses aren't running . . .'

'Like Boody told us, James can drive,' said Daniel. 'That's why he's here.'

'It's so nice to feel wanted,' James muttered. Boody looked down at her feet.

'Whose car can we get hold of?' said Hugo. 'We need the keys . . .'

'I can borrow one of the teachers' from the school drive,' said James. 'It'll be easy enough to get started and it's only a few miles into town. I'll drop Daniel outside the Alhambra, he'll sort out the reel and we'll head straight back.'

'Seems you were right, Hugo.' Daniel looked grudgingly impressed. 'Cool in a crisis.'

Hugo nodded. 'How I wish I could accompany you, boys. But three's so much more conspicuous than two . . .'

'What if the manager chooses *not* to alert the authorities?' said Boody. 'In case it brings bad publicity?'

'Nothing's guaranteed,' James agreed. 'But with the trip to consider, it makes the most sense.'

'You're actually enjoying this.' Boody was staring at him. 'Aren't you?'

James looked away. He wasn't sure where enjoyment came into it, but it did feel as if a buried part of him were rising back to life.

'I'm beginning to see why Eton wanted shot of you, James.' Daniel stared at the film can like it was poison. 'But their loss is our gain. Thanks for mucking in.'

'What if you're caught trespassing at the cinema?' Boody wasn't giving up. 'Isn't it safer to just leave the reel outside the police station, anonymously?'

'What if someone else finds it before the flatfoots?' James pointed out.

'Yes, well.' Boody looked upset. 'Just don't expect me to wish you luck. I don't believe in luck.'

'I reckon there are times when luck's all you have.' James smiled into her hostile gaze. 'Shame there's no telling if it'll be good or bad.'

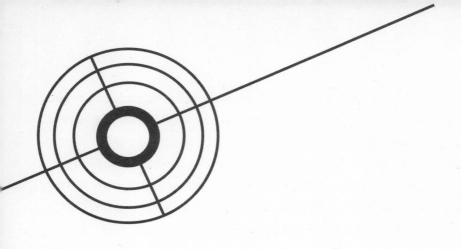

5
Killer Ending

Having told Daniel to find an open-top car parked on the school's Upper Drive, James ran to his study-bedroom and retrieved his penknife from his top drawer. He tested the sharpness of the blade with his thumb and, satisfied, he snapped it shut and dropped it in his trouser pocket.

At Eton, as a matter of course, he'd sewn razor blades and helpful tools into his uniform, insurance against whatever scrapes he might fall into. Here at Dartington, he'd not bothered.

In a matter of days, you've grown soft, he told himself. *Or you were trying to, at least.*

How quickly he'd just hurled himself on a chance of adventure! The drip, drip, drip of the commonplace had numbed his spine and he'd barely even noticed. Now he felt real purpose in his thoughts and movements.

James ran back out into the warm night, sprinting past the

Headmaster's neat, white modernist house, where lamps still burned at the windows. There was no one about save for Daniel, loitering beside a Hillman Minx in two-tone black and green.

'Sunroof's open on this one,' Dan hissed at James as he jogged up.

'This is the groundsman's car – his pride and joy.' James assessed the saloon: a ten-horsepower model, three-speed gearbox, top speed above fifty miles per hour. 'It ought to do. Not too showy. Good spot, Daniel.'

'You can call me Dan, Jim.'

'Thanks, Dan. But please don't call me Jim.' With a swift glance around, James stepped onto a wheel arch, climbed up onto the long bonnet, scrambled through the open sunroof and swung himself into the driver's seat. By the time Dan had climbed in beside him with the film can, James had torn the wires from the back of the ignition switch under the dash and was using his knife blade to remove their insulation covering.

'Is that so the wires will make a good connection?' Dan whispered.

James's answer was to touch the wires together and press the starter button. The Hillman shuddered into noisy life, and straight away, James was pulling her away, a little jerkily, down the drive.

Dan attempted a smile. 'Picked up that little skill from the movies, did you?'

'I suppose.' James flicked on the headlights but chose to keep his passenger in the dark about past adventures. Dan seemed nervous enough already.

James turned right out of the school grounds, heading

towards Totnes. The roads beyond the school perimeter were dark and silent. James found the Hillman a fair drive, but the suspension was stiff and the handling sluggish. He slowed down on the busier main road closer to town; firstly to keep their profile low, secondly because Dan delivered his directions in a last-moment gabble.

He held his breath as they drove past a police station.

Within minutes they had crossed over the railway line. A stolid Norman castle stood sentry on a hill up to their right, dark against the stars. James missed a turning when Dan piped up too late, which left them rumbling through the quaint centre of the town, down the steep hill of Fore Street, with its Tudor houses and covered streets, towards the River Dart.

'Thar she blows,' Dan announced at last as James took a left into a wide commercial street. 'The Alhambra. Dad owns thirty cinemas, but this is the largest. Converted from an old Temperance Hall. Uncle Stuart used to work here as Duty Manager.'

James parked in a quiet road round the corner and he and Dan got out. An ornate clock tower gave the time as three minutes past twelve. The Alhambra loomed high over the rooftops, large red capitals picking out its name in a floodlit challenge to the night.

Dan was looking shaky. 'I don't suppose you'd come in with me, would you? Spot of immoral support?'

James considered. 'All right. I guess it's best to know where my accomplice is at all times.' *Plus I can make sure you don't lose your bottle and dump the reel in a dustbin the moment you're out of sight.* 'Is there a side entrance?' When Dan nodded, he went

41

on: 'Lead the way, then. And try to act natural. You are an actor, after all.'

Dan grunted. 'Whereas you seem to be the real deal.'

Shying away from the streetlamps, James and Dan walked briskly along the road. James tried to calm his nerves with thoughts of more mundane trips to the pictures. He remembered usherettes in green taffeta under glittering chandeliers . . . Saturday afternoons crammed into the stifling, crowded dark of matinees . . . Sitting with his mother in the lustrous warmth of a cinema café, toast-crumbs and butter around his lips, staring out through plate glass at the skyline of some half-remembered city . . .

As the side door of the Alhambra came into sight, James focused hard on the present again. Dan pulled a clatter of keys from his trouser pocket, marched up to the door, gripped the handle, ready to unlock it . . .

But the door swung quietly open.

Dan stopped dead, flummoxed. James quickly propelled him inside and yanked the door shut after them. They stood in the dark fug of a back room, the only sound their shallow breaths.

'The cleaning ladies aren't here till seven,' Dan murmured. 'What idiots would leave the side exit unlocked?'

'They didn't.' The gloom was thick but James could feel the splintered wood around the lock. 'The door's been forced from the outside.'

Dan swallowed so hard it was audible. 'Robbers, after the takings?'

They both looked at the film canister in Dan's hands.

'Perhaps it was just some tough who wanted to save his

sixpence admission on the evening showing,' James suggested, with little conviction. He could feel his nerves tightening. 'Come on. Let's get this over with. Carefully.'

Dan crossed to an internal door. It turned out to be a store cupboard, from which he removed two usherettes' torches – James made a quick study of his: a metal tube five inches long with a bulbous tip, from Ever Ready. A good motto, he decided. As they set off through the back corridors, the torch played a smoky, atmospheric glow over the papered walls and crimson, deep-pile carpets.

Dan's torchlight soon caught a sign that said AUDITORIUM atop a green arrow, pointing up ahead, to where light pooled beneath a set of black double doors. James reached the doors first, ears straining for sounds of movement on the other side. Slowly, he edged them open.

It was light in here, and a smell of smoke, orange peel and disinfectant filled his nostrils as he stepped into an indoor recreation of some colossal Spanish courtyard. Huge plaster pillars studded each wall of the cavernous auditorium, trailing tangles of ivy. They stretched up to a ceiling of dark Mediterranean azure, freckled with starlight from hidden reflectors. To James's left was a broad, deep stage that showcased the huge rectangular screen. To his right was an ocean of plush velvet seats, waves of peacock blue trimmed with gold; you could house a thousand here, easily. At the rear of the cavernous hall, flanked by pastoral scenes picked out in embroidered satin, James could see the glint of the projectionist's window – that square glazed eye through which dreams would shine onto the screen in brilliant black and white. A smaller observation window squinted slit-like beside it.

'Why are all the lights on?' James tucked his torch into his pocket. 'Thieves wouldn't advertise their presence.'

Dan crouched suddenly beside the front row. James joined him with a quizzical look.

'Stage lighting's controlled from the Box,' Dan explained. 'Perhaps some of the projectionists are still here? Maybe it's Crispin . . .' He looked despairing. 'This is bloody madness, James. Let's just dump the reel here for the cleaners to find. They'll hand it in—'

A loud squeak and a widening crack of light signalled a door opening at the rear of the auditorium.

Dan ducked even lower, but James held absolutely still. The new arrival would see them at once if they tried to get out of the auditorium the same way they'd come. If they were caught by one of the staff, they risked waving goodbye to their zeppelin trip. But if they were caught by whoever had broken in for reasons unknown . . . that could wind up a lot more final.

Catching Dan's eye, James nodded to the far side of the auditorium. On hands and knees he began to crawl parallel to the length of the front row, grateful for the deep pile muffling his movements. He glanced back: Dan was right behind him, keeping low. Heart pounding, he turned right into the nearest gangway in the seating, and held motionless.

Was the new arrival on his way out – or aware that two boys were there, and methodically combing the stalls for them?

Then came a low sigh of hinges; it sounded to James as though the whole building had been holding its breath and was only now exhaling. James peered back through the plush and saw the same door by which they'd entered swinging shut – and heard the sound of multiple footsteps clicking on the lino, fading into the hushed thumping of his heart.

'If we'd arrived two minutes later we'd have walked right into them.' James wiped his sweaty palms on the carpet. 'Whoever they were.'

Dan looked petrified. 'You think they broke in? You think they came for this reel . . . that they're the people who phoned Crispin and told him to keep it secret?'

'Could be,' James said. 'In which case I don't suppose they're delighted to be leaving empty-handed.' Keeping low to the seats in case anyone else was about, he made for the door at the rear of the big hall. 'Is the manager's office this way?'

'Yes.' Dan followed warily. 'There's a telephone there. We can put through an anonymous call to the police . . .'

James pushed through the door into a softly lit lounge. During opening hours it would be filled with crowds impatient for the next showing, trapped until the current audience cleared out. It felt unnatural to find the room completely empty.

Except for the body.

A groan of horror, almost a death rattle, came from Dan behind him. But the man flat-out on the floor had already stopped breathing. The face looked pale and plastic, dark eyes wide, betraying the agony of his last moments. Gory hands were clutched against the crimson cut in his stomach, useless to stem the blood flooding the white folds of his shirt, drenching the crimson carpet darker still.

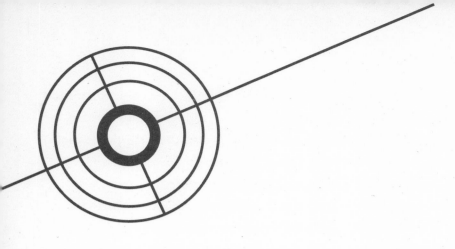

6

Rectified

James swallowed back bile. It was the wound that held him transfixed. He'd seen so much blood, stood close to death so many times. But gazing now at the tent of flesh and fluid left behind when life had fled, he felt suddenly helpless and small.

A talent for trouble – was that what Hugo had said? For a weird moment James felt almost as if it were he who'd pushed the knife into this man; and his own chest felt cold with the incision.

Dan retched behind him. 'Crispin. The projectionist. They killed him.'

While Dan stated the obvious, James tried to marshal his thoughts towards a plan of action. Then the low creak of the double doors in the auditorium carried through the absolute quiet.

The men who were just here . . . they must be coming back.

James felt the old familiar shutters inside slide down,

separating thought from feeling. Helplessness was shrugged off as the will to act took over. Skirting Crispin's corpse, he dragged Dan with him to another door; they slipped quietly through to the wide corridor beyond.

'This leads to the foyer?' James whispered.

Dan nodded distractedly. 'I don't have the keys for the front exit. We're totally sunk. We need the police!'

'If we call the police now, those men might hear us.' James put both hands on Dan's shoulders, making eye contact, willing the boy to focus. 'Hide here behind the door. I'll draw them off. As soon as they're out of sight, get the hell out, find a telephone box, call the police and wait for me back at the car. And don't let a damn thing happen to that film reel!'

Dan held the canister to his chest and sank to his haunches behind the door. Assuming the men were in the auditorium, James now had to lead them through here so Dan could get out safely. He gripped the door handle. It was smeared with blood; Crispin must have staggered some way before he'd finally collapsed.

Grimly, James inched open the door and then slammed it shut again. The hollow boom was like a starting pistol, and James sprinted away down the corridor. Even as he pushed through the next set of double doors, he heard the creak of those behind him. He glanced back to see if Dan was still hidden.

A big, dark-suited man in a fedora, a handkerchief tied around his nose and mouth, was charging towards him.

James turned and ran like hell, heart pounding like that of a racehorse closing the last thirty yards to the finish post. But where would his flight end? He had no real idea of the

Alhambra's layout, and just one dead end would mean exactly that for him.

He knew what danger did to the human system, how the body could work it to his advantage. His fear was exciting the sympathetic nerves. His adrenal glands, two small triangles just above his kidneys, were gushing adrenaline into his blood – speeding his pulse, making him sweat – and rallying sugar from his liver to fuel his body's demands for energy, sharpening every sense and reflex. James knew he had to direct and channel that vitality – or die trying.

As he pelted into the foyer, half-formed plans came in rapid snatches – and were rejected almost as fast. He passed a display of waxworks in jungle gear, promoting some new film. Hide in the foliage? *Not enough of it. Move on.* He turned to another door marked NO PUBLIC ACCESS. Thank God, it wasn't locked; James pushed through, even as the door to the foyer squealed open behind him.

The blast of a gunshot burst in his ears. A surge of adrenaline pushed James faster along the tiled, narrow corridor. Had that been a warning shot, or had his pursuer aimed to kill?

The turn in the corridor was sharp right. Not daring to slow down, James practically shoulder-charged the wall. He gasped in pain as he ricocheted off on his new course and almost overbalanced. He gritted his teeth, panting hard, blackness prickling at his temples.

Keep going, he told himself. *For God's sake, don't stop running.*

The wild sprint swept him along the next stretch of corridor. More double doors ahead. Locked? He didn't slow, launched himself into a reckless jump-kick. Twin booms came like cannon fire as the heavy doors exploded open and bounced off the walls; the impact jarred through his left foot and up his leg, and he landed badly, tumbling to the concrete floor.

Another gunshot roared out, its echoes battering at the bare walls. James risked a glance behind. The man in the fedora was racing towards him, gun raised; cold blue eyes stared out between hat-brim and handkerchief.

James scrambled to his feet and took the nearest door to his right. It gave onto a stone staircase. Ignoring the pain in his leg he took the steps three at a time to a bare white landing splashed again with blood. Crispin had been here too. The grisly trail spoiled another flight of steps leading upwards – to the Box, perhaps? Would there be another way out from there, or would James find himself trapped?

Four doors here on the landing offered a slim chance of salvation.

Hearing the rush of footsteps in the corridor downstairs, James chose the second door. The dark, box-room space beyond burned with an ultraviolet glow. James saw a glass bulb blazing within a heavy, cage-like cabinet on the wall and recognized it from Eton science lessons: a mercury-arc rectifier, converting high-voltage alternating current into direct current to feed the building's hunger for power. *This is the switch room,* he thought quickly; in the fierce, eerie light, James could see neat rows of fuse boxes and a large, two-tiered bank of chunky box-like batteries for secondary and emergency lighting.

Can I use anything here? He shook his head, starting to despair. *There must be something!* He still had the torch, but that was no advantage – if he knocked out the main electrics, the back-up lighting would kick in . . .

Inspiration hit, just as the door opened and light knifed into the room. His pursuer strode in, revolver raised. James grabbed the man's arm and forced him up against the wall, then twisted his gun-hand towards the rectifier as the man fired. The shot shattered the glass envelope in the cage.

James darted outside into the now-dimmed lighting and slammed the door behind him. Gripping the handle he clung on hard. The man on the other side yanked at the door, almost tugged it open . . .

Then the man started coughing – thick, lung-clawing barks. James felt a grim satisfaction – the broken rectifier had released toxic mercury vapour into the confined space. But would that be enough to slow the gunman down? Was he shamming even now, waiting for James to drop his guard and release the handle . . . ?

The coughing went on. James finally let go of the handle and fled back down the stairs and out into the gloomy corridor, bolting back the way he'd come. Through the foyer, down the corridor and into the lounge, past Crispin's gory body, through the fake exotica of the auditorium . . .

Finally, he was back out in the street, haring into the night cool and darkness. It was so welcome he could almost have sobbed.

He kept running all the way to the stolen Hillman. Dan burst out of the car as he approached, wringing his hands. 'James! Thank God, when I heard that gunshot I was sure you were dead. I found a police box—'

'D'you still have the reel?' James panted.

'Yes.' Dan pointed inside the car. 'I told the flatfoots a man was dead at the cinema; that the killer was still there – only I'm not sure they believed me . . .'

The distant *ring-a-ting* of police alarm-bells clamoured on the rising breeze.

'They believed you.' James bundled Dan back inside the Hillman and dived in himself as the ringing swelled and a black Wolseley raced past the end of the street. 'Let's get out of here.'

As James touched the wires together behind the ignition, his hands were shaking. Dan must've noticed. 'What happened in there?'

'I shut him in a cupboard and ran for my life,' James replied, hitting the starter. Some sluggish chugging, and the engine fired. 'With luck, the police will get him and unravel the whole bloody affair without our evidence.' He pulled away jerkily, cursing his trembling legs, willing them back under control.

'If only I'd never found that stinking reel.' Dan looked close to tears. 'Crispin is dead because I took it!'

'No. Crispin is dead because *he* took it – and because he bought into whatever the film-makers were doing.' James forced himself to concentrate on the road. 'Let's hope the coppers will sort everything while we're away. In three weeks' time we'll be back from Los Angeles. You can return to the Alhambra in daylight.'

'And get shot of this film for ever,' Dan concluded. 'Meantime, for God's sake let's tell Hugo and Boody as little of this as possible. Boody especially – after this she may crack and tell Gillian, or the Head, or worse.'

'Agreed.' James nodded. 'We'll say we couldn't get inside. The police were there ahead of us, investigating a break-in.'

They spoke no more the whole way back to Dartington Hall.

In a matter of hours, James reflected, they would be driven to the airfield at Cardington, escape real life on their glamorous transatlantic transport – while in this grey corner of England a murder inquiry would be launched and, no doubt, a family would be torn apart by grief. He glanced at the reel in the back, important enough to kill for. What if it had been collected as planned – what would have happened next?

James thought all around the incident, wanting to feel regret or anger or *something*. In the end, he found himself feeling sorriest for the cleaning ladies, who would have to scrub and mop at the whole dirty mess in the morning.

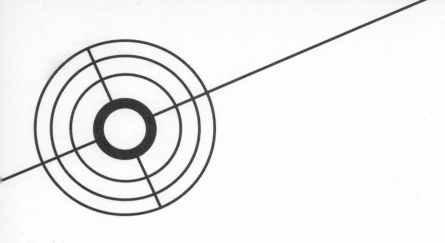

7

A Quiet Night

It was after one a.m. by the time James parked the Hillman back on the school drive. While he stayed to tidy the wires he'd left exposed to bypass the ignition, Daniel left with the film can, hurrying past the sports fields back to Foxhole.

As James locked the car and climbed back out through the sunroof, a sense of weariness and futility almost overcame him. Wherever he went, wherever he poked his nose, violence and danger lurked, twisting the sweet tang of adventure into something sour. He clutched at the thought of Kostler's zeppelin now, a grand escape route, straight up into the air.

Back at Foxhole, James walked upstairs and turned right into his corridor – to find Boody at the far end, still in her yellow summer dress, waiting outside his door.

Self-consciously, she smiled as he approached. 'I've been watching for the car from the window. I saw it, and . . .'

'What do you want?' James asked brusquely.

'To know if you're both all right.' Boody shrugged. 'Are you?'

'I thought you didn't care for our tawdry enterprise?' When she opened her mouth to reply, James jumped in first. 'Anyway, we couldn't get in. Police already there. They must have their own leads – they'll probably have the whole thing wrapped up by the time we're back.'

'Let's hope so.' Boody looked relieved. 'I was waiting in the common room, but not long after you left, Dan's uncle Stuart turned up. He's catching the motorbus with us tomorrow; Gillian's putting him up for the night in the Blacklers block, across the grounds. He wondered where Dan was.'

'And what did you tell him?'

'That I didn't know. Then I walked out. I'm a terrible liar. I blush.'

James didn't comment, locked into his private thoughts. Would Dan's uncle still be up, wanting to see his nephew? What if Dan let the truth come tumbling out – where would that leave them?

'By the way, did you see Hugo?' Boody went on. 'I saw him come up here and push something under your door.'

'Oh?' James went into his room. An envelope lay on the floor, marked with his name; he opened it and read the urgent scrawl inside:

James
Trouble. Will hide out at Queen's Marsh. Meet me at the estate road soonest – alone.
H

James felt like swearing. What the hell was happening tonight? After all he'd been through, did he really have to go running off into the wilds of the Dartington estate?

Boody was watching him closely. 'Everything all right?'

'When did Hugo leave this?'

'Maybe thirty minutes ago. He left the common room ahead of me – I thought he was going to bed. I only saw him when I was on my way to the bathroom.'

James nodded. 'How did he seem?'

'I don't know. He was too far off. I didn't want to talk after everything, so I left him to it.' Boody put a gentle hand on James's arm. 'Listen, new boy, I'm glad you didn't get yourself involved in sneaking into the cinema . . .'

Her fingers felt cool – but James flinched from the touch as if it burned. He leaned on the door, affected impatience. 'Sleep well, Boody.'

In a couple of blinks, her cool blue eyes swapped surprise for hurt, and then hardened. 'Goodnight, James. Don't over-sleep, will you.' She turned and stalked away back down the corridor, and James could almost see the glint of frost in her footsteps.

What do you care? he told himself. *She's just a girl.*

And Hugo? Was the boy's sudden plea linked to Stuart Sloman's arrival?

Or what if someone had tracked the film reel here to Dartington . . . ?

James thumped his fist against the door. Why had Hugo involved him in all this in the first place? The two of them weren't friends . . . not really . . .

He stared at the letter then tried to picture the location

from his morning runs. Queen's Marsh was to the southeast, alongside the brook. There was a footpath that led through Symon's Tree Wood to the marsh; the estate road was a good way beyond it though, close to the perimeter of the grounds. Best part of a mile . . .

Something must've scared the living daylights out of Hugo.

Heaving a long, resentful sigh, James left his room again and hurried back outside.

A dark ocean of stars stretched over the silent woods, rich and undisturbed. As he tramped through the thick under-growth in search of the footpath, James stopped every minute or so, listening for sounds of movement. The woodland, so serene in the dappled morning sunlight, had become a threatening landscape of black and blacker. He heard nothing, not even the stir of animals. The quiet seemed un-natural and played on his nerves; it heightened the crack and crunch of every step he took.

Hugo would hear him coming, at least.

Anyone might.

Finally, James fought his way through a tangle of brambles onto the overgrown footpath. Bidwell Brook murmured nearby, running alongside in the gloom. *It should be easier and quieter to navigate from here on in*, he told himself.

It took perhaps ten more minutes to traverse the boggy stretch known as Queen's Marsh and reach the unpaved furrow of the estate road that ran through it. Panting, sweat soaking the back of his thin cotton shirt, James looked all about. 'Hugo?' he hissed. 'It's me, James. Where the devil are you – and why, for God's sake?'

A dull light bobbed further along the path. James froze,

then backed away into a coppice of trees by the edge of the road. He heard the scuffle of steps. Out of the night gloom came two figures, one limping and leaning heavily on his companion, who was holding the light – the front light from a bicycle.

Abruptly the figures stopped. 'Hello there?' a male voice called as the light shone into the coppice.

James froze. Had they spotted him?

'There's been an accident.' The man's accent marked him out as a local. 'Can you help us?'

This night was shot all to hell! James hesitated. Then, self-consciously, he stepped out of hiding.

'Please.' The man helped his friend stagger towards him. 'My mate John's been hurt. Do you know the way to the nearest hospital?'

'Sorry, I don't,' James admitted.

'That's a pity.' The man paused. ''Cos you're going to need one.'

James heard the faintest movement – someone sneaking up behind – but before he could turn, something slammed into the base of his skull. The world sparked red and ringing as he fell to his knees. *Trap!* his mind was screaming. He pitched forward, just enough wits left to play dead.

John, the 'injured' man, laughed. 'You got him, Lew!' His voice was young, excited. 'Easy!'

'Let's hope he's the one,' came a low, West Country voice. 'That's him, Mitch, isn't it? Got to be.'

'Course it's him,' said Mitch, the man with the light. 'Dark, tall. That stupid curl of hair on his forehead. Just like Beatrice told us.'

Beatrice Judge . . . ? In his confusion, James almost laughed out loud. He'd been so fixated on murder and plots and men with guns, the threat of a jealous girl with a grudge and local contacts had never entered his mind.

'If it's him, you'd better earn what we're paying you,' said Lew.

Willing his eyes to focus, James saw knuckledusters glint in the light of the cycle lamp. 'He's out cold already,' Mitch said. 'Let's make it a little colder.'

The light was shone into his face. James kept up his sham of sleep, braced himself to move. If his timing was out . . .

Through the merest crack between his lids, he glimpsed Mitch raise his brass-covered knuckles.

As the fist plunged down, James rolled aside. Mitch shouted as his fist struck stone, and again as James kicked him hard in the groin. He reeled backwards and the light clattered to the ground.

The evil whistle of the spade swinging through the air gave James just enough warning to roll aside again. Too slow. The blade smashed down on his shoulder and he cried out. Anger and pain galvanized him as he grabbed the shaft of the shovel and twisted with all his strength, prising it free and throwing Lew off balance. But already, John had grabbed James by the throat, fingers wedging in against his wind-pipe. Desperately, James bit into the boy's wrist like he was chewing a tough steak. With a scream, the boy tore his hand away.

James scrambled up, turned and jabbed the spade handle into John's face, knocking him flat. But now Mitch came at him again, big arms outstretched. James brought the broad, flat blade down on the man's foot, biting through shoe leather and into the flesh beneath. Mitch yelled, until James brought up the handle of the spade under his chin; the man's jaw clapped shut and he recoiled, stumbling over his friend.

Turning to run, James wondered what had happened to Lew, the third assailant. A loud crack thundered in the darkness, and something hit his left temple. Gasping as the sting became a hot burn, James put a hand to his face and it came away bloody.

'Shot?' he muttered, then turned and stumbled away from the track, into the bushes.

'Got you!' Lew hooted.

As he ran, James heard Lew crash through the undergrowth in pursuit. His head was throbbing, and dizziness threatened to drop him with every step. He forced himself onwards, nothing left but the stubborn will to escape, to survive . . .

Clearing a thicket of trees, James dodged back and slumped against a broad trunk. It was so dark. He couldn't see through one eye, which was glued shut with blood, but he could hear careless crashing close behind. Fighting through nausea, he marshalled his anger . . .

Then Lew pushed through the bushes beside James, some kind of pistol in his hand.

James raised his fist. He knew he had next to nothing left inside him so he made the punch count – shouting with rage, first two knuckles extended, the full weight of his body behind the blow. Struck on the side of the neck, Lew went down hard, and stayed there.

The wood was quiet and calm again, the echoes of his cry

already swallowed by the dark. Shaking and sweaty with exertion, James doubled over and vomited.

When he was done, he pulled Lew's jacket from his prone body and used it to wipe blood and drool off his face. James picked up Lew's gun and stuffed it in his trouser pocket. Then, cold, he put on the oversized jacket and tried to get his bearings. He set off thinking he was heading north towards Foxhole, but soon wound up back at the track by Queen's Marsh. The brook was bubbling serenely. James's throat was burning and dry and he made unsteadily for the water – a cool drink, a proper wash . . .

But he was sleepy. The sound of the stream was close, a rushing lullaby. As he lay down and closed his eyes, James wondered if he'd slipped into the water; so cold, sinking into the blissful dark.

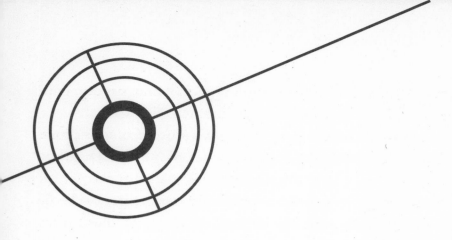

8

Space Enough at Last

When James woke he could hardly move, pain defining every muscle. He was flat on his back. Crispin's corpse jerked through confused memories, and West Country voices jeered in darkness. With sudden panic, James opened his eyes and winced. Early sunlight blazed through a large window.

Dimly, he realized the window was actually the rear doors of a van, standing open. He couldn't move because he was strapped around the waist to a trolley, half smothered with blankets. *They've got me*, he thought, pulling at the straps. *They're going to drive me away and kill me—*

'Easy, son.' A burly, grey-haired man in a peaked cap held his right arm and smiled down at him. He wore a smart dark-blue uniform bisected by a white sash, and was holding a bloodied cloth. 'I've bandaged you up. We're off to the cottage hospital.'

'This is an ambulance,' James realized.

'Old woman found you, first thing – or rather, her dog did.' The ambulance man chuckled to himself. 'She thought you were dead and called us to take you away! You've taken a couple of nasty knocks to your head, Master Judge. What happened?'

Master Judge? James was about to protest, when he dimly remembered taking his attacker's jacket last night. There must have been identification in there. 'I . . . don't remember what happened.' He coughed, and his head felt ready to split. 'Did you find any others?'

'Only you, son.'

So his attackers had got away scot-free. He reached into his jacket and pulled out a shabby wallet inscribed *LEWIS JUDGE*. Beatrice's brother, he supposed. 'What . . . time is it?'

'Seven-thirty. You've been out all night. Doctor will need to check you over.' The ambulance man patted James's arm and climbed out. 'Don't worry, I'll have you there in no time. You can get a message to your folks from the hospital. They must be worried stiff.'

'Wait! Please.' James tried to sit, tugging at his straps as the doors shut with a clunk. 'I can't go. I've got somewhere to be!'

The ambulance man didn't respond. James heard him climb into the driver's seat and start the engine. For James the scale of his predicament dawned in dreadful colours. Beatrice Judge had wanted him out of the way, unable to fly, from the moment he'd arrived at Dartington. Her first reckless attack had got her nowhere, so she'd planned last night with her brother while acting the model pupil – doubtless ready to step into James's shoes at a moment's notice.

The ambulance lurched away, but indignation burned

worse than his bruises. The letter that had lured him to the attack; Hugo must have helped to set him up . . .

Still, it did no good to speculate, to wallow in despair. The Dartington party would be on a strict schedule. They'd have left for Totnes station ninety minutes ago, and the zeppelin was due to leave at four that afternoon. If James was still to be on board, he needed a plan.

'So, think,' he breathed.

By the time the ambulance reached the hospital, James had wormed his way free of the stretcher. His clothes stank of sick, his stomach growled for food, his throat was parched. He forced himself to concentrate, to be ready.

As soon as the ambulance stopped moving, James opened the doors – just before the engine died. The hospital was as quaint as most everything else around Totnes, a quiet, shady sandstone building set in attractive grounds. He slipped outside, stepping softly on the gravel driveway, and skirted the vehicle to the left; it looked more or less new, a converted Humber Snipe 80, solid and beefy.

Through the passenger window, James saw the ambulance man get out of the vehicle; he opened the passenger door under cover of the driver's door slamming shut. Thankfully, the key was still in the ignition. James curled up in the passenger footwell, out of sight, listening to the crump of the ambulance man's feet on the gravel outside. In moments, they quickened and dwindled as the man set off towards the hospital to get help.

James clambered painfully into the driver's seat, turned the key and hit the starter button. Still warm, the big engine snarled into life first time. Fumbling with the four-speed gearbox, James turned hard on the wheel as the ambulance lurched forward in a spray of gravel, clipping a hedge as he performed an uncertain U-turn on the drive.

He was off and out of sight before anyone emerged from the hospital.

I just stole an ambulance, James marvelled, the familiar fire sparking, raising his spirits. The fuel gauge was showing nearly full. Better yet, the driver had left his lunch on the dashboard, wrapped in a tea towel – cheese sandwiches with slices of apple between the thick doorstops of white bread. James took a greedy mouthful. Heaven.

You don't have to go this alone, he told himself. *Get back to Dartington Hall. See the Head, tell him what happened. He can raise Cardington on the phone, tell them to wait for you to arrive on the next train.*

But then he caught sight of himself properly in the rear mirror – the livid welt beside his right eye, the swelling and bruising. He looked a mess. What if the Head didn't believe his story, called in the police over the hijacked ambulance, or insisted he go back to hospital for treatment? Could he seriously expect a zeppelin loaded with the most powerful moguls in the movie industry to delay take-off for one insignificant schoolboy?

There was only one sure course he could take. Switching on the alarm bells mounted on the roof, James swung the ambulance onto the main road heading north towards Exeter – and, way beyond, Bedfordshire, and Cardington airfield.

James had undergone many kinds of endurance test, but the interminable journey across England proved especially hateful. The roads were typically rutted and his arms ached from gripping the wheel. His head was pounding, making it hard to concentrate. The Snipe, with its 3500cc straight-six engine, delivered a punchy ride, and frequently he got her up to seventy miles per hour. But James knew he must resist the temptation to push the engine to its limit the whole way, and set the bells clanging permanently to warn traffic aside. If the Snipe broke down, he would stand no chance of reaching Cardington. Then again, if he played it too safe, he might not arrive in time.

And by now, the authorities must be on the lookout for him. The hospital would have called through the details of the ambulance. Police in the surrounding areas would surely be looking for it. If he passed just one on-the-ball copper . . . and if they caught him with Lew's ugly air pistol still stuffed in his trouser pocket . . .

The long hours groaned by, mauling James's nerves.

The ambulance ran out of petrol four hours into the journey, outside Reading. James found a large spare can in the rear, as well as a peaked cap, and took advantage of both; if no one looked too closely, they might think him a regular ambulance driver. He wondered how the others were faring in their own marathon journey – from Totnes station they'd have caught the train to Paddington, hailed taxis to King's Cross, headed north on the Cambridge line, changing at Hitchin for the final stretch to Cardington station . . . while here he sat, eyes blurring, arms aching and fingers numb, badgering the traffic along the back roads of Britain.

His senses sharpened at the first sign for Cardington around two o'clock, and as he saw the airfield in the distance, new vigour crept into his frame. He saw the two colossal sheds, vast hangars forged from thousands of tons of steel. But drawing the eye, massive and indomitable and so graceful in the blue, was Anton Kostler's *Allworld*.

James couldn't help but feel awed. The airship hung above the world like some vast, silvery leviathan drawn from an ocean of sky, its nose pressed up against the helter-skelter of crisscrossed girders that made the mooring mast. As he neared the site, the fuel tank needle nudging empty, crowds stood thick along the approach roads like human hedgerows; the coming and passing of a giant passenger airship still caused great excitement. James remembered the crowds breaking through the cordons in the fields at Hanworth to see the *Graf Zeppelin* up close; he'd been among them. How he'd hated the passengers on board that great craft, rising into the air for their incredible tour.

'I'm not missing out now,' he swore. 'For every curse in my life, there's a charm.' He thought of all he'd gone through last night, and of Crispin lying dead. Simply taking breath was a blessing.

James switched on those damned ambulance bells, scattering onlookers onto the grass verges, and accelerated for the final push. Boldly he drove right up to the main gate and almost smashed through the entrance barrier. 'Emergency!' he yelled at the protesting guards, brazening it out. 'Come on, let me through!'

Barely had the barrier risen than James drove the ambulance on, tearing across the asphalt, making for the *Allworld*. It held James transfixed, so colossal and yet floating so serenely about the mooring mast. The ground handlers were busy at their posts, making sense somehow of the ropes and lines and winches that grounded the airship. Beyond it, and dwarfed by its bulk, was a motorcoach, a clutch of figures standing close by. James's heart banged harder. He couldn't just drive up in a stolen ambulance and expect to hop aboard. Could he?

He switched off the deafening bells and parked up beside the large green shed-like building, a workshop or something, that was between him and the ground crew. Scrambling out, he left his peaked cap on the seat and opened the rear doors, standing in the doorway as if he'd just emerged as a patient. His legs were threatening to cramp, he was ready to drop, but the sight of the figures walking in a crocodile towards the *Allworld* tugged at the last of his resolve . . .

'Hey!' he shouted, wincing as his head threatened to split apart. 'Hey, there!'

Some of the ground crew were looking his way, and security guards had emerged from the nearest hangar. James broke into a stumbling run towards the airship. He heard shouting around the airfield. Swearing furiously, James quickened his step. 'Gillian!' he bellowed, just as the warning wail of a klaxon sounded out across the airfield. The main gate must have called in and found no emergency.

Raising his voice, James shouted again for Gillian, but it was hopeless now. He broke into a run, but found his legs would not support him and he fell.

The next thing he knew, hands were on him, he was being yanked roughly to his feet as the siren shrieked on. Grim guards' faces were pressed in all around, and—

'*James!*' Gillian de Vries pushed through the scrum. 'Leave him. Get off the poor boy, can't you? He's meant to be here.' She actually pushed one guard out of her way. 'He's one of our party. But how on earth . . . ?'

'Looks fit to drop.' One guard jerked a thumb back towards the workshop. 'Kid must have been brought here in that ambulance.'

'Where's your driver?' another demanded. 'Where'd he go?'

James did his best to look clueless and scared. Gillian pulled him to her and held him in an embrace. 'Oh, James, whatever have you been through?'

'Give the boy some space, fellows,' came a cultured male voice. 'Sounds like it's the driver you want to be after, not this poor lad.'

James looked up from Gillian's shoulder and found himself face to face with a well-dressed man with strong, scholarly features topped by a tangle of fair hair. If his horn-rimmed glasses made him look a little severe, the warmth of his smile soon undercut the impression. 'I'm Stuart Sloman. You're Daniel's friend, aren't you? James Bond? Quite a night you've had, it would seem.'

'You two, stay with the lad,' the guard captain ordered his men. 'I'll confer with Captain Breithaupt. The rest of you, fan out and search for the driver. Probably taken short . . .'

As the guards moved off, Boody, Dan and Hugo moved in, weighed down with hand luggage, full of concern. Trailing at the back came Beatrice Judge with a large suitcase, looking like she'd seen a ghost. James pulled away from Gillian and stared at her. Yes, a ghost who was out for blood.

'James!' Hugo came scurrying up. 'I knew that farewell

letter was a phoney. As if you'd run away 'cos you're too afraid to fly!'

James stared stonily. 'You were in on this.' He pulled Hugo's letter from his back pocket and passed it to Gillian. 'He wrote saying he was in trouble. Boody saw him push it under my door.'

Gillian turned to Boody, who nodded glumly.

'I went to meet him and I was attacked by three men' – James pointed at Beatrice – '*her* brother Lew among them.'

'You're lying,' Beatrice said automatically. 'That's crazy.'

'And that's not my handwriting!' Hugo was on tiptoes, straining to see the note as Gillian held it. 'Honestly, James. I got back from, um, Film Club last night and found a note addressed to you pushed under my door. So I simply delivered it to its intended recipient. What else was I to do?'

'It really isn't Hugo's writing,' Gillian confirmed. 'I mean, I can actually read this.'

'It's *hers*.' Boody had snatched the luggage tag from Beatrice's suitcase and now handed it to Gillian.

'And this belongs to Lewis Judge.' James tried to shrug off his jacket, wincing as he moved his shoulder. 'He . . . left it behind – along with this.' He pulled out the tatty wallet, the name marked with pen. 'There's identification inside.'

Stuart Sloman checked and nodded. Everyone turned to look at Beatrice, whose cheeks were burning blood-red. She looked crushed.

Gillian walked over and put an arm round her. 'I think perhaps we should have a talk on the coach, Beatrice, where it's quieter. Don't you?'

James watched them walk away. Awkwardly, he accepted

the well-meaning backslaps from Hugo and Dan, and Boody's uncertain smile. But as the questions began to fire, he turned away from them all to face his prize – the glorious silver of the *Allworld*, her shadow smeared long and dark over the airfield. He'd made it. He'd won. Where he'd expected to feel blazing triumph, all he could feel was a low toll of relief and a cold bone-weariness. The klaxon's idiot roar rang on like a lament.

'It looks to me like James could use a place to rest,' said Stuart Sloman, edging Dan and Hugo away. 'Boys, let's try to find the captain, see what's happening. I need to talk to him in any case . . .'

Boody stayed beside James and murmured in his ear: 'Something tells me the guards will have a long and fruitless search for the driver of that ambulance.'

'I couldn't tell you,' said James with a smile. 'I'm just a poor, innocent victim.'

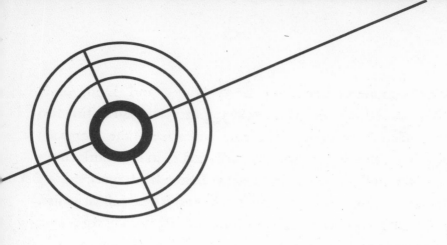

9

Scaling the Himmelstreppe

James was allowed to clean up and rest in the ground crew's quarters. A hot bath and a cold glass of water had never felt so good.

Dan lent James a change of clothes from his carry-on luggage. Checking his old pockets, James pulled out Lew Judge's pistol; *his* pistol, now, the spoils of war. Inspecting it by daylight, he saw what an ugly lash-up it was: the stock little more than a lump of wood, the trigger adapted from a belt buckle and incredibly stiff. This assembly had been strapped together and glued to the frame and barrel of a spring-piston air pistol. For ammunition, it looked as if it fired ball bearings or pellets – or, more likely, anything Lew could stuff inside! What had struck him last night? He put a finger to the wound and winced.

There was a smart knock at the door and James stashed the gun in his pocket, just as Gillian entered. 'Feeling better?'

James nodded.

'The police are driving Beatrice and her luggage back to Dartington. I imagine the Head will expel her.' Her face hardened. 'Frankly, I'm not sure you don't deserve a place on the back seat beside her. That ambulance was carrying papers from the Totnes hospital. It's been confirmed as a stolen vehicle. And you stole it, didn't you, James?'

After a moment's hesitation, James nodded again.

'Dangerous and stupid.' Gillian's face was drawn. 'For goodness' sake, James, this is an educational field trip, not a gladiatorial contest. And after this little stunt, it's not just your place on the zeppelin that's in jeopardy. With your aunt abroad, I'm responsible for you. If I get dragged into a police inquiry now, that stops me leaving with the others: the whole trip will have to be cancelled.'

'I'm sorry,' James said truthfully. 'I didn't think of that. I . . . I just really want to go to America.'

'Well, you've certainly proved that. But keep this up, it's Juvenile Court and a whipping you'll be going to, together with Beatrice Judge and her friends.' Her face softened a little, and she shook her head. 'I'll see what strings can be pulled and what half-truths told.'

James blinked. 'You'd do that for me?'

'To be quite honest, no.' Distractedly, Gillian pushed stray red locks under her headscarf. 'But I'll do it for your aunt, and I'll do it for the school.'

'Thank you.' James let out a long breath. 'Perhaps you could say that one of my attackers had a change of heart – he drove me to the airfield in the ambulance before fleeing the scene.'

'Could I, indeed.' Gillian raised both eyebrows. 'You're really quite a subject, James Bond. With the audacity and attitude you've acquired through your education, Dr Leaver will have a field day studying you.'

James watched her go to talk with Captain Heinrich Breithaupt, the German Senior Watch Officer on board the *Allworld*. Soon after, the captain, who had something of the bloodhound in his appearance as well as his attitude, came to talk to James directly. Gillian waited stoically in the background.

'There is much still to be determined,' Breithaupt pondered in mannered English, clearly dubious, staring out at the *Allworld* through the window. 'But since the ambulance is undamaged, since this trouble is clearly not of your making, and since it is our wish to leave for America without delay or inquiry . . . I suggest we leave this mystery of the driver to be investigated by your English authorities in our absence, yes?'

'Yes,' James agreed with feeling, hardly able to grasp his luck. 'Yes, that would be good.'

'Then, come. I shall escort you on board myself. Your luggage was loaded last night, of course. Are you carrying any further items that could conceivably cause fire? As you appreciate, these are not permitted.'

'My carry-on case is still in my room at Dartington. But I do have this.' Shiftily, James pulled out the lashed-up air pistol. Breithaupt and Gillian stared at it.

'It's not a real gun,' James said quickly, passing it to Breithaupt. 'Uses air and a spring to fire pellets, nothing flammable. I have no ammunition. I'm just . . . restoring it.'

'Air, we will have much of.' Breithaupt inspected the pistol and smiled thinly. 'Your "restoration project", happily, will be unique on board.'

The late afternoon sun was slowly descending as the three of them marched towards the mooring mast. James felt his stomach start to fizz. He also experienced a chafe of guilt to know he'd left behind not one crime scene in the last twenty-four hours, but two.

'Thank you, Gillian,' he breathed.

'Don't mention it,' she murmured. 'I mean it – don't mention it to anyone!'

A tall, bearded man in a peaked cap and leather coat was waiting at the foot of the mast with a clipboard; he took their names and marked them off his list. 'All present now, Captain Breithaupt!' He turned to Gillian and James. 'If you will kindly embark; once you are settled our flight can commence.'

The words made James feel dizzy as he surveyed the mast's steel staircase; it spiralled skywards perhaps two hundred feet. He started towards it, but Gillian held him back.

'I think you'll do better in the lift,' she said.

Breithaupt escorted them. The elevator car was wrought iron and open to the air. Above, the great silver ship loomed through the latticework. Instructions barked through mega-phones flew around them as the final preparations were made for launch.

The lift opened onto a passenger platform that was maybe forty feet in diameter, protected by a heavy parapet. A flexible, covered causeway led to the *Allworld*. Beside it, another member of the flight crew was waiting to welcome the passengers aboard. He was German too, and spoke more haltingly.

'Please, now climb the *Himmelstreppe*.'

'The what?' asked Gillian.

'Steps to heaven,' James translated, pointing past the man to the ramp into the airship.

Gillian smiled drily. 'I hadn't realized a visit there was on our flight plan.'

With a shrug, James stepped up the gangplank and went aboard the gondola – a structure designed like a long, wide, open rail car strapped beneath the vast body of the ship. This was the space everyone aboard would inhabit each day and night of the voyage; all clean, angular lines in black and white, with gold accents that caught the electric lights in the ceiling. A cabin boy greeted James and Gillian with layouts of the ship, menus, flight plans and passenger lists.

Breithaupt led his guests along a short corridor and through a door on the left into a crowded lounge area; it was perhaps sixteen feet square with large windows running either side. 'Our final guests,' he announced, and introduced them both to polite applause – and a loud whoop from Hugo, who was sitting on the sill beside one of the windows with Boody and Dan. Breithaupt's further announcement – 'All are aboard, we are ready for the off' – was greeted with heady enthusiasm from everyone.

As his friends made their way over, James sized up their fellow passengers in the lounge. Here were the great and good of European cinema – all middle-aged men, dressed in expensive suits, peering out of the windows or lounging in elegant chairs. James scanned the list of passengers, but the names meant nothing to him — they were the muscle behind the movies here and in Europe, the faceless shapers of their own parts of the industry. Checking the flight plan, he supposed many had come aboard at Cuers-Pierrefeu in southern France, travelling there from Spain and Italy. More were to join the party at their next stop, Lakehurst, New Jersey, before the final cross-continental push from East Coast USA to West.

On the far wall, above an interior door, a large portrait drew the eye. In vivid oils it showed a man in his prime, posed beside an old-fashioned camera pointing straight at the onlooker. He had close-cropped brown curly hair, a knowing half-smile and a voracious look in his dark eyes; the overall impression was of poise, pride and power.

'Anton Kostler.' Boody had changed into a plain powder-blue housedress with a white collar, and black ankle-strap sandals. 'Here in spirit, if not in person.'

James nodded, mildly put out to find that her heels elevated her a fraction above his own height. 'Doesn't want anyone to forget who's providing the ride.'

'I suppose we should be glad Mr Kostler likes people to travel to him and not vice versa,' Gillian noted. 'And we have Dr Leaver to thank too, for interesting Kostler in us in the first place. This is sure to be quite a trip.'

'I've heard the *Allworld*'s based on the design of the *Graf Zeppelin*,' James put in.

'It's actually bigger.' Stuart Sloman sipped his champagne. 'Mr Kostler likes to feel he's one step ahead!'

Hugo waved a tatty copy of the *Modern Boy* magazine, a special airship number. 'It says here he's obsessed with zeppelins, thinks they're the future of air travel.'

'He even has his own personal scaled-down version of the *Allworld*,' Dan added, 'for flitting between his favourite haunts.'

Gillian tutted. 'A degree of eccentricity does these moguls' reputations the world of good, I'm sure.'

'He named it *Zelda*, you know,' Hugo informed them. 'After his dead wife.'

'That's quite sad,' said Boody. 'Casts a new light on climbing the *Himmelstreppe* to Zelda, doesn't it . . . ?'

While they chattered on, James checked his plan of the airship. The door beneath the portrait led to a long passage studded with doors on either side, each opening onto one of the twenty-four sleeping cabins.

'You're down to bunk with me, James,' Hugo informed him. 'I hope you're convinced I had nothing to do with that wretched note so I'll be spared reprisals . . .'

James didn't answer. Glancing up, he'd seen a man enter from the passage – and recognition stabbed so hard that, for a moment, he couldn't breathe.

Facing him across the lounge of the airship was Fedora Man.

Suddenly, James was back racing through the passageways of the Alhambra Picture House. He turned his back on the man, heart beating so fast he felt sick.

'You look dreadful, James,' Gillian observed. 'Last-minute nerves, or have you seen a ghost?'

'I'm fine.' James said it out loud, but was chiefly trying to convince himself. He glanced back; the man was taking a cocktail from a steward. Beneath the fedora the eyes, small and blue in a hard, cold face, were sweeping the room. They were surely the same eyes that had fixed on him last night!

James stepped closer to Dan. 'Behind you,' he breathed. 'Look discreetly. I think it's the man from the Alhambra.'

Dan frowned, looked round hastily.

'See?' James whispered. 'Same hat, same eyes . . .'

'Snap out of it, Bond,' Dan muttered. 'There must be a million men with hats like that who fit his description. What would a gunman be doing here of all places?'

It was a good question. James nodded. Perhaps he was imagining things. 'What did you do with the film can? Did you tell your uncle?'

'No! I got rid of it.' Dan looked cross. 'Now drop it, can't you? I don't want to talk about it.'

An excited hubbub was building steadily in the lounge as the countdown to launch grew nearer. Whistles were being blown outside, and ground-crew voices raised in a frenzy of last-minute checks.

'*Taue los!*' The deep German holler carried through the thin walls from the control cabin at the front of the gondola, and the tow-lines were duly released.

'Here goes then.' Hugo downed an orange juice and grimaced as if it were something stronger. 'Let's all do our best not to worry we're set to travel three and a half thousand miles in a giant balloon filled with hydrogen gas that will explode spectacularly at the provocation of a single spark.'

'Thank you, Hugo.' Gillian tugged distractedly at the beads around her neck. 'I'm sure the crew know just what they're doing.'

'Of course they do.' Sloman finished his champagne. 'No one knows airships like the Germans.'

'Statistically, they've crashed the fewest.' Hugo consulted

his magazine article. 'The French *Dixmude* was struck by lightning in '23 with fifty-two dead; 1930, the British *R101* hit the ground with forty-eight dead. Last year, the USS *Akron*—'

'For God's sake, Hugo,' Dan snapped, 'you're not helping.'

'*Schiff hoch!*' came the shout from Breithaupt. 'Up ship! Up ship!'

There was a breathless moment as the *Allworld* was uncoupled from the mast. A hush fell on the lounge.

The airship began floating upwards, smoothly and steadily, as if gravity no longer applied.

In James, a moment's panic gave way to exhilaration: he had never felt anything like it. Awestruck, he crossed to the windows on the right with his party to watch the earth below fall away, while stewards attempted to direct others to the left to balance out their weight. Kostler stared out from his portrait, assured and serene. James's ears popped as the airship went on rising.

'We're so high up,' Sloman breathed.

Higher . . . higher . . . What if they never stopped? The crowds in the Cardington lanes were still waving and cheering, but no noise carried now. The ship rode the air in uncanny silence. James felt a hand grab hold of his arm; it was Boody, enraptured, staring not at the ground but at the sky all around them. She had tears in her eyes.

A distant bark from Breithaupt cut through the moment – 'Clutch in propellers. Full ahead engines!'

A hum stole into James's ears as the prop engines fired; even suspended in pods attached to the hull, shouldn't they sound louder? But clearly they were doing their job: the enormous gas cells had lifted the great zeppelin into the air, and now the propellers began to drive the ship forward.

We're underway, marvelled James, as a spontaneous cheer went up from the passengers and Hugo waved his magazine like a flag at a parade. It was incredible, surreal, to watch the ground slipping by so far below.

'Five Maybach VL-2 12-cylinder engines!' Boody was almost bouncing up and down. 'We'll be cruising at around sixty miles an hour, but our top air-speed is close to eighty!'

Her excitement was infectious. From up here the world looked ridiculously neat, like some movie special effect – the careful patchwork of fields and towns, the rivers tying the landscape together like grey ribbons. James had expected some vibration through his feet, some rocking from side to side. But there was nothing save a feeling of unreality. The excited mutterings of the crowd made a Babel about him.

'*Somos prisioneros . . .*'

'*Anyone see an angel yet?*'

'*Il fait clair, il fait doux, il fait gai!*'

'Homeward bound,' Gillian murmured.

The sun shone like a rose-coloured lamp over the broad surface of the earth. *Caged in the air for two and a half days*, thought James. *All of us – crew, passengers, whoever we may be – pressed in together, as cities and rivers and ocean slide past . . .*

James glanced over to where the man with the fedora had been standing. There was no one there now.

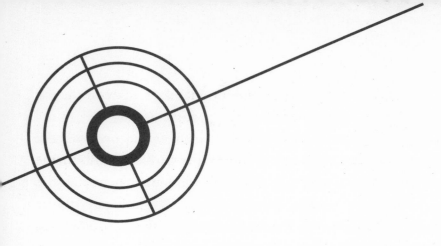

10

Voices from Nowhere

Spirits were high with the excitement of the launch and the beginning of the long voyage. More champagne was served, with orange juice for the children.

Tired, bruised and sore, James turned in early that first night. He and Hugo were to share the last cabin on the right at the far end of the passage – located furthest from the lounge, beside the passenger washrooms and toilets. Not the ideal location – since the gondola walls were little more than glazed calico stretched from floor to ceiling over a few supporting struts, you could hear pretty much everything that went on there. As he lay on his bunk beneath his blanket, he could hear soft, furtive movements from the cabin to his left. As if someone did not wish to be overheard.

James rolled onto his side. The spade-blow to the back of his head had left a lump so tender it hurt to lie on his back; it throbbed against the pillow, leaving him nauseous.

The cabins were neat and functional, like first-class sleeper compartments on a train, only scaled down and more glamorous. The back of the narrow sofa swung up from the wall to create a top bunk, where he was lying now. There was little storage space; the wardrobe was only a few inches deep, its door a stretch of fabric. And like the rest of the ship, the rooms were unheated, and at this altitude, decidedly cool. It was probably warmest in the lounge, where most people mixed and mingled.

Fedora Man hadn't returned. Was that him next door, moving around? James strained to hear over the lulling whoosh of the zeppelin's engines. The sounds almost seemed to come from over his head, above the ceiling.

It sounded like somebody hunting for something.

James tried to stay alert, but exhaustion was laying claim to his senses. He stared sleepily out through the window, at a night sky of such enormity it seemed that anyone could get to heaven.

The same window hurled bright sunlight into James's face just before six. He woke feeling better, if not exactly refreshed. Hugo was still snoozing in the bunk below. Cautious splashes came from the washroom next door – there were no baths or showers here, water was too precious; even the flushed stuff from the toilets was used as ballast.

Contemplating septic waste, it didn't take long for thoughts of Fedora Man to creep into focus.

Forget it, he told himself firmly.

Burying his unease, James vowed to do his best to settle into their cruise liner in the sky. In such enclosed surroundings, it would be easy to get the layout of the place, at least.

He got up carefully, but still Hugo awoke.

'Feeling better?' The boy yawned noisily. 'You've known some dark drama lately, eh, James. First in the Alhambra, then in the woods, then all the way to Cardington . . .'

James looked at him evenly. 'Did Dan say anything?'

'About how someone had broken in ahead of you and you couldn't move for coppers. Sounds like you and Danny were lucky not to get your collars felt. Still, a heroic try, James. You did all you could to return that film, your conscience is clear.'

'Thank you, Father, for hearing my confession.' James remembered how easily sound carried up here. 'And keep your voice down.'

'Funny coincidence,' Hugo went on, in a pantomime whisper. 'Dan's uncle Stuart said *his* place had been turned over recently.'

'Oh?' James felt suddenly alert. 'And he works for the Alhambra too, doesn't he?'

'Used to,' Hugo agreed. 'Still, it never rains but it pours.'

'That's the truth,' James muttered as Fedora Man's spectre breathed a little harder on the back of his neck. 'Are you getting up?'

Hugo closed his eyes. 'A snooze or two longer.'

Reunited with his suitcase, James dressed in his own clothes – fresh trousers and a crisp white shirt – then left Hugo in peace and padded along the passage into the lounge.

As soon as he walked in, the wonder of his surroundings struck him all over again. Boundless sky and sea lit the windows in cheerful blues; James had never seen the world from such a height. A gramophone sat on the long shelf beneath, softly spinning 'Come Josephine in My Flying

Machine'. Some of the men looked to have stayed up all night, sitting round their tables playing cards, while their patron in his portrait turned a blind eye overhead. Stuart Sloman sat at a table by himself, engrossed in a book, as if in a Lyons Corner House rather than in a glamorous flight machine.

'Ah, James!' Sloman beckoned him over. 'How are you feeling?'

'Better. Thank you.' James felt automatically for the lump on the back of his head, winced, and then accepted a coffee from a steward with a tray of hot drinks. Watching Sloman do the same, he wondered how much Dan had told him about their adventure two nights ago. 'So . . . are you going to live in Los Angeles from now on?'

'That's the plan. See how things work out for me at Allworld.' Sloman took off his horn-rimmed glasses to polish them. 'I want to get a handle on the different districts before I choose a place to live, so I'll be staying at a hotel to start with.'

'At least that way you don't have to worry about being burgled again,' James noted. 'Is that why you came to stay at Dartington the night before last?'

'You mean, was I worried the burglars might come back?' Sloman put his glasses back on and swigged his coffee. 'Not really. There was nothing in my place worth taking.'

'But that's all changing now, right, Stu?' A man with a hard New York accent appeared by their table, sharp-suited with handsome, Hispanic looks. 'Now you're on the up and up. Look out that window – sky's the limit when you're on Anton Kostler's payroll.'

Sloman didn't look delighted to see him. 'Good morning, Mr Vasquez.'

'*Great* morning! I'm telling you.' Vasquez smiled at James, his dark eyes sparkling. 'Hey, kid. Lenny Vasquez, overseas sales representative for Mr Kostler.'

'James Bond.'

'Bond, right. I've spent the last month in Britain promoting our movies.' Vasquez's voice was a rapid bark like machine-gun fire. 'You're one of Doc Leaver's special studies kids, right? At the Kostler Academy?'

'That's right,' James agreed.

'And you like motion pictures?'

'Yes. Specially when there's lots of action.'

'Mr Bond, you're a man of discernment.' Lenny turned a chair round the wrong way and sat down, leaning on the metal back, ignoring Sloman. 'I think you're gonna like this school. Mr Kostler beefed up the creative side of things – in consultation with the Prof, of course. It's a fine establishment. Fine.'

'Why did a big movie producer get involved in education?' James wondered.

Sloman cleared his throat. 'I read there's a rumour his son was thrown out of so many schools in California, Kostler had to start his own.'

Vasquez smiled fondly. 'Martyn used to be a tearaway, sure. But he's – what's the word – he's blossomed at the Academy. Old Doc Leaver, he works miracles. And by funding it all, Kostler gets to give something back to his community.' He turned to Sloman. 'And now here's you, coming out to give something to our community too. That was a hell of a deal you got for yourself, man.'

87

Sloman looked awkward. 'Well, my agent did most of the work . . .'

'No. You knew what you wanted, and you went all out to get it. I like you, Mr Sloman. You've got nerve. Nerve gets you a long way in our business.' He laughed again, like a motor starting. 'A real long way. Take it from one who knows.'

Sloman laughed; he looked uneasy. James felt there were undercurrents to the conversation he couldn't navigate. But the exchange had already ended, as Vasquez got up, slapped a palm on James's shoulder, and with a 'Catch you guys later' was gone.

James watched as Sloman drained the rest of his coffee in one gulp. 'How *did* you get the Hollywood job?'

'By being a damned good writer.' Sloman softened his defensive tone. 'That's often not enough, of course. A few years back, in between running the café in one of my brother's cinemas, I wrote *Bitter Pearl*, a stage play about the Ama divers of Kuro Island, off Japan. There were productions of it all over – did you hear of it?'

'I think so,' James lied, politely.

'My agent suggested I turn it into a motion picture screenplay, which I did. And Dan had told me how Gillian knew Dr Leaver, whose school was patronized by Anton Kostler . . .'

It's not what *you know, it's* who *you know*, thought James, remembering the old saying.

'Gillian agreed to send the screenplay to Leaver. Leaver liked it and passed it direct to Kostler – who came straight back wanting to buy the rights.'

'Sounds perfect.'

'Since silent movies died, Hollywood's been crying out for writers who can do dialogue. Well, I can do dialogue.' Sloman shrugged. 'But then Kostler's production department started to worry about how they'd stage the underwater scenes. They started getting cold feet. Well, I've been around film for years, and I knew some French shorts with amazing underwater effects, so I sent off some old film prints to demonstrate how they could do it.' Sloman was getting quite agitated. 'They sent them back. They didn't want to know. They'd decided to pull out.'

James pulled a sympathetic face. 'So, what did you do?'

'Do?' Sloman looked at James as if only just remembering he was there, and smiled. 'Why, refuse to take no for an answer, that's what I did. In the end, Kostler had to agree I was a talent worth nurturing . . .' He leaned closer, intense. 'You only get one shot at scripting yourself that happy ever after, James. You have to do whatever it takes.' Abruptly, he laughed and relaxed. 'But look who I'm talking to! You know that. That stunt you pulled with the ambulance . . .'

James couldn't help a rueful smile of acknowledgement – then Gillian and Boody came into the room, fresh coffee was poured and the subject dropped.

Later that morning, Lenny Vasquez offered to show the latest arrivals around the *Allworld*, taking them two at a time.

'Me first!' Dan cried, and Hugo got in as his partner. The two of them followed Vasquez from the lounge.

Boody looked sideways at James. 'Who gets to go next?'

Before James could answer, Fedora Man cut in, in a heavy

German accent. 'I am most keen to see around.' Those vivid blue eyes twinkled at Boody. 'Perhaps you might accompany me, young lady?'

Boody hesitated for a moment, looked awkwardly at James.

'I'll go with you, sir,' James said impulsively. Here was a way perhaps to settle his suspicions. 'My name is James Bond. And you?'

The man smiled and inclined his head. 'Rudolf Dürr, I'm a producer for the *Reichsfilmkammer*, the German state film department. And of course, young sir, I will tour this craft with you.'

Boody's smile looked a little tight. 'Have fun, James.'

James hardly heard her, heart thumping as he rose and moved over to join Dürr. 'You're a producer for the Reich,' he asked in German, 'but you came on board in London?'

Dürr answered in broken English. 'Your tongue. Is helpful practice for me, yes? I had business in London. Export meetings. Very dull, you would find it.'

'Have you heard of the Alhambra, in Totnes?'

'*Wo ist das?* I have stayed in London only . . .' Dürr smiled. 'You like the cinemas, young sir?'

Not at night, thought James. *Not running for my life.*

Dan and Hugo soon returned, buzzing from their little sightseeing trip, and Vasquez clapped his hands to summon the second group. Dürr got up stiffly and lumbered to the door. Perhaps it really wasn't the same man, James pondered. Although, Dürr was breathing quite hoarsely – could that be a consequence of inhaling the mercury vapour?

'On the other side of this lounge,' Vasquez began, 'we enter the business end of the gondola. Out of bounds usually, but for you, we make exertions.'

'Exceptions?' James suggested.

'Right. Bright kid.' Vasquez laughed again. 'Guess I should've gone to school, huh?'

You've done all right, James thought.

They stepped into the outer corridor; there was the disembarkation door down a passage to their right. Stepping past that, also to the right, there was the small galley kitchen (with electric hotplates only, James noted; flammable hydrogen and naked flame didn't mix). Across the passage was the radio room, for sending and receiving communications and getting weather reports from the world below, seemingly every few minutes.

James watched the officer listening to a transmission on headphones. There was a spare set on the table.

'May I?' asked Dürr, and Vasquez smiled expansively.

Glancing down, James noticed a set of white headphones on the floor under the radio desk. He caught a murmur of voices bleeding from the earpieces, and stooped to pick them up.

'No.' Vasquez's voice was hard, the hand on James's arm harder still. Then the smile was back. 'Sorry. That's the priority line. Anyone sees me letting a kid listen in on that – boom! I'm out of here.' He shrugged, apologetic. 'And that's a long way to drop.'

Dürr removed his own headphones and offered them to James with a smile. James put them on his head, winced as he caught his wounded temple, and listened in on a weather report. It warned of high pressure up ahead.

'Now,' said Vasquez, leading the way out, 'the information the crew gets here is marked on maps in the charts room next door . . .'

James carefully put down the headphones, glancing back at the white set on the floor.

With a start, he noticed that they weren't connected to the radio set on top of the desk. The cable was coiled on the floor beneath the headset.

Priority line?

Where had the voices come from?

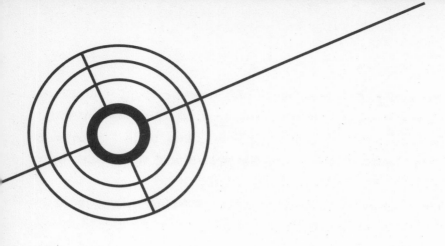

11

Trouble Is a Fellow Passenger

Still puzzled, James followed Dürr into the charts room. Captain Breithaupt was there, conferring tersely with his men. He explained briefly that by using the charts and weather reports they could not only read the circulation of the air ahead of them, but *ride* it – minimizing headwinds and catching tailwinds from the east to boost their course towards the American coast.

While busy planning flight strategies for a patch of heavy weather ahead, Breithaupt gave permission for Vasquez to show them the control room, located at the very front of the gondola.

The room, perhaps half the size of the lounge, was strung with narrow jointed girders from floor to ceiling as if the nerve centre of the ship had been built around a steel spider. The crew looked out through long, tall windows. James observed that the rudder-man stood facing forward at the front of the gondola, while his crewmate in charge of the elevator controls stood to his left. Both duties involved the turning of nautical-looking wheels. They helped re-inforce the impression that the zeppelin was a real ship afloat in a boundless ocean blanketing the world.

The tour reached its climax when James asked about a ladder leading up into a hatch in the ceiling. Vasquez informed him it was the gateway to the rest of the craft. Dürr shook his head to indicate he wouldn't go up, but James grabbed the chance.

At the top, he found himself in a vast cathedral of girders, the triangular latticework arranged in huge, sweeping circles. Huddled above were the giant gas cells, buoying the ship like huge balloons. They pulsed and quivered like living things, hanging eerily from the steel-and-canvas sky. Feeling dizzy, James shook his tender head. Ahead of him, a walkway sloped down over the passenger gondola, leading to the crew's mess, the generator room and whatever else lined the bare belly of this flying giant. The *Allworld*'s cavernous insides seemed to stretch on for ever.

He listened, but couldn't catch any more mysterious whispering voices.

Then Vasquez announced that their time was up, and the tour was over.

On board the *Allworld*, time drifted by dreamily, much like the ocean below. The window was open but no gusts blew inside; though moving at more than sixty miles per hour they were cocooned in the slipstream, the air flowing along the hull with a sound like running water.

Despite himself, James began to relax into the long, wondrous journey. It was a little easier now that he felt Herr Dürr made an unlikely Fedora Man.

He shivered. Unlikely, but not impossible.

'The crew are so dedicated, aren't they?' Dan declared over a game of rummy with James. 'I'd love to play a dashing young airship captain in a big adventure film.'

James's mind was elsewhere. 'You know, Fedora Man claims he was doing business in London.'

'Most probably because he was!' Dan put down three sevens. 'Let it rest, James, please.'

'I'd rest more easily if I knew where that film can was.'

'That film is my responsibility, not yours.' Dan looked James in the eye. 'It's safe. I hid it. I didn't tell anyone. End of subject. Now, do play your cards.'

It was a command that grew into something of a catch-phrase during the flight. *Do play your cards!* With time hanging so loosely, card games filled a good many hours. Eating filled a few more, and the remaining option was conversation. At times, James felt the chief danger on board was being bored to death by 'industry talk' from their fellow passengers. Trade quotas, censors and the dominance of American movies in foreign markets were the chief topics for discussion. His head hurt enough already without their griping.

James decided on a way to help pass the hours more con-structively. On the second day, he retrieved the scavenged airgun from his dirty trouser pocket, and brought it into the lounge.

Gillian groaned. 'Oh, not that awful weapon, James!'

'What on earth is it?' said Hugo. 'Frankenstein's pistol?'

'No. Lew Judge's,' said James. 'I want to restore it.'

Dan smirked. '"Restore it" implies it used to work.'

'It does work.' James pointed to the still-livid bruise on his temple.

'*That's* how you were hurt?' Gillian looked appalled. 'If I'd known I'd have thrown that thing away.'

'It's not the gun you have to watch for, Sweets, it's the guy who pulls the trigger.' Vasquez walked over, took the pistol and weighed it. 'Crude, but tough. You didn't get that crack on your head from no toy, Jimmy. This has seen action.' He waved it in front of some of the movie men, smiled as they flinched. 'I heard about this back-alley trick in New York, see? Cops can't touch you for carrying a kid's pop-gun, but if you add some lint soaked in pure ether to the pellet, *then* fire . . .'

'The ether would ignite,' Boody reasoned, 'and the blast would boost the speed of the pellet. But that would put terrible stresses on the workings.' She took the pistol from Vasquez and cocked it, appraising the insides as a surgeon might a fracture. 'Well, the barrel's in a bad way – the bore's filthy. The breech seal's falling apart, probably blowback into the piston area . . .'

'How come you know so much about it, Boods?' Dan was impressed. 'Ever do time as a gangster's moll?'

She shrugged. 'I just like to know how things work.'

'Well, anyway . . .' James took his pistol back from Boody. 'A regular air pistol will do me. I'd like to smarten it up a bit. Swap the muck of Queen's Marsh for some Hollywood glamour. But I'll need some tools.'

'I like your spirit, kid.' Vasquez winked and breezed away. 'I'll see what I can scare up for you.'

'Thanks,' said James.

'I . . . could give you some help with it, James,' said Boody, a bit self-consciously. 'I mean, I've got nothing more useful to do.'

Dan snorted softly. 'Never learn to play with dolls, Boods?'

'No.' Boody patted the pistol in James's hand. 'But there's time to learn to shoot straight.'

James was glad of Boody's help with the project. She went to work repairing and refining the mechanical parts; it took patience and precision, and she proved she had both.

Avoiding Dürr and the movie bigwigs aboard with their boorish shop-talk, James spent a lot of time in his cabin sanding the chunky, rough-cut stock, trying to shape it. Through the window, the cobalt ocean shifted and drifted beneath sun and moon's slow patrol.

James was blowing on blistered fingertips early on the third morning when Captain Breithaupt announced that land would soon be visible once again. There was some hubbub on board, as everyone awake crowded into the lounge and pressed faces to the windows, James included.

First, James saw seagulls, then stretches of seaweed, dark beneath the baleful Atlantic grey. Finally, there was the first glimpse of New York through the *Allworld*'s windows. A light mist was masking Sandy Hook. Skyscrapers thrust stone and steel through the murk; shapes strong and daring in the stirring sun.

America, thought James, his senses dizzied by the size and scale of all he could see from the air. It was an incredible sight. He longed to charge out and explore everything, to go everywhere – but the stop at Lakehurst in neighbouring New Jersey was timed to last just a few hours. The *Allworld* was on a tight schedule, landing only to pick up the last few passengers and top up with hydrogen and engine fuel before travelling on, this time to their final destination – Mines Field, Los Angeles.

The sensation of stillness, of *terra firma* underfoot, didn't last long. James and his friends had no opportunity to leave the naval base. Sloman made a thorough tour of the works, even talking at length to the boys in the post room – research, he explained, that would clear up a project he'd been working on. Laundry was washed, blissful hot showers were taken, and then it was back on board for another three-day flight.

The days drifted overland now, the ocean lost from sight, the nights peppered with the sliding lights of unknown towns and cities. James, his head feeling better and something of an old hand by now, enjoyed watching the new arrivals marvel at their experience. There was an Arab, a Japanese man and an Indian producer-director . . . James thought of all the different nationalities he'd mixed with at Eton, of friends left behind – distance measured not by miles, but by necessity.

'How marvellous of Kostler to bring all these representatives of world cinema together.' Sloman raised a glass to the mogul's portrait on the wall. 'We can compare markets, contrast styles, learn from each other.'

'It's an engaging atmosphere, isn't it?' Gillian leaned back in her chair looking wistful. 'Dr Leaver and I shall do the same in the sphere of education. Oh, it's been so long since I last saw him. So long since I was in California. I can't wait to talk with him, to share experiences face to face.'

Hugo groaned. 'Sounds a treat.'

'Don't knock it, Hugo,' said Sloman, mock-loftily. 'Educational theory is the reason you're here!'

Dan pulled a face. 'I'd say a trip to the movies is an education in itself.'

'Chiefly in promiscuity, crime and idleness.' Gillian looked around at the assembled company, unabashed. 'Wouldn't you agree, gentlemen?'

'God bless those noblest of occupations,' someone quipped. 'Not a damn plot without them.'

'Films are said to be the most potent influence on a country's national character,' said Sloman solemnly. 'Every week, twenty million people visit a picture house in Britain alone.'

'It's more like seventy million in America,' Rudolf Dürr put in, eavesdropping from the next table.

Why quote statistics for the USA and not Germany? James wondered dimly, fingers sore from restoring some of the blue-black lustre to his gun's barrel.

'Well, I'm sorry, Gillian, but I fully intend to quit the world of education for the world of the movies,' said Dan. 'Then it'll be glamour all the way!' His voice slipped into a clipped, American gangster accent. 'A cute dame, a thick wad of greenbacks, a fast car and all life's restrictions be hanged . . .'

'You think a film star lives a life free of restriction?' Gillian shook her head. 'Fame only makes you a prisoner.'

'I'd sooner keep my anonymity,' James agreed. 'I can think of few things worse than becoming a film star.'

The patchwork plains of middle America swept on below. Somehow the voyage took on more purpose now progress could be marked. Eagles soared about the silver giant, intruding on their space. Far below, James saw dried-up rivers in dead valleys, cattle crowding at watering holes, a landscape parched with reds and browns like it had sucked up too many sunsets. He pointed his gun-barrel at landmarks on the horizon and peered down her elevated sights, aiming at a dark and distant cloud . . .

James froze. The distant cloud was swelling like a purple bruise in the distance.

Abruptly, Captain Breithaupt stalked into the lounge. 'We are approaching a storm front from the northwest that may be quite violent,' he announced, typically matter-of-fact. 'You will close the windows, please? I'm afraid we must expect severe turbulence. We intend to reduce the stress of vertical gusts by flying low to the ground. Regretfully, waiter service is suspended until I say otherwise. I thank you for your cooperation.'

He left, and a low buzz travelled around the lounge as the seated passengers abandoned their pastimes and scattered to different windows, viewing the phenomenon for themselves. Dürr and Vasquez, together with Boody, Gillian, Dan and Sloman, crowded around James as he closed the window. The blue-black wall of cloud broiled across the horizon with frightening speed.

'If you'll excuse me,' said Hugo, looking unwell, 'I think I'm going to hide in my cabin for a week or two.'

As Hugo left the lounge, Vasquez put a hand on Sloman's shoulder. 'Hey, scribe, hope you've got a happy ending for us in hand!' He chuckled. 'Relax, troops. What's life without a little spice, huh? But I'm betting you knew that already, Miss de Vries – am I right? I know you West Coast broads.'

Gillian yawned loudly. Vasquez shot her a slightly bloody look.

'Don't worry, everyone. Kostler's crew have a fine record.' Sloman gave his nephew a reassuring smile, and extended it to James and Boody. 'They all know what they're doing.'

Tension was building in the lounge. Boody chewed at a broken fingernail, looking dead ahead. Dan pushed his hands into his pockets and puffed out his cheeks. Gillian seemed absorbed in a book, but James noticed she wasn't turning the pages.

The sky about them was darkening almost black. The hum in the engines had lowered as the airship started to drift downwards.

Abruptly the first squall hit. The *Allworld* tipped sharply, like a child's toy carelessly kicked. In a second the lounge filled with screams and flying furniture. Tables, chairs and people, all were flung like jacks across the room. James tumbled and skidded along the floor with the others in a confused scrum of limbs and blanched faces. Dürr hurtled just past him, smashed his back against the wall, gasped, 'By God!'

James crashed against a table the next moment and was showered with crockery. But all he could think was: *Dürr is meant to be German – but, taken by surprise, he swears in English with no accent . . . ?*

For a second there was breathless hush, then the airship dipped sharply as if going into a nosedive. James joined the helpless, scrabbling tide falling the other way. Boody was thrown against him; they clung together the length of the shiny floor, through a thick stream of spilled coffee, wine and marmalade. When the nightmare slide stopped at last and the room righted itself, they were lying on their sides, drenched and dishevelled. Boody looked at him, then down at herself – and burst into sudden laughter.

Her reaction broke the tension. Others laughed too as relief took hold.

Vasquez began righting chairs and helping people into them. 'Is anyone hurt?' the cry went up. Nobody seemed to be, not badly anyway.

Sloman looked up from the floor beside Dan. 'Quite an opening salvo.'

'I'll check on Hugo,' Gillian announced. She got to her feet, wiping bits of food from her clothes, and swept out of the lounge.

James pulled away from Boody, but their clothes were tangled together and she fell back against him. Their eyes met for a moment, and James could see she was afraid. So was he. The sky outside was unearthly on both sides, clouds blowing past in black tatters.

'I'll see if I can find any stewards to help clean up in here.' James disentangled himself from Boody, then got up and picked his way through the debris to the door that led onto the galley.

Two stewards were mopping up a big spill on the galley floor. One of the officers emerged from the control room, snapped for assistance and took them both into the lounge, where he faced an onslaught of passenger questions. James was suddenly left alone.

Behind him was the radio room, standing empty. He remembered the mystery of the impossible voices in the white headset, just a few days ago.

On impulse, James ran inside.

The headphones still lay under the desk. As [obscured]
up, he saw that the connecting cable actua[obscured]
hinged panel in the floor. He flipped it open[obscured]
headphone sockets in a panel beneath: two lines [obscured]

He tried a socket at random. At once a heated hubbub rose
from the tinny speakers – the same noise that was coming
from the lounge. Stunned, he sharply unplugged the 'phones
and tried two more sockets. One brought silence, but the other
allowed him to overhear Gillian soothing Hugo, who was
quietly sobbing in the cabin.

Our cabin, James realized. The crew here can listen in on
any private conversation, anywhere on the airship.

The hows and whys began to howl around his head. Then
the *Allworld* lurched to starboard, and a pounding clatter of
rain against the window reminded him that this was not the
time for thinking things out. He quickly replugged the 'phones
into their original socket, flipped down the lid of the panel,
and put the headset back as he'd found it. No sooner had he
staggered out of the radio room than Vasquez appeared in the
doorway. James remembered the hard grip, the steel in those
dark Hispanic eyes when he'd tried to use the white headphones; what would happen if Vasquez found out what he
knew?

'I slipped in the galley,' James blurted, pointing vaguely
at the mess with one hand, clutching the back of his head
with the other. 'Fell on my wound. Almost blacked out.'

'You did, huh?' Vasquez looked at James and nodded
slowly. 'Well, get yourself back inside, now. C'mon.'

'I'm OK,' James assured him, trying not to squirm. Had

verything they'd said since departure been overheard? What was the surveillance in aid of? Why was it being done?

Dürr watched as James came back in, his eyes round and bright. 'You are all right, young sir?' he asked, his accent hard and thick again, scratching at James's nerves. 'Do not be afraid. The squall will pass.'

James nodded, looked away. The darkness of the storm buffeted all around, but the weather had become the least of his concerns.

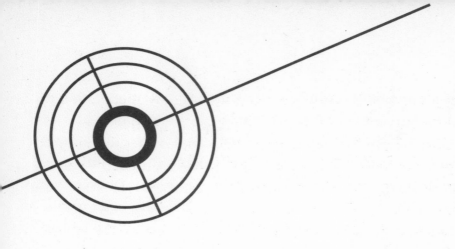

12

Among the Angelenos

The storm had spent the worst of its violence, and its dark clouds were melting into night as the airship moved on, low and slow over the land. James soon retired to his cabin to brood. Hugo lay glumly in the bunk below. The rain drummed against the window like bouts of machine-gun fire.

'I'm going to get a drink,' Hugo announced, sliding his little frame off the couch. 'Anything you want, James? Thimble of linseed oil for that pistol stock of yours, or—?'

'I'm fine,' James said, wondering who else might have heard the reply. Once Hugo had left the room, and with the racket of the rain for cover, James knelt up on the couch and placed his hands against the plasterboard ceiling. A panel that straddled the flimsy wall to the neighbouring cabin – Dan and his uncle's, empty right now – lifted a little. Forcing harder, James raised it several inches and peered hard into the murk. Sure enough, he saw a chunky microphone pressed into the recess beneath where the walkway must stretch overhead, its connecting lead snaking away towards the radio room.

James lowered the ceiling panel again. Only one microphone to cover two cabins? Well, he doubted the Dartington contingent had much to say of interest to whoever was monitoring conversation on board. But the rest of the passengers were key movers and shakers in their respective movie markets. He guessed they must have inside information that Allworld would be interested to know. And where were they more likely to talk candidly than in relaxed, luxurious surroundings, with nothing to do all day? The roofspace above *their* cabins was probably teeming with sound equipment.

James wondered if he should say something. But if he did, might it spoil Sloman's start with Kostler, or foul up the chance of funding that Dartington needed so badly?

He knew he would have to stay silent until they were off the *Allworld*, at least.

The secret sat badly with James, and cast gloom over his last hours aboard. He withdrew from his companions, sat alone, or slept, as the *Allworld* left the Rockies far behind and the high Sierras came slowly into view. He felt an impatience to return to normal life, to run again in a wider world.

By the afternoon on the third day they were over southern California. James had never seen anything like it. Sloping from epic mountain ranges down to the Pacific, the great Los Angeles plain stretched out for hundreds of square miles before them, a mosaic of rugged cliffs, forests and desert wastes, canyons gaping seawards, shores and strands and capes and bays. The city itself was spread flat, white and sun-bleached in all directions, taking whatever space could be found. From this height, the stucco buildings at the city limits seemed to break like surf over the fire-scarred foothills.

'Worth the trip, would you say?' Boody was at his shoulder.

James half smiled, rocking impatiently. 'I'm ready to get off.'

'Disembarkation will begin shortly!' Lenny Vasquez boomed as the *Allworld* drifted nose-first down over Mines Field. 'Woman and children first! Allworld limousines will be waiting to transfer you to your accommodation . . .'

Farewells were made with little fuss. Vasquez shook hands with Sloman and said he'd see him soon – then he'd tried to kiss Gillian goodbye, but she dodged smoothly and turned on her heel. James felt similarly when Herr Dürr, fedora in place, approached him to shake his hand in solemn farewell.

'Enjoy your stay in the city, young man,' he said, eyes bright. 'Take care of yourself.'

James nodded, half fearing that now, at the last, Fedora Man would finally choose to cast off this German persona, pull out a gun and try to finish what he'd started five thousand miles away. Instead, Dürr just nodded and went on his way, leaving James to mull over his paranoia once again.

The weather was warm, the sunlight like a caress on his skin. Once he'd left the mooring tower to pace the dark, packed adobe of the airfield, James looked up at the *Allworld* with mixed feelings. It had been a truly incredible trip, despite chancing on Kostler's dishonesty.

'After this, a steamer back home will be epically boring,' Dan complained.

Boody smiled. 'So follow in your uncle's footsteps and make it so big in Hollywood you never go back.'

Once Gillian had steered them through official inspections (with the 'unusual' air pistol still reduced to its component parts, it raised no eyebrows), James gave a long whistle of delight to find a fleet of smart cars outside the terminal building. One of the chauffeurs held a sign marked DE VRIES PARTY, standing beside a Cadillac V-16 landaulet-limousine.

'Our carriage awaits,' said Dan smugly. 'I suppose you've got your own limo, Uncle Stuart?'

'Actually, I'd like to ride with you all.' Sloman smiled a little awkwardly. 'We've come so far together, why split up now we've almost reached the end?'

Gillian grinned at him. 'We'll have to squeeze in.'

'So we shall,' he agreed.

James scrambled inside, his cares withering. From the chrome-plated door handles and window frames to the special disc wheel-covers and white-wall tyres, the whole automobile screamed luxury. The body was Madeira maroon, while the chassis, fenders and upper body moulding were finished in black, topped with a white leather roof. There was a collapsible roof portion over the rear quarters, folded back to allow in air, sunlight and envious glances. The spacious interior could accommodate three or four on the rear seat, with two more fold-down seats beneath the glass partition that separated them from their driver – who, of course, was on the left, not the right.

Hugo bounced in beside James and gave him such a

conspiratorial smile that he could only return it. He'd resolved to stay one step removed from the Dartington crowd, but Hugo and Boody in particular made easy companions.

That's all they are, James told himself.

'Our luggage will be sent on,' said Sloman. 'Next stop, the Hollywood Plaza!'

The limo pulled away, the warm breeze tugging at their hair as they rode in the seductive sunshine onto the asphalt sprawl of Sepulveda Boulevard. The city proper was eleven miles away, but even having come so far, James wished the noisy open-top ride could last for hours.

The first thing that struck James was the sheer *scale* of Los Angeles – the heady spaciousness of sky, land and sea gave him a sense of freedom he had never known. The city skyline was traced out in long low lines, so different from the jagged, high-rise contours he'd glimpsed in New York. The out-lying neighbourhoods whizzed by in a blur of stucco walls, red tiles, palms and eucalyptuses. After trolling along the timid backroads from Totnes to Cardington, James found the roads here superb – a vast, modern, well-maintained net-work, beetling with smooth and shiny automobiles. It was strange to see everyone driving on the wrong side of the road, stranger still to spot old-fashioned trams and trolleybuses peeping about here and there; but then James spotted mock-Tudor mansions rubbing rooftops with functional, modern residences, and traditional open-air markets mixing with busy malls. From small-town Latin charm to Hollywood glamour, Los Angeles played out to James like a massive open-air circus.

The traffic only slowed once, as a bustling crowd of men wielding placards spilled into the road. Cars started honking their horns – not in rebuke, but seemingly in support. James noted their limousine was drawing some filthy looks from some of the men.

'Demonstrators,' their chauffeur remarked, as though this were a dirty word. 'Big bunch of "have-nots" saying gimme, gimme.'

Sloman nodded as the crowd was cleared by police officers in dark, short-sleeved uniforms, and the traffic moved off again. 'It's not all glamour over here. After the Wall Street Crash back in '29, there's a lot of unemployment. The workers are trying to organize into unions and the employers don't like it.'

'This nation wasn't built on hand-outs,' the chauffeur grumbled.

'A fairer society might be,' Gillian shot back.

Besides muttering under his breath, their driver made no further comment the rest of the way to the hotel.

The Hollywood Plaza, boasting two hundred rooms across ten floors, had been built to capitalize on high-rolling visitors' need for luxury accommodation. Situated on Vine Street at Hollywood Boulevard, it soared from the pounding heartland of the movie business. However, as the Cadillac arrived outside in the dusty LA heat, James's first impression was faintly disappointing. The hotel looked unremarkable – tall and austere, the stone shone in the sunshine, a maroon canopy standing over the entrance.

An attentive concierge swooped onto Gillian as she stepped out of the landaulet onto the busy sidewalk. Soon, the party's hand baggage was stacked high on a gold-painted luggage trolley and the doorman, seven solid feet of velvet and braid, was holding open a big door and ushering them through.

Once out of the stultifying heat in a haven of marble, James was better impressed. The high, carved ceiling was studded with chandeliers, each a nest of intricate wrought iron ringed with fat, blazing bulbs. Patterned silk draperies dressed the picture windows in red and gold. Fresh floral displays all about added colour and drama, their scent as thick as the pile on the bold-patterned carpets.

As Gillian and Mr Sloman crossed to the front desk to get them checked in, a weary Dan and Boody joined Hugo on an elegant sofa in the reception area. James prowled about, exploring further. Adjacent to the lobby were a barbershop, a smoking room, a cigar counter and a beauty parlour. The prices were so high you had to crane your neck, and all about were well-heeled men and glamorous women. James felt conspicuously scruffy. He noticed Sloman was looking around as well. He seemed nervous.

Within minutes, Gillian called over that she had the room-keys. A final ascent to the fourth floor in the carpeted lift – itself as big as his old room at Eton – and James felt a bittersweet thrill to think that the odyssey from Dartington to Los Angeles was finally ended.

Dr Leaver had arranged two neighbouring family rooms for the Academy's guests – one for Boody and Gillian, and one for James, Dan and Hugo.

'As for me, I'm up on the ninth floor,' said Sloman.

'You've gone up in the world already,' joked Gillian. 'That bodes well for your first day tomorrow.'

Sloman smiled. 'I suppose so! Well, I'll leave you to settle. Mr Kostler asked me to phone him once I'd arrived.' He headed for the stairwell. 'See you later.'

No wonder he seemed nervous, thought James vaguely, but his attention was taken up by the place that would be home for the next six days – a smart, modern room with indigo walls and a carpet in French grey. Twin beds lay either side of a wide, tall window; the grumble of traffic and the singing sigh of a streetcar blew in on a breeze like hot breath from Hollywood Boulevard. He supposed he would have to fight it out with Hugo and Dan for who got relegated to the sleeper-sofa, but after their bunks on board the *Allworld*, he imagined that too would seem blissfully comfortable. There was also a reclining chair, a writing desk with a stool tucked under it, and various stylish ashtrays and magazine stands.

One extra luxurious touch was the en-suite bathroom, tiled in pastel green. James strolled in to find a fly buzzing about, exploring the white linen towels. *No paradise is perfect*, he reflected. He supposed most guests would tell the bellboy to take care of the fly, and perhaps give him a larger tip. But with the boys' bags delivered, the young porter had already moved on to settle in Gillian and Boody.

'Ahhh!' Hugo's sigh was eloquence itself as he collapsed onto one of the beds.

'We've fallen on our feet here,' Dan agreed.

'The big question is . . .' James had rolled up a towel and now thwacked at the fly. It was too fast for him. 'Who's having the sleeper-sofa?'

'Hugo,' said Dan. 'No need to turn it out into a bed, the little man'll fit on it as it is. Save the poor maid some work.'

'That's right, mock the afflicted,' said Hugo.

Comments like that must hurt, for all he makes light of it, James thought. 'With a writer in the family, I'd have thought you'd have better material, Dan.' He thwacked a little harder at the bluebottle. 'Anyway, I don't mind taking the couch.'

'Noble of you, James!' Hugo called.

'Not really. I've just had enough of you snoring in my ear.'

'What? But I never snore!'

True, but Dan doesn't know that. James smiled and carried on his deception. 'Every night in that cabin was hell. As for all the tossing and turning, the mumbling—'

'Come, now, this is fiction!'

'You know, I think I'll plump for the sleeper-sofa myself.' Through the open door, James saw Dan wrestle the couch across the room, as far from the twin beds as he could manage. 'You don't mind too much, do you, James?'

James shrugged as, with another whipcrack of the towel, the fly finally met its end on the mirror and fell to the vanity unit beneath.

'Got you,' he murmured, and strode back into the bed-room.

Hugo gave James an approving and conspiratorial wink. 'It's funny, being back on solid ground,' he remarked. 'You know, I'll never forget that journey.'

'Well, just in case you do,' said James, 'you can always ask the crew of the *Allworld* to tell you everything that was said.'

Dan and Hugo looked baffled.

'I can tell you now. There were listening devices on board the *Allworld*.' James got on with unpacking. 'I hope your uncle knows the sort of people he's working for, Dan.'

'Listening devices?' Dan shook his head. 'Nonsense!'

'There was a set of special headphones in the radio room,' James insisted, and outlined all he had found out.

'Those lumps on the head have made you delusional, James,' Dan scoffed. 'What absolute rot you talk.'

'It's true.' James folded his arms. 'There was a loose ceiling panel over our two cabins. The microphone had been placed in there. There must've been more like it all over the airship.'

Hugo looked affronted. 'And you didn't tell me?'

'Because it didn't happen,' Dan insisted. 'I *made* that ceiling panel loose the first night aboard. When I looked inside I didn't spot any—'

'It was on our side of the cabin divide, and it was dark . . .' James tailed off, thinking back. 'I heard someone creeping about that first night. It was you. *Why* did you loosen that panel?'

Dan turned away. 'Just by accident.'

'What were you up to?' James persisted.

'I . . . Look, I was just hiding something, all right?'

James stared at him. 'The reel from the Alhambra?'

Dan didn't speak. His face said it all.

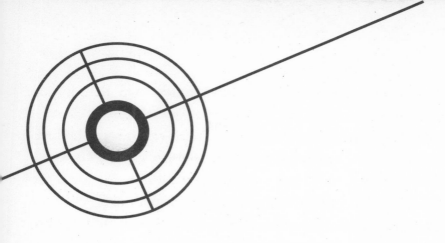

13

All the Stage Is a World

James gripped hold of Dan's arm. 'What in the world possessed you to bring that reel away with us?'

'Get off me!' Cheeks reddening, Dan pulled himself free. 'Listen . . . the morning we left England I phoned my parents to say goodbye. It came out that they'd been burgled like Uncle Stuart . . . and so had several other employees at the Alhambra, Crispin the dead projectionist included.'

'Who the dead *what*?' Hugo looked horrified.

'Never mind,' said James quickly. 'Crispin's place was most likely the first to be turned over, if whoever did it was after that film.'

'Exactly. And after all we went through with that reel, well, I didn't want to think of it being taken from Dartington Hall while we were gone. So I brought it along.' Dan shrugged. 'When you started raving that Fedora Man was on board . . . well, I thought I'd best hide the wretched thing.'

James stared. 'I thought you didn't believe me.'

'I didn't. Not really. But best to play safe, I thought.'

'You mean Alhambra Crispin is dead?' Hugo perched on his bed, ashen. 'The one you got the reel from, Dan? How did that happen?'

James cut in. 'Look, Dan, where is that reel now?'

Dan hesitated. 'I . . . took it out when we stopped at New Jersey. Got Uncle Stuart to send it back home for me.'

'Using the naval base's post room,' James realized.

'He doesn't know what it really is . . . and I thought, well, they've searched Father's house once, it should be safe by the time it arrives back there.' Dan looked at James. 'You really think you saw a microphone up there?'

'And I really heard voices through the earpiece,' James repeated. 'Kostler obviously keeps tabs on his Very Important Guests while they're on board.'

Hugo looked deep in thought. 'If Kostler's having this big meeting where they share knowledge, I suppose he wants to be sure they're telling him the truth.'

James considered. 'Yes, that makes sense. Perhaps it's not as black as I paint it.'

There was a sudden bang on the door. James held his breath. For a moment the three boys looked at each other with dread.

'Anyone there?' called Stuart Sloman, rattling the door handle.

James and Hugo fell back on their respective beds in pantomime relief, Dan quietly crossed to the door and opened it.

'Good news, boys!' Sloman burst in, arms held out

expansively. 'I've just been talking with Mr Kostler himself.' He seemed pleased and relieved now, nerves subsided. 'To welcome me to the fold, he's arranged a private, all-areas, exclusive tour of Allworld Studios first thing tomorrow morning . . . and as a thank you for taking part in Dr Leaver's tests at the Academy this week, he's invited you all to join me!'

Dan's eyes widened. 'Seriously?'

'Gillian's giving it a miss. She's hoping to meet Dr Leaver.' He smiled. 'Of course, I know tomorrow is your settling in and sort-out-your-sleep-clock day ahead of the good doctor's tests, so if you're too tired . . . ?'

'Tired?' Hugo sprang off the bed and struck an athletic pose. 'Never.'

'Thank you, Mr Sloman.' James smiled. 'That would be marvellous.'

Sloman smiled back. 'Well, we must take all the chances that come our way, mustn't we?'

As the excitement of arrival faded, and tensions sustained on the *Allworld* ebbed, James felt done in. Luggage arrived as promised, and after unpacking – and some lacklustre sanding of his pistol stock – he joined the others in an early night. But after crossing so many time zones in the airship his body clock was scrambled. Lying awake at four in the morning, it was strange to think that across the world in England it was already noon. What was Beatrice Judge doing now? Hating his guts, no doubt. Another enemy made; another who would not forget.

Sleep came finally, and when he woke the next morning it was later than planned; like Dan and Hugo he had slept through the call for breakfast. There was barely time to wash and dress before joining Boody and a sharp-suited Sloman in the back of the Cadillac.

While the others talked, James again allowed the landscape to absorb his attention. He watched a red tram rattle past, stared out at palms and sequoias and billboards, shielded his eyes from the sun's relentless glare.

The limousine passed the first of several vast, hangar-sized buildings that stood edge on to the street, beyond a chainlink fence and a parking lot. The buildings were daubed in huge letters with slogans: ALLWORLD STUDIOS – WHERE DREAMS AND ENTERTAINMENT SOAR on one, and ALLWORLD PICTURES – THE GLOBAL HIT STUDIOS on another.

Turning into the entrance, they approached a security hut where the barrier was duly raised. As the driver parked up, a big, dark-suited man approached the car.

Sloman pulled nervously at his tie. 'I think our tour guide has arrived!'

The door was opened, and the man leaned in. He was in his mid-fifties perhaps, with grey, bushy hair. The eyes beneath the heavy lids were sharp hazel. 'Mr Sloman?' The voice was deep, gravelly, mid-western. 'I'm George Barron, Head of Security.' He held out a hand to be shaken. 'Welcome to Allworld Pictures.'

Sloman took the hand and introduced his young charges as they got out of the car.

James regarded Barron with quiet wonder. The expression 'a bear of a man' came to his mind. What was he? Six-foot-six? Seven? His paunch looked set to burst through the white tailored shirt, but this extra bulk only added to an aura of strength. There was strength in his face too – weathered and pockmarked, the nose broad and broken, Barron looked as if he'd lived hard, through tough times.

'Glad to meet you in person, Mr Sloman. I've heard so much about you it feels like we already know each other.' Barron smiled reassuringly. 'Mr Kostler's looking forward to introducing himself. Asked me to show you all around.'

'Excellent, excellent.' Sloman smiled self-consciously, and James saw Dan glowing with reflected pride. 'I'm sure you're very busy, though. I'll understand if—'

'Mr Kostler asked me to show you around,' Barron repeated, 'so that's what I'll do.' He smiled. 'Would you come with me, please, people?'

'Try and stop us,' said Dan quietly as Hugo rubbed his hands. Boody gave James a sideways smile. She was looking radiant in a red cotton dress with a square neck, her hair rolling with voluptuous curls. He ignored her, and she looked away, walking on ahead of him.

Feeling a moment's regret, James trailed the party into the studio proper. It was like stumbling into a surreal village where a hundred lifestyles clashed. The roads were wide, populated with cars and catering trucks, extras and crew. A platoon of nineteenth-century guardsmen were scattered in a most unmilitary fashion by a cabriolet, honking impatiently. Fake houses, only their fronts standing, made a row before the mountains, and beyond them, kissing the black iron of a mooring mast, was the hard, bald silver of another airship: the smaller sister of the *Allworld* that Hugo had mentioned, the *Zelda*, named for the mogul's late wife. It was an icon of grace and power, floating dreamlike above the walled town's many worlds.

Anton Kostler had style, James conceded.

'Is Mr Kostler up there now?' asked Dan excitedly.

Barron nodded. 'It's his office, boardroom and bedroom all in one . . .'

'He even sleeps up there?' James marvelled.

'He doesn't like sleeping in the house any more. Ever since Zelda died, eight years back.' Barron crossed himself. 'Their old bedroom he's left just as it was. Now he sleeps among the dreams of the good people of Los Angeles. That's where he gets all his ideas and inspiration . . .' He winked at Sloman. 'Well, that's what the press boys put about, at least.'

'Did you know Zelda?' Boody asked, but Barron shook his head. 'How did she die?'

'Kidney failure. Tough break. Her dying hit the boss hard.' Barron shrugged. 'From then on, it's been just him and the kid.'

'Martyn Kostler,' James ventured. 'The boy who goes to Dr Leaver's academy?'

'The Kostler Academy,' Barron corrected him. 'That's right.'

The big man led them to a line of low-speed buggies chained together, and over the next two hours drove them into different worlds. Several sets had been built outside in the open — they drove past lakes and swampland, over bridges, through ships run aground and round the back of three-quarter-scale houses. The buggies kept moving, past machine shops, a foundry, processing labs, large administration buildings stuffed with clerks and stenographers taking care of the books and bills – and a vast workshop where props were built and sets assembled.

While Barron broke off the tour to take a telephone call, James surreptitiously helped himself to ball bearings in various sizes lying on a workbench, potential projectiles for his pistol, should he ever manage to put it back together.

'Excellent,' Boody murmured, sifting through some washers beside him. 'One of these might help shore up your pistol's broken breech seal.'

'Hope so,' said James. He supposed that Sloman was right – you had to take every chance that came.

Barron wasn't gone long. Resuming the tour, he explained that there were maybe 3,000 workers at the studios in 300 different trades, remorselessly pursuing the business of making motion pictures. But it was the vast soundstages, so character-less and industrial on the outside, but so magical within, that captured James's imagination the most. Each one was its own little world, and Barron granted them a privileged peek inside: one held a wide-open wilderness, another the hallway of a country house, still another a railway station, complete with sham train poised to pull away into the wall opposite. Each was crowded with crew members. Men held micro-phones from long poles over actors finding their marks, or steered bulky cameras about in black, soundproofed casings like miniature wagons.

Then, suddenly, the bustling scene on the main soundstage came to a stop. A man had arrived on the scene, and an electric atmosphere built as he moved. People stopped what they were doing and watched respectfully. Or perhaps a little afraid.

With a start, James recognized the man. 'Anton Kostler?'

Boody nodded. 'I'd say that portrait hanging in the *Allworld* was painted some time ago.'

Kostler looked to be in his fifties now. Lean and a little smaller than James, he nevertheless exuded a presence of power. His dark hair was greying, swept back from his head, the temples crowded with tight curls. As he walked towards the visitors he maintained a haughty aspect, eyes big and dark like those of some predatory cat. Everything, from the well-cut grey suit and black kid-leather gloves to the soft shine of his Italian shoes, suggested elegance and wealth.

Sloman had turned pale. 'Mr Kostler . . .'

Kostler smiled and scrutinized his new investment. 'Mr Sloman. Or may I call you Stuart? Welcome.' He turned to address the wider group. 'Welcome to you all. I trust you enjoyed your passage from Great Britain aboard the *Allworld*?'

James added his approval and thanks to the hubbub that followed. 'It was a real privilege.'

'An education, too, I hope.' Kostler steepled his gloved fingers. 'I believe that one day we shall all travel by sky-ship.'

Sloman looked awkwardly around at the children. 'These are the pupils from Dartington Hall School that Dr Leaver—'

'Yes. So I assumed.' Kostler swept a cool, impersonal gaze over each in turn, lingering on Hugo and Boody a little longer than on James and Dan. Then he inclined his head. 'The rising generation is of the utmost importance to us, here. Our movies must cater for your disparate tastes, your dreams, your hungers. We must speak truths to your desires . . .' He smiled again at Dan's uncle. 'And you and I must speak too, of course, Mr Sloman. We still have some terms and conditions to discuss, do we not? I'd like to settle things without delay.'

'Oh . . . ?' Sloman looked flustered, checked his watch. 'I'm sorry, I thought we had another hour until—'

'There are many matters requiring my attention, as I'm sure you appreciate.' Kostler turned to each of the children in turn. 'I'm sorry to cut short your tour, but trust you have enjoyed your time here?' James joined in the mutterings of thanks and reassurance. 'Splendid. Now, Mr Barron will escort you back to your transport.'

With that, he turned and strode away.

'Yes. Very well. Of course.' Sloman looked a little shell-shocked. 'Right. Dan, everyone, I'll . . . see you later, back at the hotel.'

'Good luck, Uncle Stuart,' Dan called as Sloman raised a hand and headed after Kostler.

Barron turned to James and the others, the big grin back in place. 'So! I'll see you guys are driven back to your hotel right away.'

'Really, there's no rush,' Hugo assured him.

'Right away,' Barron confirmed, steel behind the patient smile.

As they were led back to the main gates, James marvelled once again at the half-finished houses with perfect fronts and nothing but space and scaffolding behind their windows.

Then he was out through the metal door and into the California sunshine. Walking past a line of stuccoed offices with manicured gardens, they reached the parking lot. Their chauffeur was cleaning the Cadillac. He saw them approach and held open the rear door.

'OK, people.' Barron held up a paw-like hand in farewell. 'So long. Give my best to Dr Leaver when you see him, OK?'

'We will, sir. Thank you.' Boody stepped inside. Dan tried to sit beside her, but quick as a flash, Hugo wormed his way into the middle.

'I'm not good with cars. I need to see out clearly,' Hugo insisted. 'It's either that or I'm sick in someone's lap.' He patted Boody's hand. 'Don't worry, I'll aim Dan's way.'

Boody laughed. As James pulled down the rear-facing seat, he heard Dan mutter darkly under his breath. Then the limo pulled away, signalled right and swung out into the heavy traffic.

After a few minutes, their chauffeur was butting through the busy traffic lanes, signalling a left turn off the Boulevard.

Boody looked about. 'We didn't come this way, did we?'

James shook his head. 'I expect it's quicker, this time of day.'

After taking a couple of right turns, the sound of angry shouting rose above the wind and the engine's thrum. The chauffeur braked sharply as a scuffle on the sidewalk between two waiters and a group of men spilled into the road, angry voices rising over appeals for calm. Beyond them, the way ahead was blocked by maybe a hundred people jeering, shouting and waving banners. The slogans screamed END STARVATION WAGES and WORK PROJECTS NOW. The long wail of nearing police sirens was adding to the din.

Dan looked anxious. 'It's some sort of demonstration.'

A man with a loudhailer was standing on a chair outside an upmarket restaurant. 'See? The bosses fill their faces while the workers starve,' he shouted. 'They have more courses at a single luncheon than our families have in a week . . . !'

'Flaunting our luxury automobile in front of the impoverished masses isn't the most sensitive course of action,' Hugo noted. 'Can't we please move?'

'The engine's cut out,' James realized.

'It's broken down.' Their chauffeur climbed out of the car. 'I'm sorry. Stay here, I'll call for a tow.'

'Wait!' Dan shouted after the man as he ran off. 'You can't just leave us . . .'

But the chauffeur had already disappeared.

A big black Lincoln screamed round the corner and swerved up behind the Cadillac. It stopped so close it seemed that the silver greyhound mascot on its radiator cap was sniffing out the children. Three men, faces grey as their suits but not nearly so smart, piled out of the Lincoln and set off down the street. One of them carried a large, box-like object.

Boody stared. 'A camera?'

'Perhaps they're journalists,' said Hugo. 'Maybe it's a press car.'

The three men split up and pushed their separate ways into the thickening crowd. Some of the placard wavers were pounding on the windows of the fancy restaurant, egged on by the man with the loudhailer.

'This isn't a protest.' James gripped his seat uneasily. Angry faces had started turning towards the Cadillac. 'These people are ready to riot!'

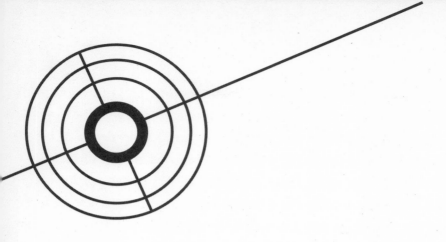

14

Down These Mean Streets

Heart beginning to race, James looked around for their chauffeur, but he was still nowhere to be seen. As Hugo had feared, their limousine was giving fresh focus for the crowd's frustrations. 'Hey, check the set of wheels!' came one jeering cry.

'Me, I can't afford to ride the tram!'

'Look at those spoiled brats thinking they're better than us!'

'Oh God,' said Dan nervously. 'What do we do?'

'We get out and run for it,' James decided, rising from his seat, reaching for the door-handle.

As he did so, one of the men from the Lincoln – the biggest of the three – reappeared to bar his way.

'Look here, it's the bosses' kids!' he hollered. 'C'mon, let's teach these fancy kids a lesson!'

James glared up at him. 'What the hell—?'

In moments, angry men were swarming around the

Cadillac, pressing up against the doors, shouting loud enough to drown out the still-approaching sirens.

Boody shrank from the hostile faces. Hugo slid down in his seat to cower on the floor, while Dan seemed frozen in shock. As the limo was rocked this way and that, James sank to his haunches between the fold-down seats, his back to the glass partition, avoiding eye contact with their attackers for fear of inciting the crowd further. He didn't know what to do. 'They're only trying to scare us,' he said uncertainly.

There was a crash of glass and a sickening cheer, and James turned in time to see the post of a placard reduce the Cadillac's windshield to glittering shrapnel. A second later, Boody screamed – James saw the big man from the Lincoln had seized Dan by the collar and was trying to haul him out.

'No!' Dan's voice was choked. 'Let me go!'

James lunged forward and grabbed Dan by the legs. 'Help me, someone, for God's sake!'

Some of the men were backing away, wanting no more part of this side-attack. Then a fierce whoosh of flames from across the street pulled more away, cheering, as a motorcar was set on fire. James choked as the oily stink scorched the back of his throat, but kept clinging onto Dan. Boody grabbed the man's arm, digging in with her nails. She yelped as he swatted her aside, but at the same moment, Hugo burst up from the floor and launched himself at the man's head.

'Hugo, be careful, you crazy—' James broke off as Dan fell back inside the car, the grip on him broken at last. Hugo was holding the big man by the ears, his torso smothering the man's face.

James jumped from the limo to help, Boody just behind

him – too late. The man tore Hugo clear and hurled him down on the sidewalk.

'No!' James felt anger flame through fear as he shoved their attacker back against the car. This bullying violence was nothing to do with protesting pay and conditions; and no matter the odds, he was ready to stand up to whoever saw fit to deal it out.

But before he could follow up, he saw Boody had whipped off one of her strappy shoes – with a grunt of anger she swung the pointed heel into the hood's forehead. He yelped, eyes shut, dropping to his knees.

Emboldened, James aimed a vicious kick at the big man's chest. There was a satisfying thump and the hood fell over backwards – and stayed there.

'Oh hell.' Boody coughed on fumes, covered her mouth, shocked eyes wide. 'We haven't killed him, have we?'

'He'll live.' James turned to help Hugo – but the boy had gone. A few men pushed past, shirtfronts pulled up over their faces, oily smoke that stung James's eyes gusting after them. A truck had now been set ablaze too. Fights were breaking out, the violence escalating. The whole street had gone to hell in what seemed like moments. One figure was calm, however – the man from the Lincoln with the camera. He was standing on a ground-floor window ledge along the street, wreathed in smoke, cranking the handle of his movie camera.

'He's filming all this. He *must* be press . . .' Boody shook her head. 'So why would his friend attack us?'

'Attack *me*, you mean.' Crouched inside the car, Dan looked badly shaken. 'It's like he brought that mob over here as cover while he grabbed me!'

'Always got to be about you, hasn't it,' James muttered. He opened the door and helped Dan climb out. 'Get out of here, both of you. I'll look for Hugo.'

'We all will,' said Boody.

'No.' He took her arm and looked meaningfully at Dan beside her, white-faced, clearly terrified. 'Do you have money for a cab?'

Boody nodded. 'But—'

'Back to the hotel, then. We'll see you there.'

'Yes, c-come on, Boody,' Dan pleaded. 'I'll . . . make sure you're all right.'

'My hero.' Boody sighed, took him by the hand and led him away. 'Watch yourself, James.'

But James had already turned, heading for the thick of things.

He crouched low, keeping tucked in to the wall as he moved, looking all about for Hugo, trying to anticipate and dodge any danger. He couldn't see the man with the camera now . . . and where the hell were the police? The question was answered when he saw two cops face down on the other side of the street. James felt sick. They couldn't have been expecting all this to kick off . . . but clearly the press were more prepared.

For a moment he flashed back to the grainy violence playing silently in the dark over the makeshift screen at Film Club. Now James felt as if he'd fallen through the screen; the fear and the clamour were all around him. He winced as a jangling, ear-splitting crash was greeted by a huge collective cheer – the plate-glass front of the fancy restaurant had shattered inwards, and one of the masked men held his bat aloft in triumph. Bells and sirens sounded — more police? An ambulance or fire engine, maybe?

Hugo, where are you?

'Listen to me!' A large police officer, his nose swollen and bloody, had climbed onto the roof of a battered cherry-red Ford. He made a dramatic figure, smoke blowing around him, holding up his bruised hands in an appeal for calm. 'There are disruptive people here who are not protestors. They are deliberately inciting the violence, and if you let them—'

James heard a dull crack. The cop's collar was suddenly crimson. Blood was flooding from his neck. 'He's been shot!' someone screamed. The cop pawed at his throat like he was trying to find the hole, gurgling and gasping. Then he lost his balance and pitched over backwards, striking the sidewalk with a smack almost at James's feet.

A flurry of shouts, and men rushed to the cop's side, pushing James aside — 'What happened?' they were asking. 'What the hell happened?'

James backed away across the street as more cops moved in, some with day-sticks, some with firearms, taking charge.

'*Up against the wall! All of you, move!*'

'*Back away! Paramedics coming through.*'

James reached the far side of the road, rubbed his stinging eyes. No sign of Hugo. The protestors were scattering now — those who were able. The street was in turmoil. Men and women lay moaning on the tarmac. Broken glass crunched underfoot. There was no sign of the cameraman from the Lincoln, but now a man in a trilby hat was taking pictures with a stills camera — a police photographer or a journalist?

Either way, James hid his face and ducked into an alley that ran alongside the beat-up restaurant.

Almost immediately he stopped, his guts jumping.

A figure stood at the far end of the alley, lurking behind another Lincoln parked there. James recognized the face beneath the fedora brim at once. It was Rudolf Dürr.

'Herr Dürr!' James called, but the man ducked nimbly out of sight – a far cry from the stiff, ponderous movements he'd employed on the *Allworld*. Why on earth was he here? James ran after him, squeezing past the black Lincoln model L, parked with its front facing him, its brawny chassis squared up to the brickwork either side. It was the twin of the motor that had roared up behind Kostler's Cadillac.

Something reached out and closed around James's ankle from behind the rear tyre. He froze at the sound of a muffled voice. 'I'd recognize those scuffed brogues anywhere.'

'Hugo?' James ducked down behind the trunk of the car. 'What the . . . ?'

'I got up from the sidewalk in a daze. Think I ran the wrong way.' The boy's head poked out from beneath the chrome bumper; a livid bruise caked in dirt and oil stained the left side of his face from temple to cheekbone. 'Didn't get very far, did I? Stout heart but short legs.' Despite the flippant tone he looked very sorry for himself, and James couldn't blame him.

'I was trying to find you,' James muttered. 'Instead, I found Rudolf Dürr.'

Hugo frowned. 'Our fedora-wearing fellow passenger?'

'And possibly the man who tried to kill me in the Alhambra.'

James was about to help Hugo out from under the Lincoln, when the sound of footfalls filled the alley. Men running from the warzone in the boulevard, coming their way. Police, protestors – or gunmen?

'Budge up,' James hissed, wriggling underneath the Lincoln beside his friend. 'Hide till they've gone.'

He held his breath as the running footsteps got nearer. Then swore silently as the doors were opened, the car rocking as several men squeezed inside. There was a hollow clatter. The undercarriage grazed against James's head and he pressed himself flat to the filthy ground. Doors closed and low voices carried:

'You should've dumped the bats, Marino. What if the cops stop and search?'

'They'll find my shooter too, won't they? Don't sweat, his lordship's got our back.'

'You sure you got it on film? If the Kid's happy, that could mean plenty extra—'

'Quit your yapping, my head's killing me.'

'Ha! That little Brit miss got you good . . .'

The engine started up, deafening in James's ears. He turned frantically to Hugo. 'They're going to pull away with us under here!'

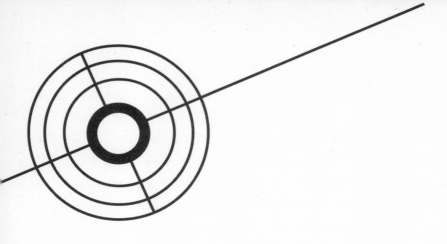

15

The Story of Tori Wo

'Hold damn still!' James hissed to Hugo – as the whole car shook with the revs and then roared away, the vehicle's transmission nearly scalping James as it tore overhead. Luckily the alley was too narrow for the Lincoln to go any way but straight forward; all four wheels missed him and Hugo. And while they were now lying out in the open, exposed, the heavy automobile took the sharp corner at the end before the driver could spot them in his mirrors.

James caught a glimpse of the licence plate – the last two numbers were 09 in white-on-black numbers, with ILL 30 printed smaller to the right, the letters stacked wonkily above the numerals.

'Oh-nine ill thirty,' James muttered under his breath, over and over.

'For my own mantra, I'll try, "Thank you, sweet Lord, for our deliverance."' Hugo groaned. 'That was too much. Were those the same men as in the other Lincoln, the one that blocked us in?'

James nodded. 'Two of them at least. The man with the camera we saw. And the one with the sore head must be the man who attacked us – Boody clobbered him.'

'Brave as her warrior-queen, correctly spelled namesake.' Hugo hugged himself. 'James, will you pinch me to prove I'm still alive? Daren't do it myself, I'm not brave enough.'

'Not brave? The way you threw yourself into the fray?'

Hugo shrugged. 'I was simply aiming for the exit. He was in my way.'

'That's brave enough.' James obliged him with a pinch on the arm, and Hugo gasped. 'There. We're not dead yet.'

'What about Dan and Boody?'

'Got a cab back to the hotel, I hope.' James got up unsteadily and jogged to the end of the alley. He surveyed the street, but there was no sign of the man in the fedora. 'Perhaps Dürr caught a cab too.'

'He might just have been dining at the restaurant, you know,' said Hugo. 'Happenstance.'

'Perhaps.' James held out a hand to Hugo. The boy got to his feet, but it was touch and go whether he'd stay there. 'If there's an ambulance nearby, perhaps we should get you into it.'

'Never!' said Hugo. 'I hate hospitals. Just the smell of them makes me feel faint.'

James caught a movement by the Boulevard end of the alley. A harried-looking police officer was positioning a wooden sign marked POLICE – CRIME SCENE, KEEP OUT. He saw James and Hugo. 'You two, beat it!' he hollered. 'Nothing to see.'

'See, be blowed! We lived *through* your crime scene!' Hugo protested. 'We're victims!'

'Button it, shorty,' the cop called back. 'We've got enough to deal with.' He walked briskly away, pursued by a small irate crowd demanding help and answers.

'I think perhaps we should talk to the police when they're less engrossed,' said Hugo. 'And when my head stops spinning.'

Keeping quiet around the police had become a habit, James reflected. 'Do you have cash for a taxi?'

'My meagre spending money's back at the hotel.' Hugo puffed out his cheeks. 'Never fret. I'll be all right.'

James checked his own pockets. 'I think you'll have to be. I only have a handful of ball bearings and some small change.'

'Wretched business.' Hugo tottered forward uncertainly. 'Hollywood, land of dreams. Ha!'

By the time James and Hugo made it round the block, the whole Boulevard had been barricaded off. A crowd had gathered to gawp; the road itself was now rammed with police cars and ambulances. Firemen had extinguished the blazing vehicles, and police were taking statements from a long queue of witnesses. Kostler's Cadillac stood where the driver had dumped it, dented and smashed, but the Lincoln that had pulled up behind was nowhere to be seen.

'We should report our chauffeur,' Hugo fumed. 'Ditching us in the middle of that.'

James nodded as he walked on with Hugo, questions biting at his mind. Had the chauffeur been *told* to bring them here and then to take off? Had Dan narrowly escaped abduction, because he knew the whereabouts of the reel? Where did their fedora-wearing friend fit into things?

'Dürr said he was high up in the *Reichsfilmkammer*,' James muttered, 'founded by the Nazis to protect German film production. And Dan said the man in the film being tortured was high up in British films . . .'

'You reckon there's a link?' Hugo hoisted an eyebrow – and winced as it stretched his bruised temple. 'I thought you'd stopped thinking of Dürr as your would-be assassin?'

'Now I've seen him again, I don't know what to think,' James admitted. 'But if our chauffeur brought us to a riot scene deliberately, he must've been following orders.'

'I hope you're letting your imagination run away with you . . .' Hugo looked pale and sweaty, which threw the dirt and bruising into sharper relief. 'Hold on. I must just . . . sit down a moment.'

James helped Hugo to a bench on the sidewalk. 'I'll scout ahead and see if there's a chemist. I'm sure I've got enough for some cotton wool and iodine – you'll feel better once you're cleaned up.'

'Thanks, James,' Hugo said gratefully.

James hurried along the street, scanning the windows on every block. A few minutes later, on the corner of Wilcox and Yucca, he found a drugstore with fancy signage promising everything from paint for hard corns to a soda fountain.

Inside, ceiling fans cooled the air. A marble countertop ran along the left side of the room, staffed by two waiters in white. A bewildering array of drinks and desserts was on offer, from banana royals to cherry-red specials – whatever they might be. James was gasping for a drink; he slapped a nickel on the counter for a lemonade and gulped it down a little guiltily. Perhaps he could buy one to take out for Hugo, if funds stretched to it after the first aid.

Smacking his lips, James crossed to the well-stocked wooden shelves on the far side of the room, scanning them for cotton wool and liniment. As he worked his way towards the back of the store he saw a woman dressed incongruously in a man's pinstripe suit with short, straight black hair. She was using the coin phone: a dark-green box mounted on the wall inside a booth. Waving the conical earpiece around her head, she was speaking into the receiver with mounting impatience.

'Come on, Oscar, what kind of an editor are you? You think I ran the whole way from the riot to this two-bit drug-store for my health? This angle will set the *Record* apart from every other paper! Before he got shot, "Iron Cop" Peters knew someone was stirring up the violence – just like at that demo in Old Chinatown last month. You know he's about the only captain in the whole damn force who won't take bribes from the mob – taking him out sends a big-time message to every other honest cop. Dammit, I'm out of pennies.' She looked behind her, noticed James. And James certainly noticed her. She was in her late twenties, perhaps, with honey-coloured skin and striking oriental features. 'Hey, you! Got any pennies?'

He looked at her blankly. 'Er, you mean, British money?'

'Why the hell would I be asking you for British money?' She turned her dark eyes heavenwards. 'I'm talking one-cent pieces for the phone so I can call through this story to my dumbass editor before the evening edition hits the presses.' She held out her hand, expectantly. 'Come on! Pennies!'

Taken aback, James found himself offering her both of the 'pennies' he'd found in his pocket. The woman took them distractedly without thanks and rammed them into the phone-box coin slot. 'You still there, Oscar? Yes, I did call you a dumbass. At least I tell it to you straight instead of behind your back like all the others, right? Now, will you listen? One of Allworld's limousines was at the scene of the crime . . .'

James turned back to the rows of lotions and liniments, but all his attention was on the woman's words.

'That ties it all in, don't you get it? Everyone knows the Chicago mob's active in Los Angeles now. Everyone knows Hollywood and gangsters got a mutual love-thing going. And our friend Junior lets gangsters pick him up from school! All right, *alleged* gangsters . . . all right, alleged by *me . . .*'

James thought gangsters made it all sound like something out of the pictures. But who was 'Junior'?

'What d'you mean, no hard evidence? I got you pictures. I got someone on the case in Chicago working to ID those hoods so we can dig up all the bad stuff they did, and blam! There's your link. And Tori Wo, star reporter, gets a *sensational* scoop.' The woman drummed her fingers against the wall impatiently. 'You can quit with the cheap shots. C'mon, am I the only one who thinks shifting some copies of our paper is a good idea—?' She broke off into a groan of frustration. 'Hey, you, Limey, making out like you're not listening in. Talk's not cheap. You got another penny?'

James turned, and this time shook his head.

'Hey, what about you guys?' she hollered over to the customers at the counter, but they ignored her. The waiters shook their heads. 'Anyone got a . . . Hello, Oscar? Hello? Aww, nuts.' She banged the earpiece against the wall in frustration, then slung it back down on its hook. 'I work my backside off for peanuts – and for an idiot!' She came out of the booth, shaking her head. Then she looked at James and her face grew more imperious. 'Why the eavesdropping, Limey? You sent by *The Times* to snoop on Tori Wo's scoop, huh? Or by the *Examiner*? They sending kids after stories now?'

'I've never heard of you or your paper!' James protested. 'Look, I should go, my friend got hurt in that riot you're talking about.'

'Oh, sure.'

'We were in that limousine you saw, on our way back from an Allworld studio tour.' James glared at her. 'We got caught up in the protest as things kicked off.'

James could see he had Tori's interest now. 'You were touring *Allworld*?' she said. 'How come?'

'We're over here visiting Anton Kostler's academy and had a tour of the studios before our work there starts.'

'The Kostler Allworld Academy?' Tori was rapt. 'You been there?'

'Not till tomorrow. Why?' James tried to reason out her eager attention. 'Hold on – is *that* the school where you saw those gangsters pick someone up?'

She folded her arms. 'Ask me something easier.'

'All right.' He nodded to her suit. 'Are you dressed like a man so you could fit in with the protesters? Did you know there would be trouble?'

'I heard a whisper.' Tori looked at him dubiously. 'Hey, what is this, an interview? My time is precious.'

'I did just give you two cents for your call.' James smiled hopefully.

'I guess you did. So, Tori Wo goes from undercover reporter to the cheapest informant in town?' She laughed, a sort of dirty, sniggering laugh. 'I'm sorry, I know it wasn't funny back there. But you know how it is. If you don't laugh . . .'

'Yes. I do know.' James selected a bottle of iodine, a small tin of Germoline, a bottle of Molloy's aspirin and some sticking plaster from the shelves. 'Who did you mean when you said "you-know-who"?'

'You trying to scoop me?'

'No. But I think I can help you with your story.' He held the first-aid kit out to Tori. 'If you were to cover my expenses . . . ?'

'You've got some front, I'll say that.' Tori was either amused or impressed, it was hard to say. 'What else you got, Limey?'

'A black Lincoln drove up. Three men got out. The driver attacked me and my friends . . .' James hesitated. 'For no reason.'

'I already know there were mob boys leading that violence. Luring out the cops and taking down the good apples.' Tori checked her watch. 'Where'd these guys you saw go?'

'They took off in another Lincoln. One had a "shooter", one had a bat – and one had a camera. They were filming that cop being killed, I bet.'

'Shooting the shooting, huh?' Tori reflected. 'I saw that camera guy. Figured he worked for one of the newsreels, that he'd heard the same whisper I did. How'd you find out this stuff you're spouting?'

'I wound up stuck underneath their car! The number plate – licence plate, I mean – ended 09, ILL 30.'

The effect on Tori was electric. '*ILL?* You sure it said ILL?'

James nodded. 'I wish I'd had a chance to remember the rest. I wasn't expecting to see little letters there—'

'ILL is short for Illinois.' Tori's smile grew broad and knowing. 'Illinois, the Prairie State. Homeland of our great president Abe Lincoln – if you still had those pennies you'd find his face on every one of them.' She sniggered again, triumphantly. 'And up in the northwest of Illinois we find Chicago, home to these damn gangsters I've been trailing the last few months. Can't be coincidence, right?'

'Right,' James agreed, feeling slightly silly as he realized Tori was only thinking aloud.

'So the plate ended in oh-nine. Doesn't give me much to go on. Can't check records with the cops, can't take the chance of tipping off the mob – you know how many officers Police Chief Davis has sacked for corruption since he took charge of the LAPD?'

James didn't, of course. But suddenly he was glad he and Hugo hadn't spoken to the police.

'You got anything else? Anything at all? Think. C'mon. Anything?'

Tori's abrasive chatter was like a Tommy gun through James's thoughts. 'I . . . don't know. It's . . . all a bit of a blur, right now.'

'Sure, you've been through a lot, you and your friend. But this has been good. My lucky day. And something else might occur to you, right? What's your name?'

'James Bond.'

'Well, congrats, James Bond, boy in the right places at kind of the right times. You just joined Tori Wo's network of informants. Where you staying?'

'The Hollywood Plaza, do you know it?'

'What am I, big spender, a tourist?' Tori pulled a pen and a crumpled dollar bill from her jacket pocket – then wrote busily over it. 'Here're my details if anything else comes back to you. Day or night, get in touch. And you only tell me, OK? You know how hungry those staffers at the *Record* are for a big-time story like this?' She tucked the money into the pocket of his jacket. 'Be good at school. Your big, exclusive, Kostler-funded school.' She walked swiftly to the door, the bell on top jangling as she left.

'A dollar!' James grinned at his sudden windfall. On the note was written VICTORIA WO and two phone numbers.

After quickly committing the information to memory, James bought the first-aid supplies and a bottle of Coca-Cola with two straws. That bit hard into fifty cents. Keeping the rest in his pocket, he went and rejoined the dismal Hugo.

'Here.' James handed over the Coke. 'According to the sign in there, it's the pause that refreshes.'

'I'm so hoarse I'd drink a camel's spit, right now.' Hugo slurped at his straw and eyed the brown bag of supplies with some suspicion. 'This first aid is going to hurt, isn't it?'

'Probably,' James admitted, producing two quarters. 'But at least we can ride back to the hotel in style.'

Hugo stared. 'Did you hold up the place or something?'

'No. I met a journalist,' James said distantly, his memory searching each last detail of the riot. 'I hope very much I can pay her back.'

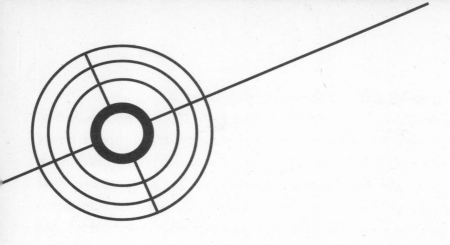

16
You Will Enjoy Dinner

James did his best on Hugo's injuries, but his every dab of iodine was greeted by a froth of melodramatic agony, and the tar was hard to shift with a damp handkerchief. So with their new-found riches, he hailed a yellow cab to take the two of them the twenty-cent ride back to the Hollywood Plaza.

'With any luck, Gillian's still out with Leaver,' James remarked. 'If she sees us in this state she'll throw a fit.'

The doorman's top lip twitched as James and Hugo approached, dirty and dishevelled. But still he opened the door, and once James had gained their key from the lobby it was up to the fourth floor, stagger down the corridor, throw open the door and finally collapse onto their beds with much noise and abandon. There was no sign that Dan had returned to the room ahead of them.

'Surely he and Boody should be back by now?' said Hugo.

The answer came seconds later as with a curt knock the

door opened and Gillian swept inside, features pinched with worry. 'We heard you arrive,' she said, and James saw Boody and Dan hovering in the doorway. 'When I heard what happened . . .! Thank heavens you're all right.' She saw Hugo's face and her own blanched. 'You're not all right! Look at you!'

'It's not so bad, Gillian,' said James quickly. 'Most of it's dirt from the road.'

'Turns out the streets here aren't paved with gold after all,' Hugo quipped ruefully. 'We hoped — I mean, we thought you were out with Dr Leaver.'

'I couldn't see him. He had meetings all day. Lousy timing.' Gillian's tone was matter-of-fact, but her face betrayed her disappointment. 'If only I'd gone along with you, perhaps this wouldn't have happened.'

'There was nothing you could have done.' Boody was hugging herself. 'Thank God you found Hugo, James.'

'Never any doubt, was there?' Dan muttered.

Spying the improvised first-aid kit, Gillian laid into it with grim determination. She proved a more effective nurse than James, though Hugo resisted her repeated suggestion that he go to the County General Hospital for X-rays.

Boody wanted to report the incident to the police, and Gillian said she would accompany her — provided the boys vowed to stay put in the hotel. Leaving Hugo to rest, James and Dan followed Gillian and Boody as far as the lobby. The concerned concierge booked a cab to take the ladies to the new police station on Wilcox Avenue, and smiled when his concern brought him another penny in his tip.

Everyone's an actor here, thought James.

'That fellow filming the violence in the street,' said Dan suddenly. 'It made me think . . . of the reel we watched.'

'Me too.' James looked him in the eye. 'And another thing – Dürr was there today in the alley.'

Dan's eyes widened. 'You saw him?'

'It made me think that . . . maybe it really *was* him who chased me at the Alhambra. And maybe that thug in the Lincoln came specifically to grab you.'

'No!' Dan sat down miserably on the couch. 'There can't be a killer coming after us. There *can't*!'

James bit his lip. It wouldn't help anything to make Dan more frightened than he already was. 'No. I guess you're right. After all, how would Dürr have got passage on the zeppelin so quickly?'

Dan brightened. 'And how would anyone in Hollywood know about the reel in Totnes, let alone my involvement?'

'Right . . .' James didn't let on that he could think of a couple of simple explanations: if Dürr was close to Kostler, or had some sort of hold over him – or even a hold on whoever coordinated travel plans for the big party – he could have commandeered a place on board. After all, there had been room for the school contingent. And if the reel *was* Dürr's, that would explain its presence in England . . .

Am I just being paranoid? James wondered. After all he had been through these last months, was he now finding conspiracies in shadows?

His internal sleep-clock still uncertain, James spent the afternoon dozing on a bench on the Patio de Las Palmas, one of the hotel's two enclosed gardens, crowded with dense, woody date palms. Jazz music was playing on a gramophone somewhere. That and the gurgling of water in the large stone fountain did their best to drown out the drone of traffic in the nearby streets.

Presently, James went up to check on Hugo, and found Dan in the room too, lying pensively on the couch, clearly still troubled. Hugo, at least, was in better spirits for his sleep; better spirits than Boody and Gillian, certainly, who returned from the police station around five, miserable and exhausted.

'They didn't seem to take me very seriously,' Boody said. 'I suppose with the murder of that poor policeman and all that other violence . . .'

James pictured again the gout of blood bursting from the officer's neck. An honest cop, shot dead as a warning to others. *A job well done, 'your lordship'*, James thought bitterly, *whoever you are.*

'We did the right thing in going, anyway,' Gillian affirmed. 'These monsters who attacked you need to be caught. And as for the chauffeur who left you, ha! He should lose his job! I'm going to contact this Mr Barron character and tell him to take action.'

James wished he could take action himself. Right now he felt helpless.

He wound up sanding the grip of his air pistol again, with hard, savage strokes.

Stuart Sloman didn't make it back to the Plaza until gone seven thirty. He looked wired, his smile twitching like it was caught on a hook. He insisted on treating everyone to dinner at Klemtner's Blue Plate Café, the hotel's celebrated eaterie.

Gillian protested at the prices, and no one felt much like

eating, but Sloman wouldn't take no for an answer. They'd all had a terrible experience, and he was going to make sure the day ended on a high. He was almost belligerent about it.

James ordered a steak sandwich with eggs. The eggs proved less straightforward than he'd imagined; they were offered to him sunny-side up, over-easy, over-medium, over-well, hard or overcooked. He chose the first option because it was the only one he could remember, and was somewhat disappointed to find they were simply fried. Boody opted for lobster Newburg; she stirred the creamy concoction distractedly around her bowl. Gillian ordered a crabmeat salad while Dan and Hugo both opted for the veal scaloppine with brown butter and capers. Dan had brightened somewhat, basking in his special relationship with the provider of their feast, perhaps.

As for Sloman, he ordered the most expensive dish on the menu, the *filet mignon jardinière* – or, 'the daintiest part of the cow served with vegetables', as the young, attractive waitress helpfully explained to the table. Sloman chuckled at that, said he would use that line sometime. He ordered a martini for himself and lime rickeys for everyone else – a refreshingly sharp combination of lime juice, sugar syrup and club soda over ice.

I could get a taste for cocktails, James decided.

'So.' Gillian looked at Sloman. 'I take it *you* had a good first day?'

'Better than I had any right to expect.' Sloman beamed. 'I'm getting my own office. They want me to rewrite existing screenplays, to start with. And I can't say I blame them.' He gulped at his martini and put on a bad American accent. 'Man, some of that dialogue . . . pure baloney!'

'How was Mr Kostler?' Dan asked through a mouthful of veal. 'Was he scary?'

'He's a powerful man. Gets things done.' Sloman sawed calmly through his steak. 'But you need men like that in a creative business. Someone who'll cut through the quarrel to take the decisions.'

James nodded. 'Did Mr Kostler's chauffeur tell you he dropped us in the middle of that riot?'

'I didn't hear about it until later. Mr Barron gave him a real talking to, don't you worry.'

'Is that all?' Gillian slammed down her cutlery. 'What that driver did was criminal!'

'I agree.' Sloman drained what was left of his martini and motioned to a waiter to bring another. 'I hate to think of the children exposed to such violence.'

Some of us are used to it, thought James darkly.

'Well, I'm happy to say that Dr Leaver has arranged his own transport for us tomorrow morning,' Gillian said. 'It will take us straight to the Academy.'

'What do we have to do there?' said Hugo hesitantly.

'You'll have a tour of the place, and I expect you'll be asked to take part in some of his tests.' Gillian smiled quickly. 'Remember, Dr Leaver is one of the most respected educationalists in the world. We could use him at Dartington Hall—'

'And you could use Kostler's money?' Sloman broke in, smiling.

'Of course.' Gillian was unapologetic. 'In England, truly independent schools are seen as a fad, an experiment. If we're to survive and replace the orthodox way of teaching, we need proper funds for promotion as well as resources – or we'll never truly challenge the public schools of Britain that expel a boy like James for not fitting into their outdated, barbaric traditions . . .'

James felt his cheeks prickle. 'I'd sooner not think about school at the moment.'

'Yes, Fettes awaits you, doesn't it?' Dan smiled a little waspishly and swigged his lime rickey. 'Soon have you strait-jacketed by rules and regulations again, won't we?'

Boody glanced over at James. 'I doubt it.'

'Rules and regulations have their uses in any case.' Sloman winked at James. 'They give you something to rebel against, eh?' He smiled a thank you as the waiter brought his martini on a silver tray. 'Well, here's hoping you all enjoy a happier tomorrow. And in the evening it's Anton Kostler's big celebration party over at his mansion house. I'm going, and I've got a "plus one" ticket . . .'

'Me!' Dan piped up. 'Let it be me, Uncle Stuart?'

Sloman smiled. 'As blood of my blood, Mr Kostler has generously granted you an invitation.'

'Yes!' Dan grinned at Gillian. 'Thank God you forced us to bring dinner dress.'

'I imagined you might need it for educational functions.' Gillian shook her head. 'Ha! I'm pleased you'll be able to put it to better use.'

'What's more,' Sloman went on, 'your invitation entitles you to bring one guest.'

'Boody,' said Dan immediately.

'Me?' Boody's face lit up. 'Are you sure, Dan?'

'It's hardly a difficult choice, is it?' Dan turned to James and Hugo, his face a pantomime of pity. 'Sorry, boys, no offence.'

'None taken,' said James truthfully. He had hardly expected to be chosen. But seeing Boody looking so starstruck at the prospect, he felt a sudden twinge of unhappiness.

'I should inform you, Dan, I look better in evening dress than Boudicca,' Hugo told him. 'I suggest you take me.'

'In my pocket, perhaps?' Dan retorted.

'Oh, how droll.' Hugo shook his head. 'On second thoughts, Boody, you're welcome to him.'

'Now, now, boys.' Sloman looked over at Gillian. 'Miss de Vries. Would you care to attend as my guest?'

'Me? Good God, no!' Gillian laughed, leaned forward and pressed Sloman's hand fondly. 'I mean, forgive me, bless you, but I'm not one for chasing glamour. I wouldn't know a Hollywood star if one fell on me.'

'Well, that's settled then.' Sloman seemed almost relieved. 'I felt I had to ask you, but Mr Kostler did mention a rising Allworld starlet was free to accompany me for the evening.'

'I'm doing you a good turn then.' Gillian looked embarrassed, cleared her throat. 'Well, anyway, after what happened today, it's best I stay and look after the boys.'

'Be sure to have them tucked up by ten o'clock!' Dan smirked and raised his glass as if toasting the pair of them. Boody glanced away, covering her smile.

James and Hugo looked at each other, and sighed.

Rest came uneasily to James that night, violence flaring at the corners of his dreams, waking him in a sweat, though he was unable to remember why. Around five a.m., the rhythmic rasp of Dan's breathing on the couch kept sleep away for even longer. He lay stewing at the thought of Boody tripping off to the ball like Cinderella, with Dan as her Prince Charming.

What do you care? he told himself. *The further away you stay from girls, the better.*

He was still thinking about Boody when sleep finally returned for him.

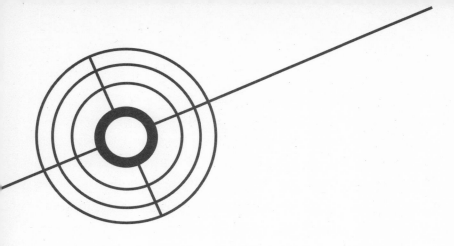

17

Reality or the Vision

Eyes scratchy and screwed up against the Californian sunshine, James peered out of the window as the private motorbus carried them along the San Diego Freeway. They were heading for Kostler's academy, out to the west of the city in the woody sprawl of Rustic Canyon. Its natural geography, cut into the Santa Monica Mountains, left it separated from the well-heeled surrounding districts of Malibu and Pacific Palisades.

Dan leaned forward in the aisle, calling to Boody at the front of the bus. 'What will you be wearing to the party tonight, Boods?'

'The black dress I wore that last night on the *Allworld*, I suppose,' she called back. 'It's being dry cleaned.'

'That dress will impress the great and good of Hollywood, I have no doubt,' said Dan with enthusiasm. 'Don't you reckon, fellows?'

Hugo, sprawled in the seat opposite, muttered darkly.

Dan swung himself into the seat beside James. 'Seriously . . . no hard feelings over not coming along tonight, I hope?'

'None.' James lowered his voice. 'But what if the men in that Lincoln attacked you because they wanted to know where that reel's gone? If they could get at our chauffeur, they may have other links to Allworld Studios. If you go to that party, you could be putting yourself and Boody in danger.'

For a moment Dan looked shaken. Then, slowly, he smiled. 'I see what you're trying to do. Scare me into not going so I miss out. Going to volunteer bravely to go in my place, I suppose? That's weak, Bond.' Dan moved forward to sit next to Boody. 'We just have to get today out of the way, then we'll have us the night of our lives . . .'

'I suppose I *am* just being paranoid,' James brooded. 'If only I had more to go on . . .' After sighting Dürr at the scene, he couldn't help feeling that wheels were in motion around them.

It was a disquieting feeling.

The palms waved lazily over Sunset Boulevard and its neat white houses, the Spanish-style façades bleaching in the sunlight. Then the bus turned off and the neighbourhood grew more rural. The avenue slowly shrank from the land-scaping around it. A few more turns and intersections and it became a fire road, a black asphalt scar scored through the hillside, thickly wooded either side with oak, sycamore and eucalyptus. Patches of fog steamed silently about them.

It felt a world away from downtown LA, and yet they'd

barely been driving for thirty minutes. Here and there James glimpsed millionaires' mansions, serene and secluded.

'Imagine going to school here,' Boody marvelled.

'It's an impressive location,' Gillian agreed. 'It enhances the exclusive feel of the Academy. I'm sure after a time, the pupils all take the scenery for granted.'

The bus turned onto a paved track lined with chaparral and cypresses. It led to a set of wide-open wrought-iron gates. The sign beside them stated boldly that they had arrived at THE KOSTLER ALLWORLD ACADEMY FOR EXCELLENCE IN THE ARTS, with a motto in Latin:

RES VERA
REIQUE IMAGO
RE ALTIOR
AEQUE PETENDAE

'Rather a mouthful,' Dan observed.

'What does it mean?' James wondered.

'Let's see . . . We must pursue reality but also its vision – a loftier goal – in equal measure,' Hugo translated. 'Or something like that, anyway.'

James shrugged. 'I still don't know what it means.'

The bus trundled onwards into a large metal parking lot. A taxi cab drove past them in the opposite direction, leaving the school.

Gillian turned to the driver. 'I understand only about sixty per cent of the children board here, is that right? A good many come from the surrounding community, I suppose.'

'Local kids with rich parents,' the driver translated. 'Yeah, they love it. Playing at making movies, you know.'

'Ha! Vocational training is far better for a child than learn-ing stuffy old classics by heart,' said Gillian. 'Since the local area's key industry is movie-making, and it's expanding all the time, it's sensible to specialize, wouldn't you say? Hmm?'

James caught the driver's rueful raising of his eyebrows in the rear-view mirror. 'Lady, I think you're going to get along with Doc Leaver just fine.'

Hugo leaned over to James confidentially. 'While I suspect he's going to bore *us* to death.'

James and his fellow guinea pigs had to wait a while before they could test either prediction. They'd been about to follow signs to Reception when a boy and a girl of fourteen or so came out to greet them. They weren't wearing uniform as such, but both sported trousers and a short-sleeved shirt. As far as James could see, glimpsing through classroom windows, all the pupils did.

The Academy was a far cry from the fading grandeur of Dartington Hall. The buildings looked new, designed and built in clean, modernist lines, much like the *Allworld*. The grounds looked to stretch on for miles, framed in the distance by the scrub and chaparral of the mountains.

James followed the others into the welcome cool of a large, imposing building. There was no clutter here, no worn carpet or chipped paintwork; it felt more like a workplace than any sort of school. At the reception desk they took turns to sign their names in an immaculate leather-bound book, and were led on to a waiting area outside a closed mahogany door. The boy and the girl excused themselves politely and left.

Wooden chairs lined the walls of the waiting area. James

perched on the one nearest the door, on which a brass plaque read:

DR TOBIAS LEAVER
DIRECTOR OF EDUCATION

Right now, voices could be heard inside the office.

'Parents have complained about him' – the first voice was hoarse and stentorian – 'and as Director here they expect me to do something about it.'

The second voice sounded familiar. 'Mr Kostler won't like that, Leaver.'

'That's *Dr* Leaver, *Mr* Vasquez. And the running of this Academy is still my responsibility . . .'

The argument went on. 'He's got Lenny Vasquez from the *Allworld* in there,' Hugo realized.

James nodded. 'I thought he was Kostler's movie promoter abroad. What's he doing here?'

Points of red were warming Gillian's cheeks. 'Now, now. We shouldn't be eavesdropping. Perhaps we should wait back at the reception.'

Dr Leaver seemed to be losing patience. 'I've signed what you wanted me to. Perhaps you might allow me to run the rest of my affairs without interference. You were supposed to be getting hold of the latest reports from the Nairobi academy.'

'Mr Kostler told you not to bother yourself with those.'

'It's my *business* to bother with them. These schools were founded in my name, to embody my educational principles, and yet I'm not permitted to visit, I have been told nothing of how—'

159

'Like Australia, Nairobi's a long way away, Leaver. And we can't have you neglecting your work here, right?' The door opened and Vasquez sauntered out. The dark eyes zeroed in on James and the big smile was back at once. 'Hey, hey!' He looked round at the others. 'It's my fellow travellers. How are we all today? Good? That's good! Well, I've got to run back to the office now.' Vasquez tapped Dan lightly on the shoulder. 'Be seeing you tonight, right? Pays to have your uncle on Mr Kostler's payroll, huh? Sure it does.' He walked away with a final cheery salute. 'Adios, amigos! Keep your noses clean!'

Dr Leaver came to the door, watching Vasquez go. The doctor was a short, portly man in a crumpled tweed suit, and might have looked quite comical, but for the strength in his face. His bristling moustache was like scrub growing down from his nostrils. The high forehead was furrowed, the grey eyes peering suspiciously through round, wire-frame glasses. With him came a waft of sweat and chalk and tobacco.

'Tobias . . . ?' Gillian was on her feet, her uncertain smile growing stronger as he turned to her and took her in. 'Ah, Tobias, it's been so long!'

A change came over Dr Leaver as he gazed at his visitor. 'Gillian!' His face relaxed as he shambled forward to embrace her. 'You came! You're here! Thank heavens.'

'I'm so happy to see you.' Gillian seemed a little over-whelmed as Leaver clung to her. 'You're looking tired. You've been overdoing it, haven't you? Ha! You have, you can't stop yourself. Oh, Tobias.'

'It's splendid to see you, my dear.' He recovered himself a little and stared round at the children. 'And here are your proud examples, eh? Quite a journey you've all been on. Forgive me, I wasn't expecting you here so soon.'

He relinquished his grip on Gillian and started shaking hands with her pupils, starting with Hugo and Boody. 'I recognize you all from the reports Gillian sent. Quite an enterprise, this. Let us hope for a good outcome. Ah!' Leaver shook James's hand warmly. 'James Bond, your aunt is an old and dear friend of mine. Her anthropological investigations were of great use to me when it came to setting up schools in different cultures.'

James smiled and nodded. 'Why was Mr Vasquez here, sir?'

'Not now, James,' Gillian began.

'Now, now, my dear Gillian. We should be the last people to object to an enquiring mind, eh?' Leaver smiled, pulled a handkerchief from his pocket and dabbed at the sweat on his domed forehead. 'I had to sign a purchase agreement for screening motion pictures at the Kostler Academy in Nairobi. And as well as promoting Allworld movies abroad, Mr Vasquez is godfather to Mr Kostler's son, Martyn.'

'No wonder he got protective about Martyn on the *Allworld*,' Hugo murmured. Leaver looked over sharply, and Hugo blushed. 'Er, Mr Vasquez mentioned he'd had problems with schools in the past, but was fitting in here well.'

'Mr Vasquez should respect pupil confidentiality.' Leaver turned quickly to Dan. 'Ah! Now then, Daniel Sloman, the writer's nephew? So fortunate there was room aboard the *Allworld* for the whole lot of you. Quite a family outing, eh? Splendid, splendid.' He seemed distracted, but kept up a smiling front. 'Well, I'm sure these meetings will be very useful for us all. Very useful.'

'I know we're early.' Gillian seemed suddenly flustered around her old mentor. 'If you need time to compose yourself after your, er, last appointment—'

'No, no! I've only just set eyes on you, I'll not have you leave so . . . so soon.' Leaver smiled again and squeezed Gillian's hands. 'Have you enjoyed your stay in the city so far?'

'It's getting better all the time,' Dan piped up. 'We're going to Mr Kostler's party tonight. Aren't we, Boody?'

'Oh, hell, I was asked to that as well.' Leaver tutted. 'I despise the empty glamour of these showbusiness affairs.'

'Well, I'm staying in at the hotel with James and Hugo.' Gillian smiled. 'You'd be most welcome to join me instead—'

'So we could talk? Catch up properly?' Leaver looked delighted. 'Oh, my dear girl, yes! A hundred times, yes. Now, all of you, come into my office.'

James followed the others inside. Dr Leaver telephoned a secretary for tea, and was soon deep in conversation with Gillian.

'Mr Kostler approached me to set up this academy four years ago,' Leaver explained. 'His funding is most generous. With it, I had hoped to achieve a radical reinvention of the educational curriculum.'

'With the emphasis on letting children choose for themselves what they wish to learn rather than teachers thrusting dry facts and figures down their throats,' Gillian agreed. 'Well, you've made a lot of progress, no? The film-making disciplines taught here make the school unique.'

Leaver nodded. 'Yes, yes, I can see how from the outside looking in, it must seem like a successful experiment. And Mr

Kostler is keen to create new academies on a similar pattern in many countries, Great Britain included.'

'That's wonderful news,' Gillian said slowly. 'But you know, of course, that at Dartington we value our independence and our own curriculum . . .'

'Oh, quite, quite.' He smiled. 'That's why we shall test and compare our pupils, explore our philosophies and consider what we can learn from each other's approaches and atti-tudes.'

Gillian's smile for him had grown fonder still. 'Thank you.'

'Excuse me, sir,' James broke into the conversation. 'What sorts of tests and comparisons?'

'Brisk and incisive, eh, James? So much like your aunt.' Leaver dabbed again at his forehead. 'Well, I'd like to talk to you all about your experiences. I'll be asking you to sit in on some classes, and also participate in some intelligence tests, so I get a feel for your different stages of development. Some physical trials too, of course.' Dr Leaver glanced up and smiled as a stocky, good-looking boy walked up smartly to the doorway. 'But first, I've arranged a guided tour of our premises here, in the company of one of our highest achievers – Brad Cummings.'

'Brad asked me to tag along and help, Tobias.'

James saw Leaver stiffen as another boy appeared in the doorway. He was tall and lithe with a shock of white-blond hair, muscles taut beneath his short-sleeved shirt. High cheek-bones accentuated his almost feminine beauty – dark eyes, a straight nose and full lips that looked painted onto his pale face. To James, he looked somehow more like a product than a person.

'Martyn A. Kostler,' the boy introduced himself. 'A hearty welcome to our guests from England.'

'Now, Martyn,' Leaver began, 'I'm not sure it requires two of you to show our guests round the Academy—'

'It's my pleasure to help, Tobias.' Martyn turned to Boody, his smile inching wider. 'Shall we begin?'

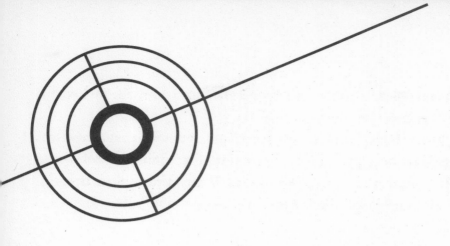

18
Hell of a Tour

The Academy was set in sixty acres of land, a mix of manicured lawn and mud-banks, of hills and trails and wild, scrubby borders. A single-track road cut across the landscape. To the east, distant downtown LA could be glimpsed, a shimmering phantom in the shadow of clouds and mountains.

The classroom buildings were set well apart, the areas in between carefully landscaped. Boody wondered why.

'That was my father's idea, Boudicca,' said Martyn, striding across the grass. 'It gives us time to reflect on one lesson before arriving at the next. And a brisk walk gets the blood flowing, increases oxygen to the brain, makes you more receptive. Puts you at your best.'

They looked in at one of the classrooms. Students were huddled on the floor in groups, notes laid out beside them.

'Everyone wears the same kind of clothes,' James had

noticed, 'almost like a uniform. Isn't that a bit old-fashioned in a modern school?'

'Not at all.' Brad was surprisingly soft-spoken for such a well-built boy. 'It's simply a template for what to wear, freeing pupils from burdensome choice. If the mind isn't distracted by trivialities like, "What shall I wear?" it can better focus on what's important.'

'Makes sense,' said Dan.

'Does it?' James shrugged. 'I've never found freedom of choice a burden.'

'You sound so old-fashioned.' Martyn seemed amused. 'I bet your school's, like, a hundred years old.'

'Actually, the Great Hall is over five hundred years old,' Boody informed him.

'I visited England once,' Brad said. 'Or was it Scotland?'

'They're pretty much the same speck on the map,' Martyn assured him. 'Ancient and damp.'

'Yes! While over here, it's warm and dry and *new*,' said Dan with enthusiasm. 'It makes England seem so dreary.'

'No wonder you Brits love our movies so much,' said Martyn. 'What other excitement can you find over there?'

'You'd be surprised,' said James mildly.

'I'm going to your father's celebration tonight,' Dan blurted. 'That's real excitement.'

'I've heard.' Martyn turned and looked Boody up and down. 'And you're to accompany him. What will you wear?'

Boody frowned. 'I . . . I haven't decided.'

Martyn went on looking like he was deciding for her. 'You will look beautiful. I'm certain of it.'

'I'm not in competition with any starlets,' Boody said

coolly. James saw dots of red dimpled in her cheeks. He'd known pretty much at first glance that he wouldn't care for Martyn Kostler; now he was really starting to hate him for his self-assured arrogance.

Hugo pointed past them to a circular building in the distance, on the way to what looked like an athletics track. 'What's that building over there?'

'That's our concert hall. It has its own recording suite,' said Brad. 'Students score their own scenes and movie themes and record them with state-of-the-art equipment.'

James was impressed. 'They make their own gramophone records?'

'Compact magnetic tape, actually.' Brad smiled. 'It's a new development from Germany.'

'I suppose you could use tapes like that for recording conversations, too,' James ventured, watching Martyn for a reaction.

But the boy merely smiled blandly and nodded. 'Suppose you could.'

To the south, perhaps a quarter of a mile away, James noted a tall metal tower, fashioned from crisscrossed girders, dominating a wide paved area almost like a landing strip. 'Is that a mooring mast for your father's airship?'

'Of course. One mast here, one at the studio, one above the house. About the only three places he goes. That's all *his* world.'

'And he really has a bedroom up there?' Dan asked.

Martyn smiled. 'You expect the shepherd to sleep among the sheep?'

James saw that on one side of the mooring mast there was

a hangar, and on the other, a very large single-storey building of a noticeably different style from the classrooms they'd seen. The white walls were stained and dust-blown. A large chimney pointed up from the roof, dark smoke wisping into the sky.

'What's that?' he asked.

'The old Allworld Studios,' said Martyn. 'Built in 1914 when Father was on the way up. Within five years he'd outgrown it—'

'I actually meant, what's that smoke coming out the chimney?' James broke in. 'It's a hot day . . .'

'Big furnace,' said Brad. 'It's part of the system that's used to heat the water here.'

Hugo was surprised. 'What, and it's kept all that way away from the other buildings? Doesn't seem very efficient.'

Martyn smiled patronizingly. 'It works just fine, sonny.'

'Can we visit the old studio?' asked Boody.

'Sorry, sweets. No can do.'

James frowned. 'But isn't this a tour?'

'Of the Academy, Bond, yes. Not of my father's private property.' Martyn shrugged. 'He keeps it as a shrine to the old days. But we have a *new* studio here at the Academy. We make our own movies, and watch the dailies in a special viewing theatre.'

Dan chuckled. 'Makes Dartington Film Club's sheet-in-the-basement seem a bit dismal, doesn't it?'

James, Boody and Dan followed Martyn and Brad across the field at a fair pace, Hugo scurrying to keep up. The Academy studio was the biggest building they'd been in so far. The insides smelled of paint and sawdust. Martyn led the party into a viewing gallery, overlooking the studio like a box at the opera. An impressive set – a dark, wet street – was bathed with the spotlight of a moon shining down on a boy and a girl dressed in raincoats. The girl was beating her fists against the wall, and the boy put a restraining hand on her shoulder. A small huddle of pupils surrounded the director and his film camera, mounted on a wooden tripod, as a melodrama played out.

'They're trapped in there!' The girl sounded hysterical. 'They'll be hunted down and killed!'

'They got what they deserve,' said the boy, putting on a deep, gruff voice. 'They went against the boss . . . so the boss has *got* to do this. If he goes easy on them, his lieutenants lose respect.'

'But this is murder!'

'It's execution, lady.'

'Are you going to just stand by and let it happen?'

'It's got to happen.' He spun her round, took her wrists, looked down into her frightened eyes. 'In this dark, crazy world of ours, death is the only thing you can count on . . . You know that.'

'Who writes this stuff?' James scoffed.

'*I* wrote it,' said Martyn, staring out into the darkness. 'That ham's saying it all wrong.'

'It's great, Mart,' said Brad quickly. 'It's just rehearsals.'

'No!' Martyn's shout rang out across the studio. 'It's all *wrong*!'

'And – cut!' The director – a lanky boy with a blaze of red hair – turned from his players and peered angrily up at the gallery. 'Could you keep your voice down? We're on our fifth take here—'

'You want to tell *me* what to do?' Martyn exploded. 'You really want to mess with me?'

'Martyn?' The director held up his hands like a terrified crook who'd just been busted. 'I – I'm sorry, didn't recognize you.'

'Well, I didn't recognize my script.' Martyn gestured angrily at the actors on the set. 'I want *them* dumped. Get someone better. Someone who appreciates language and what it can do.'

James could think of a couple of choice words to tell Martyn what *he* could do. But the director merely nodded dumbly as the young actors stalked from the set. Martyn turned on his heel and stormed out of the gallery. Brad, his face neutral and composed, gestured that Dan, Hugo, Boody and James should follow.

'That was awkward,' Hugo muttered.

'Horrible,' Boody agreed.

James nodded. 'It's his daddy's place, so he thinks he can act however he likes.'

Outside, Martyn was standing relaxed and composed as if nothing had happened. 'It sickens me,' he declared, 'that in the midst of this recession, people waste indecent sums sending their talentless children here.'

'Sick,' Brad agreed.

Dan jumped in: 'I could do the lines, Martyn. I'm an actor.'

Everyone looked at him; James had to admire the boy's nerve: far from feeling outraged or embarrassed by Martyn's outburst, Dan was seizing it as a chance to audition.

'I'm good,' Dan went on.

Martyn bared his teeth in something like a smile. 'You think so?'

'I don't have to be British. I can do accents.' He added an East Coast twang to his voice: 'I can talk like this . . . or pretty much however you like.'

He went on with his impromptu performance, quoting lines from his favourite movies in a range of accents and impressions. Martyn watched him like a cat watches a mouse, while Boody looked down at her feet. James swapped an uncomfortable look with Hugo.

'Thank you, Dan,' Martyn broke in at last. 'I think we've seen enough. That was quite something. Don't you think so, Brad?'

Brad looked as if he were trying to read Martyn's mood; he nodded carefully.

'Really?' Dan smiled round at his friends. 'I can do much more—'

'No need,' Martyn assured him. 'You've convinced me. I'll get you a script before you go home today.'

James was waiting for the killer punch – for the sneering, sarcastic put-down he thought would follow. But there was nothing.

'Thank you.' Dan's smile was big enough to split his face in two. 'Hey, just think – I'll be able to say I've acted in Hollywood in a genuine Kostler production!'

'You will, at that.' Martyn stood up. 'OK, enough here. We'll finish up with a trip to the sports track.'

Again, Martyn set the pace a little faster than was comfortable – though perhaps not for Dan, who seemed to be walking on air – heading north this time to a large athletics arena. They passed the concert hall. Music was swelling out from inside, distinctive and jazzy with a mid-tempo beat, brasses and strings and needling steel guitars. James didn't recognize the tune, but felt a sense of anticipation and danger in its ominous swagger; right now it felt as if the musicians were scoring his mood.

At the arena there was a large oval track for circuit training. The middle section was laden with mats, and boys and girls in loose white jackets and trousers were circling, coming together, and throwing each other to the ground, moving almost in time to the distant twang of the music.

'What are they doing?' asked Boody.

'Judo,' said Brad simply.

'It's a martial art,' James added.

'No, no, Bond.' Martyn tutted. 'Jujitsu was the art. Judo is more of a philosophy; the word means *gentle way*.' He looked at Boody. 'Kind of spiritual, see?'

Boody shrugged. 'What's the point of it?'

'You grapple with your opponent and then throw or pin him to the ground,' James said coolly. 'Isn't that right?'

Martyn turned to him. 'Or you grip your opponent close and force him to submit.'

'Judo was demonstrated at the Summer Olympics here two years ago,' Brad put in. 'It's grown really popular. We have our own club.'

'Of course, that's mainly down to me.' Martyn smiled. 'Father hired an instructor who trained under Kano Jigoro himself at the Kodokan in Tokyo.'

Dan frowned. 'Jiggery who at the what?'

'Kano was the founder of judo,' said Hugo. 'The Kodokan

is the movement's headquarters. I read about it in the *Modern Boy*.'

Martyn clapped sarcastically, gave a knowing look to Brad. 'And do you play many contests yourself, dwarf?'

James frowned at his rudeness, but Hugo only smiled. 'Oh dear, perhaps you misheard me earlier? My name isn't "Dwarf", Martyn.' He offered his hand to shake. 'It's Hugo.'

'I'm so very sorry, *Hu*-go.' Martyn made a great show of bending over to take Hugo's hand – and in a sudden blur, Hugo gripped his wrist, hooked his right leg around Martyn's left, twisted and pulled. Caught off-balance, Martyn gasped, lost his footing and went sprawling to the grass. In the astounded silence, James's snort of laughter came out louder than he'd intended.

Martyn jumped up and rounded on Hugo. 'What the hell was that?'

'I *think* that was me getting under your centre of gravity and turning your own momentum against you.' Hugo looked solemn. 'I've got a brother about your height, you see, and we've never got along.'

'You little runt!' Martyn spat. 'I'll pound you.' He started towards Hugo, but James stepped forward and barred his way.

'That's enough,' James said.

In response, Martyn grabbed James's right elbow and twisted viciously. James felt his legs knocked from under him and before he knew what was happening, he was face down on the grass. Martyn's knee was in the small of his back and his right arm was being forced to bend the wrong way. He gasped with pain. He realized the music had stopped.

'Feel that, Bond?' Martyn hissed in his ear, the words thick and savage. 'That's your arm, ready to snap. Would you care to submit?'

James shook his head.

'A little more pressure, then . . .' Martyn levered downwards.

'For heaven's sake,' said Boody. 'Stop it!'

'Oh, Bond's a big man, he can take it. Can't you, Bond?'

James felt his elbow strain and creak. The pain was excruciating, but he wasn't about to give Martyn the satisfaction of submitting.

'Let him go!' Boody insisted.

A pause – then the pressure on James's arm was relieved. 'As milady commands.'

Now he could breathe again, James got to his feet and brushed himself down with his good arm. His cheeks felt hot, his elbow burned, but the anger inside was stone cold.

Martyn only smiled. 'You know, the dwarf's a better fighter than you, Bond. Perhaps next time, you'll stick to sparring with him.'

'Next time, I'll stick something—' James began, but Hugo held up a hand and shook his head.

'The tour is over,' Martyn announced. 'Brad, walk our British visitors back to Leaver's office, huh? I'm being picked up.'

'Um, you won't forget the script?' Dan mumbled.

'I don't say what I don't mean.' Martyn looked at Boody. 'I'll see you tonight – and you'll look quite charming.'

With that, he strode away towards the exit. Boody gave a mock salute. 'Aye-aye, Captain Kostler Junior.'

Brad eyed her coldly. 'You want to come this way?'

Dan offered his arm to Boody, who refused it, choosing to take Hugo's hand instead. James looked over at the judo class still in progress. He'd learned some jujitsu in the past, how to strike and block, but Martyn was clearly an expert at judo, with its emphasis on throws and holds. James wanted to learn and practise hard now, to discover for himself how to unleash hell on someone like that.

It'll be your face in the mud next time, Kostler, James vowed. *One way or another.*

Suddenly, Boody's choice of words chimed in James's head. He remembered Tori Wo on the phone to her editor in the drugstore: *Our friend Junior lets gangsters pick him up from school!*

James almost swore aloud. *Kostler* Junior?

While Brad marched away, leading the others, James sloped off to follow Martyn at a discreet distance. Ducking and dashing between trees and bushes, he watched Martyn stride across the parking lot – to where a familiar black Lincoln was waiting. He squinted for the Illinois licence plate. It ended in 09.

Someone opened the rear door for Martyn and he slid inside. The Lincoln drove away.

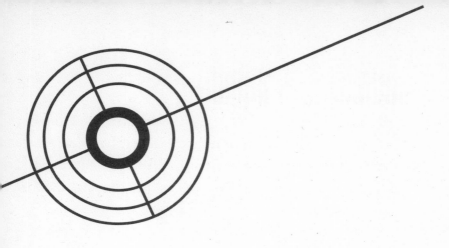

19

First Evidence

The rest of the day at the Academy passed slowly as Dr Leaver carried out his educational tests. James sat in an office opposite the old man's and stared at psychological evaluations, general knowledge tests, multiple-choice papers, challenges in logic and lateral thinking . . .

He still ached from his punishment at Martyn Kostler's hands. The answers he scrawled were grudging, cursory. James didn't much care what Dr Leaver made of his academic ability. He was dwelling on the information gleaned from his impulsive spying mission.

Martyn Kostler had got into a car owned by Chicago gangsters. Tori's 'scoop' seemed about right; on top of being a general creep, the movie mogul's son was playing gangsters. But with his father's permission, or otherwise?

He vowed to telephone Tori Wo the moment he got back to the Plaza.

As James worked on, he wondered if Anton Kostler was proud of the son he had raised. The mogul's wife had died before Martyn was even old enough to remember her . . . Had Kostler been a positive influence in Martyn's life, or a distant figure, giving wealth and status to his son but little else?

James felt the old familiar pangs of loneliness for his own parents. Not knowing them at all would perhaps make things less painful – but at the same time, those well-worn, embroidered memories were among his most treasured possessions. He felt a flicker of pity for Martyn Kostler, but it was soon gone, an ember thrown from the fire, falling as ash while the flames of his anger licked on.

The bell went at three, sounding home time for the day pupils. Boody and Hugo swapped mournful stories on their written trials as they returned to the parking lot with Gillian, where the motorbus was waiting. James kept his own counsel. Dan held back, too, keeping a deliberate distance. The drive was busy with yellow cabs and motorcars come to collect those lucky pupils escaping back to their homes in the hills or downtown.

James sat on the back seat of the bus and Hugo plonked himself down beside him. Boody sat in the row in front, while Dan sat opposite, apparently absorbed in some neatly typed pages.

'You got your script from Martyn, then,' Boody noted.

'Hand-delivered by Brad.' Dan looked pleased with himself. 'I think I must've made quite an impression.'

'A very fine impression,' Hugo agreed, 'of someone bowing and scraping to the little dictator. He thinks he can treat people any way he likes.'

Dan lowered his script and turned a cold eye on Hugo. 'He

knows what he wants and won't stop till he gets it. Those are decent qualities.'

'For the Hitler Youth,' Hugo suggested.

'You're just jealous,' said Dan. 'You almost ruined everything back there. Why did you have to drop Martyn on his behind like that?'

'So you could kiss it better.' Hugo turned to James. 'How are you feeling?'

'I'm fine,' James muttered.

'Only thanks to Boody stepping in,' Dan put in. 'You put us both in an embarrassing position.'

'The only person who embarrassed me was you,' said Boody. 'I'm not sure which is your stronger suit – showing off or boot-licking.'

'I simply dared to take a golden opportunity.' Dan brandished his script and stalked away to a seat in the middle of the bus with his back to them.

It was a long journey back to the Hollywood Plaza.

When the coach finally arrived, it had to manoeuvre round a battered, dark-blue Plymouth parked at the side of the road. The doorman leaped to escort the party inside, and Gillian tipped him as usual. James followed her to the reception desk to pick up the keys – and today, a telegram.

'Hell,' she said, frowning. 'It's from the Head. There's been a spate of break-ins at Dartington Hall. Several of the rooms, yours included. Nothing was taken, but . . .'

'It must be Beatrice Judge,' said Boody. 'Or that brother of hers.'

Hugo nodded thoughtfully. 'Trying to get back at us for going without her?'

'That does seem likely.' Gillian was clearly upset. 'What a business. I'll freshen up in the room, then I'd better call the Head, though it's rather late back home . . .'

She and Boody walked away. Dan seemed almost pleased as he murmured to James: 'This rather sabotages your conspiracy theories, doesn't it? If Herr Dürr and his fedora are behind things, using the *Allworld* to listen to every word we say, who's tearing Dartington apart looking for that reel? I didn't tell anyone I'd sent it back home.'

'It's an obvious place to check,' James persisted. 'Dürr could have left people behind in England to keep searching.'

'Well, then, they've muffed it,' said Dan. 'I sent the reel away last week, and specified second class by steamship. It won't reach England for days yet.'

He walked away to the lift. Looking worried, Hugo followed him.

'I'm just going to make a telephone call,' James called. He crossed to the payphone. The nearest was occupied by a woman in a white-and-fawn trouser suit and dark glasses. She turned round and smiled. 'Sorry, Jimmy-boy. This one's occupied.'

James grinned. 'Tori! I was coming to call you.'

'I'm all ears.' She held up the receiver. 'Well, I'm one ear. The other's trying to get through to the mailroom at work. I'm expecting a package. Your pretty friend just received one here, and I'm jealous. Mine hasn't shown yet. It stinks.' A voice squawked from the phone receiver at last, and she turned to the mouthpiece. 'No, I wasn't talking to you. But I should've been! You gonna be reunited with your brain anytime soon, sugar? Yeah, wiseguy, same to you.' She hung up, shook her head. 'No package yet.'

'But Boudicca's had one delivered?' James was puzzled. 'Or did you mean Gillian?'

'My, my, Jimmy, so many ladies.' She pulled out a cigarette. 'This is how it is. I was snooping round the Kostler Academy parking lot on the trail of Junior—'

'Martyn Kostler, you mean,' James broke in. 'He left in the black Lincoln with the Illinois plates.'

'Right. You were following him too?'

'I have to say, I don't like him.'

'Well, he sure likes your pretty friend.' Tori lit up with a match from a Plaza matchbook. 'So, here's the story. The guy who showed in the Lincoln goes by the name of McGee. Took Junior to a fancy department store. Junior bought something, gave it to McGee, then took off on foot. I was in the car, so I trailed McGee here. Figured I might as well wait for you, see if you got any more info for me.' She pulled out a crumpled photograph. 'See, here's McGee's mugshot. You ever see him before? Maybe at the riot scene? Didn't see him myself, but maybe . . . ?'

James took in the dark marks on the man's neck and around the jaw to his ear, caught his breath.

It was the man from the torture reel. The man who'd cut the helpless Alexander Roberts, his image projected in the basement at Dartington.

'You *have* seen him.' Tori was watching him closely. 'Where'd you see him, James?'

'On film,' James murmured. 'Using a knife on someone.'

Tori stared. 'Film? You mean, he was acting?'

'More like a documentary.' James took a deep breath. 'Long story, but back home there was this reel of film a friend

181

found, with real-life violence on it. That hood McGee was one of the ones dishing it out.'

'You're kidding me.' She grabbed his wrists. 'And you've got this film reel?'

'No,' James confessed. 'It's on its way back to England.'

'Aww!' With an impatient groan, Tori pushed him away. 'McGee is the only one of the Chicago gang I can find with any form. Twelve months inside eight years back, for robbery and assault.' She leaned forward, snatched back the picture and stuffed it into her pocket. 'When he's not driving a Lincoln, know where you'll find him? On the staff of George Barron's private security firm.'

James let the sudden rush of information sink in. 'Barron is Kostler's right-hand man,' he said. 'You think he knows that McGee's a crook?'

'*Was* a crook, Jimmy-boy. Seems he's keeping his nose clean these days.'

'He's not,' James assured her. 'I told you, that movie reel—'

'Thing is, I kind of need evidence, you see, Jimmy-boy. I'm waiting on some to come in right now – the lowdown on McGee and any known associate of George Barron. And that's what I should be getting in this package.' Tori took a long drag on her cigarette and pushed out the smoke with a sigh. 'Just swim back to Limey-land and fetch that reel, will you? I need to really push my story, and for that I need positive proof – proof that the mob is involved with Kostler through Barron and his men. Don't you see, that's not just one sensational headline; it's a whole bunch: *Gangsters in Hollywood – Chicago Mobsters Work for Top Producer*. Even your fancy

Allworld Academy is implicated. We're talking hold the front page for the next two weeks, Pulitzer Prizes, and Tori Wo's one-stop hitch to the stratosphere . . .'

'How is the Academy implicated?' James demanded.

'On the level? OK. Dr Leaver is well-respected. He's, like, an instant mark of top quality – with his name attached, Allworld schools can get established real quick, anywhere in the world. But get this.' She blew a smoke ring and leaned in closer to James. 'There was this cheap crook, Mac Reagan. Good with a camera. Word is, he took home movies for the mob, with blackmail in mind. Then, one night, he disappeared, the same night a known friend of his was killed, shot in the head from clear across Fifth Street – motive unknown.'

'So? What's this got to do with Dr Leaver?'

'Point is, the police didn't look too hard for Reagan when he disappeared. Turns out he'd had this nice little job offer from the Kostler Academy – they wanted him to give camera-work lessons at a new school in Nairobi, and had sent him a one-way plane ticket. I got hold of the letter the cops found in Reagan's two-bit room out on Olive Street – it was signed by Dr Tobias Leaver and dated the day of that homicide.'

'That's odd,' James conceded.

'So just watch yourself around there, OK? Now, I've got to run before they tow my car. I got a big date tonight – at Anton Kostler's party.'

James was impressed. 'You're going?'

'My boss wangled an invite. But he's got the worst diarrhoea. Such a shame – must be something he ate.' She smiled slyly. 'Something he ate about an hour from now, when I go get it for him and spike it with laxatives.'

'So you get to go there in his place?'

'I've got to. Because who's going to be running security at Kostler's mansion tonight, huh? You got it, George Barron. And it's the hottest party in town, so you can bet he'll bring out his whole gang of toughs – I mean, staff.' Tori tapped her nose. 'Very obliging – I can put faces to names and names to faces, know for sure who's on the payroll. And if my evidence comes through in the way I hope, I'll have enough for a front page that'll land some crooks in jail, the most powerful producer in Hollywood in the dirt, and me in clover.' With a squeal of excitement, she patted James on the cheek. 'Meantime, if you see Junior up to anything again, you call and let me know. And be careful, OK?'

'OK . . .' James watched her sweep away across the reception, his thoughts conflicted. That damned reel that had haunted his thoughts for days, that had almost got him killed – one of the stars of its footage was here, and who was to say how many others were involved? Which meant that tonight, Dan could be placing his head inside the tiger's jaws – and Boody's too.

James sighed. He'd been so determined to stay out of things after leaving Eton. To chase the quiet life for a change. And yet the urge was on him to storm this party tonight and thrust his own head down the wild beast's throat, in the hope of uncovering the truth of things.

Why can't I change? he thought. *How much further can I push my luck?*

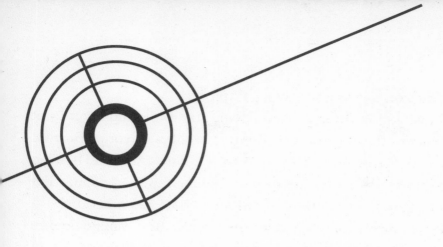

20
The Full Package

Feeling weary and disquieted, James made his way up the stairs to the fourth floor. He heard angry voices carrying down the corridor. Boody, Gillian, Dan and Hugo were standing outside the girls' room.

'Who does he think he is?' Boody sounded angry. 'He can forget it, I'm not wearing it.'

'It's a fine dress,' Dan was arguing. 'It looks like it cost a lot.'

'Well, I hope he kept his receipt!'

James hurried down the corridor to see what was going on. In the doorway to the room lay a large, fancy box, coloured tissue paper spilling from it like guts.

So that's the package McGee delivered, James realized.

'I found this in our room,' Boody told him, 'waiting on my bed. It's a dress by Vionnet, must have cost a fortune. And this note was on top of it.' She thrust a white card into James's hand.

Boudicca
I said you would look beautiful tonight.
Martyn

Hugo sighed. 'He didn't waste much time finding out where you were staying, did he?'

'Ha! The boy's just showing off,' said Gillian, picking up the box and folding the tissue paper back in. 'I doubt his life has ever been conventional. He probably thinks everyone makes such gestures.'

James wasn't so sure. 'Perhaps you shouldn't go tonight.'

'Don't be ridiculous,' said Dan. 'If you don't go, Boody, and if you don't wear it, Martyn will be really offended.'

Boody's eyes narrowed. 'So offended he might stop you playing in his stupid scene?'

'I sometimes think there's an L missing from your name,' Dan muttered.

'Let's all take a little time out, yes?' Gillian said. 'Expressing how we feel is good—'

'Not always,' said Dan, stalking off to the adjoining room.

James followed him and closed the door. 'Listen, Dan, I really do think you should reconsider going tonight. I just talked with that journalist I met. Remember the man with the knife from the film, the man with the birthmark on his neck? He's been seen with Martyn Kostler—'

'For God's sake, Bond!' Dan snapped. 'You're jealous that I'm friends with Martyn and you're jealous that I'm going to the party, so now you're making up a lot of bosh to try and scare me.'

'You should be scared,' James told him quietly. 'We don't know how big this thing is. How far it goes.'

'I thought you knew it all,' Dan sneered. 'For heaven's sake, the brightest stars in Hollywood are coming out for this party! What could possibly happen in such company?'

'I'm only saying—'

'Well, don't! Just forget it.' Dan threw the door open and stamped out of the room.

Hugo poked his head round the door. 'I take it that didn't go so well?'

'No. This whole bloody mess is pretty much down to him, and yet he won't . . .' James trailed off, shook his head. Of course, it wasn't all down to Dan. It was down to the likes of McGee, and whichever sadist gave him his orders.

Today, that had been Martyn Kostler.

James's bruised arm burned all the more as he clenched his fists, feeling utterly helpless.

The world seemed a grey place for James that afternoon.

He lay down and brooded for an hour. Then, for something to do, he decided to see if any of the ball bearings he'd taken from the studio would serve as projectiles in his air gun. Boody had been working on the barrel, shimming the breech seal – but she wasn't in her room any longer, and nor was Gillian.

Perhaps they're sending the dress back to Allworld Academy, James thought hopefully.

He opted instead to work on the stock, only to find it was missing from his drawer.

'Oh, yes. Forgot to say. Boody wanted it,' Hugo informed him.

'Why? It's my pistol.'

'Beats me.' Hugo shrugged, eyes wide.

James's eyes narrowed. 'Hugo Grande, you know something.'

'I don't!' Hugo protested, his voice going high-pitched. 'I'm as empty-headed as they come.'

'I'll ask the concierge if he's seen her,' James decided.

'Really? Oh, I wouldn't bother . . .'

But as James went out, he ran into Boody walking back to her room, holding her white leather bag. She was wearing the same yellow dress as when they'd talked on the lawn at Dartington. It seemed such a long time ago.

'I was just looking for you,' James began. 'And for my airgun.'

'Oh.' Now Boody looked shifty. 'Sorry, I've been working on it. The bore wasn't uniform, which will hamper the pistol's accuracy when firing over distance—'

'Lewis managed to hit me.'

'I imagine he hit you from close range.' She looked at him. 'Obviously, up close is how you cause the most damage.'

Even as she spoke, James found himself taking a step away from her. 'Well, thanks for taking a look. But you needn't do all the work.'

'I didn't mean to take over your pet project.' Boody looked genuinely contrite. 'I'll reassemble it and let you have it back.'

James felt suddenly awkward. 'Thanks,' he managed. 'So, have you decided about tonight?'

'I'm going. As Gillian says, it's only one evening – but a once-in-a-lifetime experience.' She looked wistful. 'Something to look back on.'

'Martyn and Dan will be pleased.'

'But you're not?' Her eyes were questioning.

'It's down to you,' said James flatly. 'Just watch out for Martyn.'

'If he bothers me, I can always get help from the nearest Hollywood A-lister.' Tentatively she reached out and gently stroked his bad arm. 'Poor James. How is your elbow?'

The touch of her fingers felt good. James didn't want it to, and pulled away. 'Oh . . . not as bruised as my pride. You know.'

'Yes, James.' Boody turned and withdrew back into her room. 'Yes, I do know.'

As the door closed, Hugo, who'd been keeping a respectful distance in the corridor, cleared his throat. 'Ever wonder if you've been focusing on projects in place of people?'

James looked at him. 'What's that supposed to mean?'

'Nothing very clever. Just that life is short. Take it from one who knows.'

'I don't want to take it from anyone.' James leaned moodily against the wall.

'Look, how about we cheer ourselves up tonight.' Hugo smiled slyly. 'While Gillian talks shop with old Leaver, we can sneak out. Find a drugstore with a pinball machine and play it all night, or fill our faces with a dozen banana sundaes. Sally forth down the Boulevard, buy ourselves a beer, take in a movie at the Chinese Theatre . . . ?'

James smiled grudgingly. 'I suppose life *may* be just too short not to.'

It was already five thirty, and James and Hugo retired to the plaza downstairs rather than endure Dan, who had returned to the room to get ready, singing in the bathroom. 'You might be deaf to reason,' Hugo yelled at him, 'but there's no need to inflict the condition on us!'

An hour later, James watched as Gillian escorted Boody down the spiral steps into the lobby. Whatever Martyn's several faults, he had some taste: Boudicca looked amazing in the dress, a flattering concoction in white satin and crêpe de Chine, with an asymmetric hem that swept about her knees. Dan came down behind Boody, dapper in his dress suit, looking thoroughly pleased with himself.

'So, you decided to wear it after all.' Hugo dragged his eyes to her face and smiled apologetically. 'Sorry, I like to state the obvious. Saves having to put any real thought into a conversation.'

'I'm wearing it under sufferance.' Boody smiled at Hugo, but ignored James entirely. 'I don't want a scene. I'd quite like one trip out in this city not to end in disaster.'

'I don't suppose he'd dare act up in front of his father,' James assured her.

Boody kept her gaze on Hugo. 'I was thinking of the violence I might do to him.'

'Where's your uncle, Dan?' asked Hugo.

'He's been busy buying a new suit and hiring a suitable car for us.' Dan was preening like a peacock. 'Aha! Here he is now.'

Stuart Sloman came into the lobby, looking elegant in a white double-breasted dinner jacket, nipped in at the waist, with a black bow tie and black dress trousers trimmed with braid. He kissed Gillian's hand, bowed to Boody and ruffled Dan's hair affectionately. James glimpsed a huge motorcar outside in the street with a long, louvred bonnet – a Rolls-Royce Phantom II in black over burgundy; Sloman, Boody and Dan would be showing up in style.

Hugo tugged on James's arm. 'D'you think if I hid in the boot . . . ?'

But James's attention had been taken by the concierge approaching Sloman. 'Excuse me, sir, but a parcel has been delivered,' he said. 'It's at the front desk. Would you like it delivered to your room?'

'Immediately, please,' said Sloman, with a taut smile. 'Now, we must be away.'

Dan tried to take Boody's arm, and with a glance back at James she consented. The doorman held the door open for Sloman as he led the way out to his hired Rolls, Gillian wishing them a lovely time.

'Good luck,' James muttered.

Gillian turned to them. 'Well now, boys. Try not to be too downhearted, hmm? I'd ask you to join Dr Leaver and me, but it seems he wants to discuss a "delicate matter" away from familiar haunts. Just how delicate, I'm not sure. To do with the funding, perhaps.'

Or perhaps not, thought James, remembering Tori's warning. He remembered how unhappy the old man had seemed, how tightly he'd embraced his loyal former student. 'Is Dr Leaver all right, do you think?'

'He's insisting on taking me next door to the Studio Theatre for a show.' Gillian shook her head fondly, as if bemused by the little eccentricity. 'I'm not sure if we'll be listening to Hoagy perform, or simply using him to cover our voices!'

'Who?' Hugo looked blank.

'Hoagy Carmichael. Oh, he's good. A piano-playing singer from New York. I saw him in San Francisco a few times when he was a good deal less well known.' Gillian looked James up and down. 'Now that I come to think of it, there's quite a resemblance, James. Oh, you wouldn't know, you haven't seen him. Well, take my word for it. Anyway, before I leave you, would you care for a game of cards, or . . . ?'

'No, thanks,' said Hugo, with a conspiratorial look at James. 'We might turn in and sulk quietly in our room all evening.'

'Try to use your time well.' She smiled kindly. 'And I know you're both very capable, but you can ask the concierge to fetch me from next door if you need anything. Anything at all. Just stay out of trouble, and don't start any of your own, yes?'

James smiled in compliance.

Hugo mooched away across the lobby. As James followed him, he noticed a bellboy in a tan jacket with white trim fetch a parcel from the front desk and take it over to the lift. Something in the size and shape of it sparked warning bells in James's head.

'Come on.' He grabbed Hugo and dragged him over to the steps. 'Move, as fast as you can. The ninth floor.'

'The *ninth*?'

'We've got to reach Sloman's room ahead of that lift.'

Hugo may have had shorter legs, but they moved in a blur. James explained his plan as he went, finishing as they emerged onto the plush corridor of the ninth floor.

'Do you know Sloman's room number?' James hissed.

'Room 929, I *think* Dan said . . .'

They'd got as far as 921 when there was a ping from the lift. James pushed Hugo in front of him, shielding him from view. He hovered at the door, patting his pockets as if for the key. The bellboy went quietly past with the parcel, opened the door to 929 and went inside.

'Get ready,' James murmured, walking towards Sloman's room.

His timing was good. As the bellboy came out again, James barrelled into him, knocking him to the floor. 'I'm so sorry!' James crouched over the young man, obscuring his view of room 929's doorway, fussing over him for far longer than was necessary. 'Are you all right? Let me help you up.'

'I'm fine, sir. Really.' Shrinking from James's attentions, the bellboy smoothed out his uniform, went back to Room 929, closed and locked the door, and then went on his way with only the briefest backward glance.

And so he didn't notice Hugo lurking in the doorway opposite, the parcel clutched to his chest.

'Good work, Hugo,' James murmured.

'Call me The Shadow.' Hugo seemed pleased with himself too. 'Mind you, we're lucky he put it down by the door and not all the way over on the bed. Now, do you want to tell me *why* I just stole Mr Sloman's package?'

'You'll see.' James pulled out his penknife and carefully cut through the thick brown paper wrapping, leaving minimal signs of trespass. But he already knew what was inside. The scrawled address on the outside was in Dan's handwriting.

And on the inside was a familiar film canister, with a reel of film inside.

'Dan lied.' Hugo shook his head wonderingly. 'He didn't send the evidence home. He sent it here to the hotel. But why, for God's sake? You'd think he'd want to get shot of it.'

'You're missing the biggest thing.' James straightened up. 'Dan didn't send it to himself, but to his uncle. Which presumably means that Sloman knows about it. Dan *did* confide in him after all, even though he told us he didn't.'

'That's a true actor for you — a professional liar.' Hugo looked at James. 'Well, what are *we* going to do with it? Take it for safekeeping?'

'I'm going to show it to Tori Wo first thing tomorrow,' said James. 'She's been wanting hard evidence that the man who drove Martyn Kostler around today is a crook — well, now we've got it. Let her see the proof shown here on film and print *that* in her paper.'

Hugo smiled. 'If it brings a proper end to things and no more madness, then, hallelujah!'

'In fact, why should I wait until tomorrow? When Sloman gets back, he'll want to know where his package is . . . Awkward questions could be asked.' James nodded to himself. 'I'll go and see her now — at the party.'

'At the party?' Hugo looked appalled. 'You can't. You'll never get in.'

'Never say never.' James half smiled. 'I'll think of something.'

'It's a terrible idea, James. If you're right about things, you'll be delivering yourself straight into the lion's den.'

'I've hardly been safe outside it,' James pointed out. 'Since finding this film, trouble's been sprung on me most everywhere I've gone. I'm sick of rolling with the punches. I'm ready to swing a few of my own.'

'But the danger!'

'What's life without a little danger?'

'Longer,' Hugo suggested.

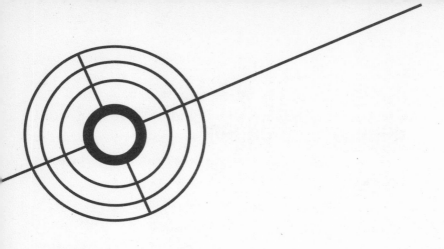

21

How to Crash a Party

James sat sweating in the cracked leather rear seat of the cab, pulling at the starched wing-collar of his shirt. Gillian had warned of dull and official functions that might require a tuxedo; he doubted she'd ever had *this* in mind. The suit was the fine work of Norton & Sons of Savile Row, a firm in existence for over one hundred years. It felt strange to be wearing that badge of old tradition here in the super-modern thrust of Beverly Hills, the Gold Coast of the cinema world, eight miles west of Los Angeles.

Sliding open the window, James cooled his face in the dusty evening breeze as the cab sped along the Hollywood Freeway. In the distance to his right he could see the huge white capitals spelling HOLLYWOODLAND set into the rugged hillside. He'd heard talk of the sign while on board the *Allworld*. It had been put up originally to promote real estate in the area, and expected to stand only eighteen months, but the rise of the movie industry had given the letters fresh meaning: Hollywoodland had become a by-word for intrigue, glamour and wonder. The moon hovered above the 'A' as if it didn't want to stray far from the luminous stars gathered below.

I've got to get a whole lot closer, James realized.

The queasiness building in his stomach was two parts excitement, two parts nerves and one part the swinging motion of the cab as it chewed up the white lines on Mulholland Drive, stealing into the exclusive heart of Hollywood's elite. James hoped Hugo would be all right, waiting back at the hotel alone. He'd talked through his plan with his friend, and Hugo had grudgingly agreed that it might possibly work . . .

Yes. His friend.

It was impossible not to make connections, James supposed. Whatever Boody might think, he wasn't always watching, aloof. He might never hold many close friendships, but he would prize those he had.

The car rounded a bend and a fantastical sight greeted them – the good airship *Zelda* floating above the high walls and treeline, picked out gold and silver in roving spotlights, gloating over the darkened landscape below. 'Kostler's private suite,' he murmured. 'But tonight he's come down to breathe everyone else's air . . .'

The cab turned onto a road that opened up to their left. Kostler's place came into sight slowly, and James marvelled at just how much there was of it. Huge and white, a neo-classical symphony of straight lines and fluted columns, the magnificent mansion looked to James like a wedding cake crossed with a mausoleum; above it, the airship, tethered to its mast, drifted this way and that as if hoping to escape the spot-lights.

'Hey.' The cab driver slowed as they approached a junction. 'You want to be slung out through the main gate to our left or the tradesman's entrance to our right?'

'You can just drop me here.' James felt his pulse quickening, handed the driver a dollar.

'I give you three minutes till you're out on your ear. Want me to wait for you?'

'No. Keep the change.'

The mission was on.

As James got out, the metal film canister dug into his ribs; Hugo had fashioned a kind of harness for him from a pillow-case, so the can was hidden under his shirtfront. It was uncomfortable, but the bulk was mostly disguised by his jacket, and it left both hands free. He'd had plenty of practice sneaking in and out of grand buildings over the last year, and guessed he'd need every scrap of experience to triumph now. The challenge sent a sizzle of exhilaration through him.

James continued along the path, keeping to the scrubby sides. Rounding a corner, he found a set of silver gates stand-ing open in the glare of floodlights, with a smart little cabin to the left – a checkpoint. Two burly men in security-guard uniforms were smoking outside.

James heard a vehicle trundling cautiously up the track, still some way distant. He ran back round the corner and ducked out of sight on the right-hand side of the track.

Finally, a beautiful Pierce-Arrow motorcar came into sight

– broad, elegant and luxurious, it was grey with burgundy fenders. A man and a woman sat in the back, driven by their uniformed driver. James let the Pierce-Arrow pass, then scuttled after it.

As he'd expected, the big car slowed down as it approached the floodlit gate. Keeping low, James jumped lightly onto the running board on the passenger side, the vehicle's bulk between him and the guards. He crouched down, holding on tight, praying the couple in the back wouldn't notice his brazen tag-along in the dark.

'That's in order, ma'am,' a guard said. 'Drive towards the house – a valet will meet you and park up for you. Enjoy your evening.'

'Thanks,' James breathed, clinging to the running board as the car set off again. When the road ahead forked and the driver slowed to maybe five or ten miles an hour, James took his chance and rolled off the running board, striking the asphalt on his side. He rolled over and over to the side of the road, almost crying out as the film can bit into his ribs. The Pierce-Arrow trundled on, oblivious, and once it was out of sight, James made for the other path, which he reasoned would lead to the rear of the house.

His reasoning proved sound, which comforted James as fear and doubt gnawed at his resolve. Ahead, vehicles were clustered on a vast semi-circular swathe of floodlit concrete outside the kitchens. One truck stood near the entrance. A couple of lads his age in tuxes were unloading boxes from inside under the bored scrutiny of a more senior staff member. As James crept closer, using the parked cars as cover, he realized with a shiver that he'd seen the man on the makeshift screen at Dartington. The same man Tori Wo had identified: McGee.

James picked up a stone and threw it at a window at the corner of the kitchen block. He missed; it bounced off the wall. He tried again with another pebble — and this time the impact made a loud retort. McGee turned at the sound and moved to study the window.

As he did so, James darted out of hiding towards the truck. He joined the boys unloading as casually as he could. One of them eyed him without interest, the other ignored him altogether. James picked up a box marked CAVIAR and followed the boys towards the kitchen entrance. McGee glanced back their way, and James had to fight the instinct to freeze. But the thug seemed to have noticed nothing untoward.

Sweating now, James followed the boys inside. Unlike them, after he'd dumped his box he didn't go back for another. Boldly, he picked up a half-empty silver platter of fancy canapés left on a worktop, and strode along a corridor towards the sound of conversation and music.

He was in.

At last, the corridor opened onto a large atrium. A five-piece jazz band was playing a lively ragtime number beside a grand staircase that swept upward out of sight to the first floor. Some guests were dancing, others talking. A tall, handsome man took a canapé from James's tray. With a shock James realized it was Douglas Fairbanks Jr, an actor whose big-screen adventures had always filled him with wonder. He gaped in astonishment; Fairbanks Jr popped the bite-sized snack in his mouth, winked at James, and walked out through a set of French windows.

James wanted to laugh out loud. Then he glanced around nervously, imagining the scene if Dan were to take one of his canapés and start screaming blue murder at the sight of him. But the spectacle was intoxicating, and it was hard not to lower his guard. The more he looked around, the more glamorous he found both the setting and the company. The floor was pink marble inlaid with quartz crystal that shone in the glow from the chandeliers, with doors of solid oak inlaid with claret-dark panels of rosewood. There really were stars here; huge names like Joan Crawford and Clark Gable (who had bigger ears than James would've imagined). To his left, screen Tarzan Johnny Weissmuller was leaning against a broad, fluted column, holding court with an entourage of smiling sycophants. James wanted to go over and offer his platter, but found himself frozen, unexpectedly starstruck. It was a weird, disorientating collision between dreamworld and real life.

What the hell am I doing here? thought James, trying to control his nerves. *Find Tori.*

James held the platter at shoulder-height, as he'd seen the caterers do once at a house party; if it was good enough for the landed gentry, it was good enough for Hollywood. He left the atrium and drifted from room to elegant room, looking for his friend, then came to a sudden stop at the sound of familiar voices from a dark blue study.

Martyn Kostler was in there with Boody and Brad.

'Please, Martyn.' Boody's voice was as cold as her manner. 'I've accepted your "private tour", now I'd like to return to my chaperone.'

'Come on, be a sport,' said Martyn. 'It's not far to the pine grove, and your friend Daniel is longing to see you.'

'I don't want to go outside with you to see anyone, thanks.'

Martyn looked at her wonderingly, a disquieting smile on his face. 'You're being very stupid, you know that? You think I offer what I'm offering you to just anyone?'

'He doesn't,' Brad confirmed seriously. 'You, he likes.'

James shifted his position outside the door, so he could see the reflection of the three in a large picture frame.

'You only just met me,' Boody said.

'I know when I want something.'

'And then you buy it, I suppose.' Boody brushed crossly at the flared hem of her dress. 'Like this was supposed to buy me? I only wore it as a courtesy to you, as I'm a guest in your home.'

'But you like it, right? C'mon, stop playing the prude.' Martyn leaned forward, his voice cajoling. 'I know you love this attention. This is the chance of a lifetime I'm giving you.'

James longed to step out of hiding, tap Martyn on the shoulder and strike him. But Boody had hesitated.

'The chance of a lifetime,' she murmured. 'I suppose it is.' Slowly, she leaned her face closer to his; he smirked, mouth widening like an animal ready to bite. But inches from his lips, Boody stopped. 'It'll be a cold day in hell,' she said softly, 'before I waste another second on a boorish, spoiled little bully like you.'

She turned to storm out, but with a snarl, Martyn caught her arm. James tensed, ready to act and damn the consequences.

'What are you going to do, Martyn?' Boody said softly. 'Use your judo and throw me to the floor? Shall we ask some of your movie-star friends to watch?'

'You'll be sorry for this.' Martyn let her go. 'Like your friend Dan's going to be sorry, in the morning . . .'

James turned discreetly aside with his tray as Boody stalked out of the study, returning polite nods to the several guests who looked her way. He held his breath as Martyn stepped outside with Brad, just a few feet away.

'What're you going to do?' Brad asked softly.

'Don't worry. I'll have her eating out of my palm soon enough, like the dog she is.' With that, Martyn sloped away, and Brad, as ever, followed.

James let out a breath, watching them leave, contemplating murder. What did Martyn mean, Dan would be sorry in the morning? Had that only been an excuse to lure Boody outside, or . . . ?

He decided to follow Boody, to check she was all right.

The corridor gave onto a full-blown reception hallway with a second, still more enormous spiralling staircase in the same glittering marble; James could imagine Fred Astaire and Ginger Rogers dancing up it to some secret celluloid heaven. People were drifting into the hall now as if at some unspoken command. Where was Boody? The strains of the jazz band faded away, and an expectant buzz filled the air. James looked around to find that Anton Kostler was climbing the stairs towards a microphone on a stand beside a loudspeaker. Dressed simply but elegantly in black velvet with a white tie, he turned halfway up the staircase and stood, arms wide, like a priest embracing his flock. A ripple of applause swiftly grew into a rapturous roar. The reflected lights of the chandelier made the marble dance with hypnotic sparks as he smiled around in gracious acknowledgement of the crowd's acclaim, a Caesar before the common folk.

'Dear friends,' he announced, his tone Shakespearian, gloved hands now clasped together. 'I stand here tonight surrounded by colleagues and peers, friends and family, by stars of the screen and creators of legend . . .'

A murmuring of further applause. Even the other waiters were watching, spellbound. James stood behind a huddle of guests, shielded as he looked around the room. There was no sign of Tori, but with a thump of the heart he saw Stuart Sloman across the room, sipping champagne, his eyes on Kostler, while two men stood close behind him, as if keeping watch.

James backed away, heading for the atrium. With Kostler making the most of his moment, it was the perfect chance to take the staircase he'd seen to the rear and look for Tori upstairs.

He put the platter down on a table in the deserted atrium and darted up the marble steps, Kostler's voice carrying, faint but audible:

'*You are all here because I have asked you to help me celebrate my twentieth year with Allworld Studios.*' A ripple of applause. '*Those who have known me during that time are aware of the changes that have not only befallen our industry, but which have befallen me personally . . .*'

The landing had a white tiled floor, with walls accented in black and gold. Beautifully carved doors studded the smooth façade. Exploring, James tried the first one; it opened onto an imposing boardroom with a huge polished oak table and chairs enough for twenty.

'*The passing of my dearest Zelda . . . the growing up of Martyn, my dear son, of whom I am so proud . . .'*

James glanced at the framed prints of Allworld productions from the last two decades on the walls. It was easy to imagine the cinema high-ups from around the world sitting in here for their grand discussions.

'But this is not a time to look back, nor even to celebrate the growth of Allworld Studios from a ramshackle enterprise to a colossus of production that dominates Hollywood. It is a time to look forward to new enterprises . . .'

A creak from somewhere. James peered around, but the landing seemed all clear. He tried the next door. It was locked.

'. . . to look forward to a time when the silver screen blooms with full and radiant colour . . .'

The next door along stood ajar.

'. . . a time that is coming, when Allworld Studios takes the lead in creating movies that will transfix a global audience as never before . . .'

A hand slapped down on James's shoulder.

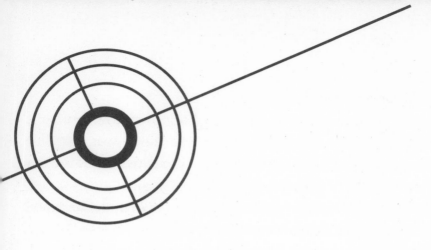

22
Paths Will Cross

'Get in, Jimmy-boy!' Tori Wo bundled James into the room, which was a nondescript, tidy office. 'There're gorillas patrolling up here.'

Heart hammering, James glared at Tori. She looked a far cry from her suited self, in a black silk damask dress, holding a clutch bag. 'God, Tori, you nearly killed me!'

'If I didn't, someone else will if they catch you here. Especially once that gorilla realizes he somehow lost his keys after I "fell into his arms".' She closed the door and held up some keys. 'I thought you were him coming, so I ducked out ready to pretend I was looking for the powder room.'

'Sorry. But I'm glad I found you.' James glanced around – there was a desk with an electric lamp, a bookcase lined with files, not much else.

Tori swung herself round behind the desk, grabbed a file and opened it to a particular page. 'Let me finish up here.

Hit the light. C'mon, move.'

James turned on the desk lamp. 'What are all these files?'

'Dirt on pretty much everyone in the movie business.' Tori pulled from her bag a tiny camera, dominated by a circular lens in the centre. 'Everyone in the world, maybe.' James stared, transfixed, as she held the camera between finger and thumb and started taking pictures. 'It's not mine, it's the paper's. A Fotofex Minifex. Cost a mint.' She turned the papers, peered through the little viewfinder on top of the camera body, and clicked and wound on the film in a swift, efficient manner. 'Takes 16mm film and you get thirty-six exposures across the width of the film. Are you impressed yet? You're impressed, right?'

'I'm impressed,' James admitted. 'What's in the file?'

'Barron's staff payroll.' Tori went on clicking and winding. 'Proof that he's paying all kinds of lowlife to undertake unspecified "security work". My source came through with police files thought "lost" on most of these characters. Including a real nice guy called Leonard Vasquez.'

'Lenny Vasquez?' James felt a tremor shake his chest. 'But he's a promoter – publicizes Allworld's films abroad.'

'He's a con merchant, an extortionist and a murderer,' Tori corrected him. 'I don't know what story he told you, but he's on Barron's private security payroll.'

James leaned heavily against the wall, thinking back over all the easy conversations he'd shared with the man. 'What was he doing in England?'

'Wish I knew.' She lowered the camera and shook her head. 'There again, maybe I don't.'

'Do you think Mr Kostler knows he's employing gangsters for security?'

'I'd like to ask him that myself.' Tori shrugged. 'Of course, Barron's owned a legit private security firm for years. There's nothing on paper in this state to say that Barron and his buddies have criminal form, besides those files I just got hold of.' Tori bit her lip. 'Trouble is, there's no *real* dirt on Barron himself. Sure, there's circumstantial stuff. We know he consorted with these guys back in Chicago, he knew what they were like, but aside from that . . .'

James's breath caught in his throat. 'Wait a moment. "His lordship's got our backs" . . .'

Tori put down the camera, started flicking through another file. ''Scuse me?'

'One of McGee's friends — when Hugo and I were hiding underneath that Lincoln in the alley — when someone got jumpy about the cops coming after them, this guy said, *His lordship's got our backs.*' James looked at her. 'And who would you address as "lordship"?'

'An English lord, or . . .' Tori groaned softly. 'A baron — George Barron!' She looked up from the file. 'That's cute, Jimmy, but I don't think it'll quite stand as evidence in a court of law, you know?'

'Maybe this will.' James tapped the canister strapped to his stomach; it made a dull clang.

Tori raised an eyebrow. 'Should I get out my camera again?'

'It's that film reel I told you about. I didn't have to swim for it after all . . .' Breathlessly, James explained more about the reel of film — about McGee's torture of the British film producer, of the lengths to which Rudolf Dürr, or whoever he was, had gone to get hold of it. 'We were watching it on an old projector with a sheet as a screen, it was foggy and not so clear, but maybe George Barron might feature on it somewhere . . . ?'

'Jeez, Jimmy, I had no idea what you'd been through with this.' Tori shook her head. 'Well, I guess you may be right. And I guess we ought to get the hell out of here so we can see.'

A wave of enthusiastic applause carried from the main hall. 'Sounds like Kostler's finished his speech,' James noted – then broke off as he heard soft, furtive sounds from outside.

Tori heard them too. Hastily, as soundlessly as she could, she packed away the files, while James crossed to the window and opened it. The wooden frame moved freely. Below was a small courtyard, not overlooked. But there seemed to be no way down.

A door along the corridor – the boardroom, maybe – was thrown open with a crash. The hard, sudden sound reverberated through the wall.

'You think they noticed a journalist's been missing from the party longer than it takes to powder your typical nose?' Tori whispered.

'I think,' James agreed. He pushed his head out of the window and craned all around for a drainpipe, or ivy or . . .

Black-coated cables?

They ran in a bundle up the wall beside the window and disappeared somewhere inside the brickwork. With a sinking feeling, James turned to the shelf beside the desk and moved some of the files – to expose a small, concealed microphone.

'Just like on the *Allworld* . . .' James felt sick, dropped his voice to a whisper. 'And I just said all that about the film reel.

210

I'll bet every conversation in this house is being overheard, transcribed or recorded.'

'For blackmail? Inside information . . .' Tori shook her head. 'Well, I guess no one was listening in on us, or they'd have come and got us straight away—'

The door smashed open and the man from the Lincoln burst inside. A welt on his forehead from Boody's pointed heel burned like a third eye.

James strained with all his strength and managed to tip the desk over. The edge struck the man's foot and he snarled, stooped to free himself. James snatched up the desk lamp and smashed it over his head. The man fell back, eyes closed.

James turned back to Tori – but she'd gone. He rushed to the window and saw her scrambling nimbly down the cables.

'I know I'm gorgeous,' she hissed, 'but quit staring and haul yourself down here after me!'

James quickly did as she advised, his hands fumbling for a grip on the cables. Tori's weight must have loosened them; they pulled away from the wall, but they still held. He caught a shaky glimpse of similar wires snaking around the board-room window. Then his soles were slapping down on the ground, and Tori was dragging him away into the cover of some bushes.

'We'd better split up,' she said. 'That guy you creamed is the only one who saw you. You might slip out OK.'

'I won't get far without wheels. Did you bring your car?'

'Ford Plymouth. Blue. Well, two-tone blue and rust. Not fancy enough to be parked up front – security told the valet to park it with the service cars and catering trucks out behind the kitchens.'

'Perfect,' said James. 'Less far to run.'

'Always plan for a quick getaway.' Tori moved away, deeper into the bushes. 'I'll meet you there, Jimmy, OK?'

She was swallowed by shadows before he had a chance to answer.

Palms sweating, James checked to see if anyone was looking from the upper windows. When he saw no one, he broke cover and skirted the perimeter of the mansion, the airship drifting eerily above like some great silver phantom.

He passed some French windows standing ajar; the murmur and tinkle of voices and laughter carried from within. James stepped inside and was clocked at once by a wine waiter across the room. The man looked at him dubiously before hurrying away.

To fetch his superior?

Cursing, James stepped back outside into the warm night and disappeared through a line of trees into a small patio area, bounded by jacaranda and pepper trees, their blue and scarlet blooms full and fragrant. Cicadas thrummed like the night's unseen engine. Branches waved as if signalling a warning. James took their advice and moved on, down a path, through a gap in some saplings, over some crazy paving . . .

Then he heard groans from the other side of a line of pine trees.

Pushing through quickly, James found Dan, sprawled on the ground, fingers locked around a large medicine bottle and his head propped against a tree. He saw James and squinted. 'Wha . . . the hell you doin' . . . ?'

'Dan?' James crouched beside him. 'God, what happened?'

'Tonic. For my voice . . .' Dan smiled and tapped his nose. 'Martyn's decent, whate'er you say. Gave me a tonic to help my voice.'

James sniffed the glass and recoiled. 'It's straight gin.' So this was the 'hilarious' joke that Martyn had played, that he'd wanted Boody to see. 'How much did you have?'

'All the big stars drink this before they perform,' Dan slurred, his eyes unfocused. 'I'm going to act for Anton Kostler! Martyn said so. He's going to bring his father out here to see me . . .'

James shook his head. 'Oh, Dan. You idiot.'

'And . . . he knows about the reel, James!' Dan was still smiling. 'He knows who wants it. Knows how to get them off our backs.'

'Did you tell him the truth?' James tried to keep a lid on his anger. 'Did you say that you sent it to the hotel?'

Dan nodded. 'He can deal with it, you see. He wants to help me, James! I'm gonna be . . . star!' He belched with a nasty, liquid noise. 'I'm . . . gonna be . . .'

'You're going to be sick.' Looking around, James struggled to help Dan sit up. Time was against him; he couldn't just leave. He knew to his cost what it was like to be poisoned by drink. Dan mumbled something incoherent, tried to shake off James's hold. Then James heard furtive move-ments on the other side of a thick drift of yellow acacia, a sound like scuffling.

A voice: 'Get off me!'

James swore. It was Tori.

'Real wildcat, aren't you?' That sounded like George

Barron. 'You bust into my office and think you've still got rights? McGee – knock some of the fight out of her.'

A smack of fist against flesh, and Tori gasped. 'You think you're so tough,' she wheezed, 'don't you?'

'You've abused Mr Kostler's hospitality, young lady,' said Barron quietly. 'Press were told no pictures, and yet you bring a camera.'

'I just snapped a few movie stars. For my paper. I know it was wrong, but—'

'Come on. We both know you were snooping. I ought to write to your boss,' Barron went on. 'Letting a pretty woman like you do a man's work. I know you newshounds have to poke your noses where they're not wanted . . . but you've got to remember, that means, sometimes, your nose is going to get broke.'

Tori gave a muffled cry as another smack hit home. Trying to keep calm, James parted the furry yellow flowers and peered through into a kind of natural arbour. A man was holding Tori's arms behind her back. The gaunt, grizzled form of George Barron towered over her; McGee was at his side with one fist raised. Blood was dripping from Tori's nostrils, and she sniffed noisily.

'You boys are a class act,' she hissed. 'Lay another finger on me and that's it – I won't cut a deal with you.'

'Deal?' Barron scoffed. 'What deal? You've got nothing on us.'

'Really?' She paused. 'Charles "Redneck" McGee, I know you got your kicks beating up on women back in Chicago. I know you've done time for aggravated assault and robbery. I know you picked up that cute "birthmark" of yours in a shootout with the cops back in '28 when one of your home-made firebombs went up in your face . . . and that you tortured that British producer guy on film.'

'So.' Barron's voice was predictably cold. 'How do you know all this? Who've you been talking to?'

'I got hold of those criminal records you paid some flatfoot clerk with the Chicago PD to burn. Turns out he made copies as insurance for a rainy day. I left them with a colleague of mine. If anything happens to me, that information will go straight to the District Attorney's office.'

Barron sneered. 'You think we don't know how to get hold of that reel of film?'

James looked around nervously. Besides Dan moaning softly to himself, all was quiet.

And then it hit him: Martyn's pretended friendship, his getting Dan drunk — it had to be more than just a prank. It was a softening up, prepping Dan to spill all he knew about the reel and its location.

'Now tell me, Tori Wo,' Barron was growling, 'where are these police files?'

'I told you, with a colleague of mine,' she hissed. 'So, like I say, if you let me go, I'll cut you a deal . . .'

Barron laughed softly. 'Know what I think, Tori? I think you didn't share a single page of those files. You're a lone wolf. Got to be — only girl on the team, all that competition, right?'

Tori was glaring up at him. 'I . . . left written instructions before I came out here tonight.'

'Oh, so you're changing your story now? This is bull.' Barron nodded to McGee, who kicked Tori in the right kneecap. The man holding her shoved a hand over her mouth to muffle her scream.

I've got to stop them, James thought. *But how?*

'Poor Tori Wo. The brave little girl, fighting to get the scoop in a man's world.' Barron shook his head, tutted. 'Could make a good movie, don't you think?'

'I'll tell you what'll make a good movie,' Tori hissed, teeth gritted. 'The tale of how you went to jail, Georgie Porgie. How you handed nice fat jobs to the old Midwest Mob, like you were giving out candy bars . . . Helping a bunch of vicious gangsters with their slates wiped clean to play it legit. So clean they can even work someplace as fancy as Kostler's, and become best buddies with his psycho kid . . .'

James saw a large, flinty rock in the soil at his feet. As weapons went it wasn't much, but if his aim was good enough . . .

'Where are the files now, Tori? You tell me, maybe we *can* deal. If you don't, you're going to die for sure.'

'Here at this fancypants party, where any A-lister could walk in on us, any moment?'

'No,' Barron told her. 'Not here . . .'

Suddenly, Dan jerked forward and threw up, noisily and messily, all over himself. James turned in horror, the stench of the sick catching in his nostrils, turning his guts. Dan moaned, shaking, a thick string of drool hanging from his chin, vomit all over his lap and trousers.

Next moment, McGee had pushed through the yellow blooms to investigate. James turned and brought up the rock – but the big man knocked it aside and closed in.

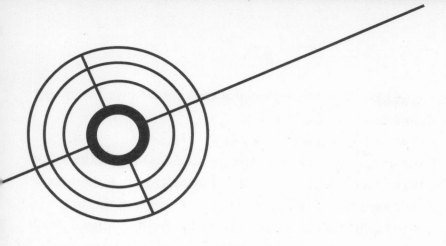

23
Chasing Hollywood

James tried to dodge, but was too slow to avoid a punch to the guts – McGee's fist connected with the film canister. James fell to the ground winded, but as the big man staggered back, he slipped in Dan's vomit and crashed to the ground. Dan groaned and threw up again, all over the man's legs.

As McGee moaned in disgust, James snatched up his rock and pushed through the trees. The man holding Tori stepped forward at the intrusion, trying to shield her from sight.

James hurled the stone into the man's face. He cried out, staggered back, and Tori twisted free.

Barron didn't know who to go for first. The hesitation cost him; Tori kicked him in the groin as hard as she could, and James followed her lead, running over and kicking him there again. Barron sank to his knees, hissing for breath.

Before James could say a word, McGee crashed back through the acacia, out for blood. James stamped down with his heel on the big man's foot and then pushed him into the undergrowth with all his strength.

'Come on!' Tori hissed at James.

'You go. I'll catch you up.' Heart pumping, a metallic taste in his mouth, James darted back to where Dan was kneeling, wretched and shivering on the ground. Grabbing the boy by the collar of his jacket, James hauled him to his feet and propelled him across the lawn towards the house at a fast stagger. He had to get the film away from here to a place of safety.

Tori was already hobbling through the French windows, keeping up the pace though her knee was bloody. James followed, manhandling Dan into the atrium. Guests were whispering, heads were turning their way, and James was glad – with witnesses around, Barron surely wouldn't dare act.

But he'll be planning something, James knew.

He marched Dan along the corridor after Tori, heading for the kitchens. A waitress tried to pass the other way. James stopped her, pushing Dan into her arms. 'His uncle's Stuart Sloman – find him, or a girl called Boudicca Pryce . . .'

The girl fell to her knees under Dan's dead weight as he collapsed to the floor, groaning. But James had no time to stop and apologize, no time for anything but getting the hell away. He hurried after Tori, caught up with her as she was hobbling out through the kitchens and back into the cool night. Her knee looked a mess, almost as blue and battered as her Plymouth.

'I can drive,' she insisted as they reached the car.

'So can I,' James told her.

Tori grimaced at her knee. 'Oh, all right.' She climbed into the car with some difficulty.

James suddenly remembered the car would be left-hand drive, with the gearshift on the right – the opposite of all he was used to.

'How hard can it be?' he muttered, jumping into the driver's seat. The valet had left the key in the ignition so James turned it, hit the starter, searched for the handbrake and released it. As the engine juddered into life, James stamped on the gas. The heavy petrol roar of the accelerator was joined by a squeal of tyres as the Plymouth lurched forwards.

'What do we do about the guards on the drive?' said James. 'If they're onto us . . .'

Tori smiled gorily through bloody lips. 'You think one more dent in this rust-pile's going to show?'

The checkpoint was in sight already. The two guards must have been telephoned – they stood with their guns trained. Two hollow cracks rang out; James ducked down, aiming for the barrier, hitting the accelerator and hoping for the best. There was a jarring impact as the Plymouth struck the bar and smashed it clear. James sat up again, pulling hard on the wheel to stop them careering off the path. He glimpsed two sprawled figures beside the remains of the checkpoint.

'Don't sweat it,' Tori shouted over the roar of the engine. 'They jumped clear.'

James nodded, changed up a gear. Barely braking, he swung the car out onto Mulholland Drive.

'On the right!' Tori yelled, as headlights came swooping towards them round the corner. 'Drive on the right, you dumb Limey!'

James jerked the wheel and the Plymouth dodged a collision

at the last second. James fumbled for a lower gear as he took the tight corner ahead, forced himself to stay calm.

'You think they'll come after us?' he said breathlessly. 'I mean, they're supposed to be looking after Mr Kostler's big party . . .'

Tori wiped at her bloody nose. 'They'll come after us.'

Mulholland, with its ghostly palms swaying slowly in the night breeze, twisted and turned in treacherous darkness. The engine groaned and rattled as he shifted gears, up and down with the constant curves and corners. To his right the LA lights burned in the blackness, while to his left he could see only the unclaimed shadows of the San Fernando Valley. Gripping the wheel, James felt he was taking a tightrope between the two.

Finally, Mulholland gave onto the Hollywood Freeway. It was close to midnight, and the roads were still busy. A set of traffic lights turned red as they approached, and Tori swore.

'Company, Jimmy-boy. Catching up fast.'

James swore too. A black Lincoln was tearing towards them. Fear pushing him into action, James revved the engine and thundered away through the red lights. A van swerved out of their way, horn honking impotently. The Lincoln ran the lights too, looming larger in the wing mirror.

James hurled the Plymouth to the right, almost sideswiping a cabriolet. The driver shouted and made rude signals.

'Can't this thing go any faster?' James shouted.

'No, it damn well can't!' Tori shouted back. 'But slower traffic keeps right here – so move left!'

But the Lincoln was already starting to pull past in the left lane. James saw McGee behind the wheel, with a couple more men in the back. One was sliding down the side window.

A gun barrel edged into sight; the Lincoln swerved towards him . . .

'If we can't go faster, let's try slower!' James stamped on the brakes. The Lincoln shot past, while the Plymouth's loud protesting squeal of tyres on tarmac was almost lost in the clamour of horns that met James's hard left turn on the wheel. Now they were travelling just behind the Lincoln.

James tried to accelerate but the engine grunted and spluttered. *You're still in high gear!* Hand slick with sweat, James grabbed the gear shift, drove his foot down hard on the clutch, heaved the stick into second, while steering hard left with his other hand. The Plymouth went piling across the lanes towards a freeway exit, a reckless move that was met with an insane chorus of screeching tyres, honked horns, the crunch and smash of collisions as cars tried to get out of his way, only to run into others.

Tori groaned. 'You're gonna do their job for them.'

By some miracle, the Plymouth made it through unscathed and onto the exit road. Red lights stared balefully, but James knew he couldn't stop now. He accelerated, roared out into the street beyond, forcing another car to mount the pavement and sideswipe a palm tree. Terrified, muttering apologies and prayers under his breath, he kept on going. A rush of dreadful imaginings whirled through James's mind – breaking down suddenly, helpless as the Lincoln drove at breakneck speed after them . . . patrol cars combing the city for an out-of-control Plymouth, closing in – a whole squad of officers, bribed by Barron to take them straight to the gangsters . . .

James realized a high-pitched metallic noise was fluttering under the acceleration. He was over-revving her. If the

Plymouth threw a rod, the whole engine would be shot.

Stay focused, he told himself.

James turned the car hard right down a wide-open avenue – and as he did, caught a glimpse of a big black car behind. *It's them. They're never giving up.* His hands ached from gripping the heavy wheel, white knuckles set to pop through the skin. The Plymouth thundered past a darkened church, and James prayed for a miracle.

But he'd got himself into this, and knew that only he could get himself out.

'Hollywood Boulevard,' James said quickly. 'Tori, which way is it? If we can get to my hotel . . .'

'Take a right at the lights.'

The lights were green, for once. Without signalling, he swung the car right and took care not to overwork the engine as he accelerated again. 'Where now?'

'Another right, onto Whitley,' she said.

James wished he could close his eyes; the Lincoln was gaining on them like a ravening beast, a note of triumph in the howl of its engine. The lights ahead were red, and pedestrians were milling at the crosswalk. James had no choice but to brake hard as the black Lincoln hurtled closer . . .

At the last moment, a green Corvette shot out from a side-street, inserting itself between the two cars. There was a short, fierce bark of brakes as the Lincoln tried to stop – and smacked into the Corvette.

'Just when I thought our luck was all bad!' James crowed.

McGee started banging his horn, the pedestrians scattered and James took off again, leaving the Lincoln for lost.

Tori laughed out loud. 'I feel way better now. Turn right

onto North Cherokee, then left at the next corner down to Hollywood.'

'Then what?'

'Then you hand me that can of film and you get the hell out of my car, Jimmy-boy. Head east back to the Plaza. You warn your friend and your guardian there are some bad people coming for you. Take a cab to the precinct house down on Wilcox Avenue.'

'The police station, you mean? Yes, Gillian's been there. She knows it.' He swung the Plymouth right, arms really aching now. 'Sure your leg is up to driving?'

'You saying I'm not tough? I'm tough, little man – and I'm all rested up. Trust me, I'll make it. And I need to grab my files from my apartment. I'm going to take them and the film to my office. There's a night watch and guys working the presses for the morning edition – I'll be safe enough there. I'll phone the District Attorney's office first thing, then I'll come find you. Deal?'

James said nothing as he turned left onto Hollywood Boulevard at last. Then he pulled in at a clear stretch of kerb-side, undid his shirt and, with some difficulty, manoeuvred out the film from its pillowcase and passed it to Tori. 'Deal.'

Their eyes met. She had to know it was a big thing for him to hand over the reel. She nodded silently.

'Good luck,' said James, getting out of the car. Tori edged over, wincing with the pain. He shut the door, and the Plymouth was away again, barging into the traffic. James watched her go, standing on the sidewalk, rubbing his bruised ribs. Without the film can, he felt lighter, but slightly lost.

On instinct, he turned. The Corvette had shifted and the

Lincoln, like a vengeful phantom not to be denied, was back on the trail. James ducked behind a streetlamp, watched the big car go past.

'Keep your foot down, Tori,' James murmured.

He stepped out from behind the streetlamp. Then he saw someone running towards him. His guts twisted to see it was Barron. He must have bailed from the Lincoln to go after James on foot – and now he had found his target.

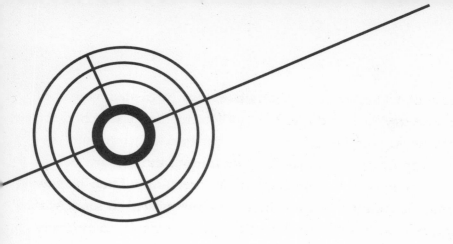

24

What's the Damage?

At that moment, in the great surge of adrenaline, time seemed to slow. With a stab of horror, James saw Dürr, sprinting behind Barron.

So Dürr is one of them, he thought. *He must have been Fedora Man all along.*

Desperation pushed James into madness: he bolted straight out into the busy street. A white truck bore down on him, horn pumping harder than its brakes, headlights glaring. Half blinded, James dodged past it – and almost bounced off the hood of a Bugatti steaming past. There was barely a gap between that and the car behind, but James took it, rushing forwards, only to stop again as another truck thundered past, a whisker from scraping his face off. The familiar soundtrack of squealing brakes and honking horns seared James's ears while headlights, streetlamps and neon hoardings flashed and dazzled wherever he looked. As he scrambled for the central reservation it felt like the whole city was bent on his destruction.

James stumbled up to the concrete barrier separating the opposing streams of traffic, pressed himself flat against it, felt its coolness on his cheek. He didn't dare chance a glance behind; the horns and shouting couldn't all be for him. He hauled himself up the grimy concrete wall, slithered over the top and dropped feet first onto the other side. A huge lorry thundered past, way over the speed limit for sure; its slipstream almost dragged James after it, out into the road. A black Ford followed close behind, but James cut across the lane in front of it, and the central lane too. At the final lane he had to stop as a motorbike roared past, its driver making rude hand signals that James returned as he darted over the last stretch of tarmac and dived onto the sidewalk like a man in the desert reaching cool oasis waters.

But there was no respite here. Passers-by scowled at him, calling him drunk, asking what the hell was he doing?

He forced himself onwards, running down the street at full pelt. His breath was coming in ragged gasps, stripping the back of his throat. He must've sprinted two blocks. Hoping for cover, he ducked down a side-alley beside a grim-looking hotel on Cosmo Street. It led through darkness and drunks to the back of a club, bounded by a high chainlink fence. Without hesitation, James threw himself at it and started to climb, feverishly, his feet scrabbling for purchase as he pulled himself up and over. It was a dizzying drop down, but James took it, landing awkwardly. Pain flared through his ankle, but he refused to heed it, ran towards the beat and twang of music and light from across the yard.

A big black bouncer loomed up, blocking his way. 'Whoa, whoa, boy, where's the fire? You've got to pay to come in.'

Too exhausted to speak, James pulled dollar bills from his inside pocket, pushed them into the big man's hands.

'Oh, so the fire's coming after you, huh?' The big man took the bills, gripped James's arm and pulled him inside. James tried to pull away – *I can't be caught, not now!* – but the bouncer twisted him round so James was behind, hidden from view.

James bent over, tried to breathe deeply. He could glimpse the outside through a thin gap between the bouncer's legs. Breath stopped in his chest as he saw Dürr jog up to the fence, his face a garish red and green in the neon light, looking all around. His black eyes fixed on the bouncer.

'Hey, buddy.' The accent now was American, not German. 'You see a boy come down here, dark hair, lean, little scar on one cheek?'

'No boys in this club, mister,' the bouncer called back. 'Just live ladies dancing. You want a piece of it, entrance is round on Selma.'

'Some other time, maybe.' Dürr – or rather, Fedora Man – looked around again, as if scenting James on the smoky air. Then he turned and walked smartly away into the shadows of the alley.

The bouncer hauled James back out of the darkness and glared down. 'So what gives, little man? That's a lot of green you pressed in my paw, and you ain't exactly dressed for climbing fences. You rob that guy? Is that it?'

'No!' James shook his head fiercely. 'I . . .' He smoothed his hair back from his forehead and took a stab at an

American accent. 'If you have to know, I'm Hoagy Carmichael's son.'

'Carmichael . . . ain't he that piano guy?'

'Right. We're here from New York. Dad's playing the Studio Theatre tonight, left me on my own. Thought I'd take a look around by myself.' James paused, mind racing. 'Uh . . . that guy after me is my minder. I spend a lot of time running from him.'

The bouncer smiled. 'Your old man is pretty rich, huh?'

'We do OK, sir.'

'Then I will keep your kind donation, little man.' The bouncer slapped James heartily on the back. 'You can slip out through the front.'

James grinned. 'Uh . . . is the Studio Theatre far from here?'

'About six blocks south-ways. Watch out for men in fedoras.'

Yes, thought James, pushing through the cramped, smoky din of the dancefloor. *I'll watch out for them.*

James made his way south. He hoped for the hundredth time that Tori really was OK to drive . . . that she'd made it to her place, and on to the newspaper.

How he wished that with a single yell of 'Cut!' the disturbing movie his life had become would simply stop, ready for a more agreeable retake.

If only life were like the movies.

His heart jumped as he saw the Plaza soaring up above the street. With a last effort, James pushed himself towards the hotel. The doorman greeted him.

'Have you seen Miss de Vries?' he panted. 'She was next door at the Studio Theatre with an older man.'

'They came back a while ago. Said they were having a nightcap in the bar.' The doorman was all smiles – until James explained he had no money left for a tip.

Looking all around as he entered the lobby, James prayed he wasn't still being followed. Everything seemed normal. Well-heeled men and women populated the place as usual. It was suddenly hard to believe that his nightmares tonight had even happened.

Aside from the aches and the blisters, the cold sweat that left his clothes plastered to his body, and all his money gone, of course.

Gillian and Leaver were not in the bar. With rising unease, he went up to the fourth floor to check on Hugo.

The door had been left unlocked.

Inside, James saw that Hugo's luggage had gone.

'No,' James breathed, his stomach churning anew. 'Oh, no.'

There's got to be a note, he thought. *Where?* He searched the dresser, went through empty drawers. In desperation he threw back the covers of Hugo's unslept-in bed and his own.

Beneath his pillow, James found a parcel wrapped in tissue paper. He snatched it up and tore it open.

Inside he found Lewis Judge's cannibalized air pistol, back in one piece and fully restored. The barrel assembly gleamed blue-black, as new, not a trace of rust or residue remaining. The belt-buckle trigger had been properly weighted, its action firm but smooth, and the chunky stock he'd spent so long sanding had been stained and varnished. Carved carefully into the base of the stock in small, discreet capitals was the word QUEENSMARSH.

James saw there was a note on the tissue paper; it was

unsigned, but the neat, precise handwriting was unmistakably Boody's.

Something to occupy you once Gillian's tucked you in. You realize I had to raid the Plaza's maintenance supplies to finish it? I know it's presumptuous of me to give your pistol a name – it's not exactly Excalibur and I'm not exactly the Lady of the Lake – but it's the place you got hold of this thing, and the place you escaped.

I think you can probably escape anything, James Bond. Anything but yourself.

Told you I like to know how machines work.

Escape, yes, James thought, with a guilt that seared. *And I left you behind, with Martyn making sick threats.*

He wondered where Dan was right now – if Mr Sloman had learned yet what had happened to his nephew. What the fallout would be.

Feeling sick, James dropped the note on the bed, stuffed the pistol in his trouser pocket and padded down the corridor towards the girls' room, praying Gillian and Hugo would be there.

They weren't. But Dr Leaver was, sitting on the edge of the bed, a cup of cold-looking coffee at his side. He raised his head slowly as he registered James's presence. The old man looked terrible – sweating and pale.

James felt awkward. 'I . . . I was looking for Gillian. I thought you two . . . ?'

'We talked,' he said dully. 'In the theatre. It was so noisy, I thought we'd be safe there. I thought no one would hear.'

James felt a bad taste grow in his mouth. 'What's

happened?' He looked around in bewilderment. 'Where is she?'

'She's not here.' Leaver shook his head. 'When we got back, an hour or so ago, she came upstairs to check on you and Hugo. She didn't return. I went looking, in the end. The door was open . . . she wasn't here.'

'Hugo's gone too. Even his luggage.' James crossed to a wardrobe, nerves sparking in his belly; he recognized plenty of Boody's clothes hanging there but none of Gillian's. 'Dr Leaver, I think someone's got to them. Most likely on the say-so of George Barron from Allworld.'

Dr Leaver looked shaken. 'What's that?'

'I think you heard me.' James walked further into the room. 'Barron's involved with Chicago gangsters.'

'Don't . . . don't be ridiculous, boy.'

James remembered Tori's tale. 'Why did you write to a criminal called Mac Reagan, offering him a job at the Nairobi Academy the day he disappeared?'

'You can't know about that . . .' The old man's head bowed, until his bald pate was like a big, pink eye aimed his way. 'You can't.'

'It's going to come out. All of it.' James didn't like goading the old man, but right now there was nothing else he could do. 'Unless you help me.'

'I can't. This is all beyond help now. And it's my fault!' Leaver's thick fingers knitted clumsily together. 'My last chance of catching a lifeline. Oh, Gillian, you were always such a compassionate student . . .'

'Sir, please,' James said slowly. 'What do you mean, it's your fault?'

'I persuaded Gillian to come out here. I thought she could

231

help me get away to England – help me escape him . . .'
Leaver was starting to weep. 'But he knows I've talked to her,
don't you see? That's why he's taken her. He knows, and now
he'll punish me again.'

'He? You mean Barron?'

'I . . .' The old man wiped his eyes. 'I mean Kostler.'

James felt chills turn through his body.

'I made one mistake. Just one indiscretion! There was a
student, you see, such a bright boy . . . He was in debt, and to
try to get out of it he was doing . . . bad things. I went to
him, hoped I could help him.' Leaver shook his head, sent
tears plopping to his lap. 'Kostler got wind of the business
through Barron's contacts. He filmed me coming and
going, twisted everything, incriminated me. Said he'd send
the film to my colleagues at the faculty . . . shame me in the
eyes of the world.' Leaver shook his head, clawed at his
damp eyes. 'He made me his puppet. Well, it's gone too far,
James.'

'Come with me to the police, Dr Leaver,' James urged him.
'You'll be safe there—'

'There is no safety.' Leaver wiped his nose on the back of
his hand, a schoolboy gesture, and a bitter laugh escaped his
lips. '"Come weep with me," said Shakespeare's Juliet. "Past
hope, past cure, past help . . ."'

The words died on his lips. He was looking past James.

To someone else, standing in the doorway behind him.

James spun round to find Lenny Vasquez, all smiles – as he
smashed a fist into James's stomach. Caught by surprise, the
air punched from his lungs, James hit the floor hard. He rolled
over, trying to get out of range. But Lenny planted a boot on

James's chest, the heel digging under the breastbone, pinning him to the ground.

Unable to breathe, pressure building and buzzing behind his eyes, James looked helplessly at Leaver. But the old man was shielding his eyes with his hands, quietly sobbing.

'Having to do this to a nice kid like you, it pains me. It really does.' Vasquez pressed his foot down a little harder. 'A lot of things can happen to a kid, this far from home. Bad things.'

Lenny raised his boot, and for James it was like an anvil had been lifted. He gasped for air, as the foot shifted to hover above his forehead.

Then the heel stamped down hard, and James knew nothing more.

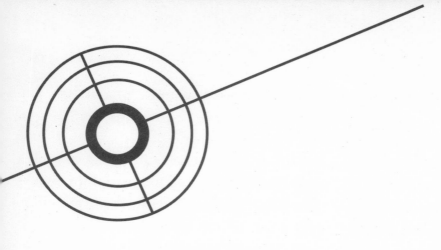

25

Director's Cut

Hearing was the first of James's senses to return; distantly in the blackness he thought he could hear water rushing. He was by a stream. His head was drumming.

I must be back at Queen's Marsh, he thought, in a daze. For a precious moment, he was certain that all he'd lived through in LA had been some fevered dream. The moss beneath him was soft but the fragrance was wrong. He could smell must and cigarette smoke.

No dream.

James tried to open his eyes but a tight, bruised burning made him wince. The noise had resolved into a rushing, flickering whirr, not water going by but film spooling over the lamp of a projector. The moss was a rich, crimson carpet; he was lying on it, on his side − in the front row of a cinema. The smoke was coiling in the silvery dark above him; its smell made him nauseous. He tried to push himself into a sitting position. No good.

His hands were tied behind his back.

James turned his head towards the blur of a big screen and forced himself to focus. He recognized the footage of the film producer, Alexander Roberts, being stabbed in the arm, and McGee's grinning face.

'Funny how Roberts changed his tune about signing that contract, handing power in his movie company to you.' Vasquez was giving a commentary. 'And he's a shoe-in for the British government committee on censorship in movies. He's well respected, got a lot of say – and he'll say whatever you tell him to.'

'He shows pain exquisitely well . . .' That sounded like Kostler. 'Run that part again.'

In a bilious blur James remembered the violence that had brought him into blackness, and felt chilled to the core. They'd got hold of the reel. They must have found Tori. There was a thunk of machinery, a change in the whirring. The images ran backwards, then forwards again, then paused, capturing Roberts' silent scream.

'We should get someone to dub a real cry over that,' Kostler said softly. 'You could ask one of your students, perhaps, Tobias?'

So Leaver's here too? thought James. At once, he remembered Queensmarsh. Maybe he could use it, try to bluff his captors? He tried discreetly to reach it, but no – it was gone from his pocket.

'Ah, Master Bond, you're awake,' said Kostler at once. 'Quite a party last night, wasn't it? Sit up, please.'

James did as he was told – he wanted to get the lay of the

land – and struggled into a sitting position. The world seemed to turn on a pivot, and he winced. He realized he'd been dumped beside the front row of a small cinema. Ten rows of eight plush fold-down chairs filled most of the space. Sitting right at the front was Anton Kostler, flanked on either side by Barron and Vasquez. All three were wearing the same clothes they'd worn last night; and judging by the four o'clock shadows and bags under their eyes, they'd not slept. Seated at the back, looking abject and defeated, was Dr Leaver, while Boody was lying on the floor at Barron's feet, trussed up like a joint at the butcher's.

'Where are we?' James said croakily.

'In the viewing theatre of the old Allworld Studios.' Kostler's eyes remained riveted to the screen. 'My crimson velvet shrine to times past.'

That explains the smell of age, James thought. *I'm back at the Academy. In the part Martyn didn't want us to see.* 'Where are Hugo and Gillian? And Tori? If you've got the reel, I suppose you must have her too.'

'Your little group has vexed me greatly,' said Kostler quietly. 'But one by one, we are dealing with you. Tori Wo, Mr Sloman and Daniel have already learned what awaits them. But you and the girl are sounder sleepers.'

'That pig Martyn . . . put something in my drink.' Boody shifted on the floor, her voice slurred. 'Knocked me out. Woke up here.'

'We should've dumped them in the arena all together,' Barron opined.

'Come, Mr Barron,' Kostler chided. 'It's important our young friends understand their motivation.'

Motivation? James puzzled blankly over the ominous word. His only motivation right now was to get himself and Boody the hell away from here. There were two exits, he noted – one near the front, to the right of the screen, and one at the rear to the left. James found his legs were not tied up and thought briefly of running to get help. But Barron was holding a revolver, and in any case – what help could he hope to find outside, particularly while his friends were being held?

Kostler raised a gloved hand and the film rolled on to show the man being beaten in the underground car park.

'Now, these guys show potential,' said Barron. 'That one really getting into it, I told you about him. Goes by the name of Jack Strap; he's made some pretty big ripples in New York. He's real ambitious and he's in town, so I've brought him in for the exercise today.'

'I look forward to your further assessment,' said Kostler languidly. 'The man on the ground is from the British government's Board of Trade, I understand. He'll agree to increase movie imports from us by thirty per cent?'

'Sure. He was real easy to convince,' said Vasquez. 'Can't you see?'

'Your camerawork improves, Mr Vasquez. I'm glad this footage has been recovered. It should help convince those we aim to work with and those we seek to intimidate that we mean business.'

'Thank you, sir.' Vasquez sounded genuinely proud as the violence continued on the screen in sickening detail. 'Hey, and there's his lordship giving us his best side!'

James saw that in the corner of the scene, Barron's face was clearly visible.

'That's enough,' came the gravelly voice. 'I *knew* you'd got me in shot. How many times have I told you – you never – ever – get me in shot.'

'I know, I know.' Vasquez sounded unrepentant. 'Look, it wasn't me who sent out the wrong goddamned reel to that chump Sloman . . .'

'Poor old Mac Reagan.' Barron did not sound remorseful. 'Gets in a friend to help him out, friend screws up. Both of them end up sorry.'

'I've seen exactly how sorry they were,' Kostler said quietly. 'Many times.'

'Wait.' James stared. '*Sloman* got sent the reel? He told me he sent you some film prints of underwater scenes, but you sent them back.'

'That's what Sloman should've got,' said Vasquez.

'It was an accident he tried to turn to his advantage.' Kostler signalled and the film stopped playing. As the house lights were raised, he rose from his seat and turned his other-worldly eyes to James. 'Poor, foolish Sloman. He thought to blackmail me into giving him a career.'

'*He* was the one who asked Crispin to keep it for him at the Alhambra.' Boody closed her eyes. 'He used to work there, of course.'

James glanced at Vasquez. 'And he must've known some-one would be looking to take it from him.'

Vasquez nodded. 'I always knew it was just a matter of time till we got it back safely.'

'Before or after you killed that kid projectionist?' Barron retorted.

'I thought he was playing me for a dope!' Vasquez

whined. 'How was I supposed to know Sloman's brat had taken it?'

'So you murdered him. A foolish, attention-drawing waste.' Kostler sounded petulant. 'You didn't even *film* it.'

'How can you do this?' Crumpled and tearstained, Boody sounded defeated. 'How can you live with yourselves?'

'I truly don't see how we can take the blame,' said Kostler smoothly. 'If Stuart Sloman hadn't chosen to try to blackmail me into giving him a position here in Hollywood, the projectionist would've lived. If his dreary nephew Daniel hadn't taken that reel and shared it with you and your friends, you would not have to die. And if dear Tobias hadn't told your tutor everything in the hope he could run away to England and live happily ever after—'

'Stop it!' James hissed. 'You're a madman.'

'Not at all,' said Kostler. 'I am simply the director, taking responsibility for his story. Stepping in to tie up the loose ends.'

Boody looked at James; he thought of how he'd brushed her touch away yesterday and felt a fool. 'What are we going to do?' she whispered.

'I rather think that's for me to decide.' Kostler smiled and steepled his fingers. 'My productions always deliver a memorable climax.'

James glared at him. 'Why are you working with gangsters?'

'Just a means to an end,' said Kostler mildly. 'You know, the Bolshevist Russians have long cited cinema as the most important of the arts. The Nazis, too, cherish its power of propaganda, its scope of influence, while the fascist movement in Italy claims, *Il cinema è l'arma più forte* – "cinema is the most powerful weapon". You see, movies influence the mind, manipulate the feelings . . . they can tell people what to think. And while the United States stays out of world affairs as a rule, its movies have more reach and impact around the globe than any other power.' He laughed, an almost girlish sound. 'The trouble is, there are too many film-makers, too many voices. Too many studios at cross-purposes—'

James shrugged moodily. 'So what, you want to become the voice of them all?'

'Don't interrupt,' snarled Barron.

'No, it's all right.' Kostler held up a hand to stay his hench-man. 'This young man is surprisingly astute. You see, what I require in life is . . . control.' He nodded, as if satisfied that this was indeed the case. 'Knowledge of my opponents, acquired through surveillance by hidden camera or microphone, helps me to gain it . . . and my relationship with Barron and his men allows me to enforce it. Blackmail, intimidation, exploitation . . . it's the stuff of movies, is it not?' He gave another effete laugh. 'From other studio heads to the owners of the biggest cinema chains – in this country and any coun-try – *I* will control which movies get made and shown, right across the world.'

'So you didn't just fly out those movie bigwigs for a celebration,' Boody muttered.

James shook his head. 'I saw the microphones on board the *Allworld*, like the ones in your house.'

'You smart-assed little . . .' Vasquez's small dark eyes flashed for a moment. Then he shrugged. 'People say a whole lot when they're relaxed and well-oiled and got nothing to do but talk. And when they think things are private, a whole lot of secrets spill.'

Barron nodded. 'We couldn't blackmail them if they didn't do this stuff in the first place.'

'And as for those few who lead blameless lives, well . . . they're the ones we show the footage to, such as the reel you've tried so hard to protect. Footage which my dear son shows a real flair for producing.'

'You must be so proud of him,' James muttered.

Kostler smiled benignly. 'They see that Mr Barron and his men are not playing games . . . and they take us seriously.'

'You really enjoy watching those . . . those horrible scenes?' Boody shuddered. 'You're sick.'

'Hey.' Vasquez lashed out with a foot and kicked her thigh, making her gasp. 'Respect.'

'Why should I respect him?' James could hear Boody was trying to keep the shake from her voice. 'He's sick. Him *and* his son.'

'You're swift to judge us, my dear,' Kostler chided, apparently unperturbed. 'I suppose many would. But over time, we can use our movies to shift perceptions, to show what might be, to change how people think and feel. At the same time, I'll be founding influential academies all around the world that will reinforce my values in the psyche of the emerging generations . . .' He gestured to Leaver, still slouched at the back. 'With a respected educational authority like dear Tobias attached, and the touch of Hollywood glamour my film-making classes bring, we can't fail to have enormous reach and impact.'

'Meantime, the schools in Nairobi and down under are a good way to lose people,' Vasquez chipped in. 'Like you and your friends, James. Doc Leaver's gonna put in writing how useful it would be for you to visit there as part of your trip . . . but then, guess what? Your plane's gonna go down over the ocean. No survivors.'

James turned up his nose. 'Who'd believe that story?'

'Who would doubt someone as fine and upstanding as Doc Leaver, huh?' Barron smiled. 'Besides, they'd have to scour an awful lot of ocean to prove him wrong. And by then your bones will have spent so long in our furnace here, you'll be nothing but ash.'

'Don't.' Boody had closed her eyes. 'Please.'

Vasquez ignored her, affecting deep thought. 'What about Sloman, though, boss? I guess you should let him go on the trip too, to look out for his nephew?'

'Or perhaps it's for research?' Kostler suggested. 'An African epic I hoped he would write for me—'

'Just stop it, can't you?' James shouted.

'It will never stop,' said Dr Leaver quietly.

'Oh, you accept that now, Tobias? At last!' Kostler sighed. 'It's such a shame you felt you had to confide your unhappiness to the charming Miss de Vries. Especially after I facilitated her expedition here as a reward for your . . . loyalty.'

'Nonsense,' Leaver murmured. 'You knew I was desperate, knew she was my only hope. You agreed to fly her out here with the others simply to take that hope away from me . . . to show me I'll always be your puppet.'

'The former student teaches the tutor a lesson,' Kostler agreed. 'That's a neat narrative twist, don't you agree?'

'You're a monster, Kostler!' Leaver stood up, stabbing a finger, anger overcoming his fear at last. 'A filthy, twisted—'

'Sit down, Tobias!' Kostler thundered. James saw he'd turned white with fury; in his grey suit he looked like he'd just jumped out of his own monochrome movie. 'Now. You will watch the freshly shot footage of our latest private production with me here.'

Leaver shook his head. 'No!'

'You will, I assure you.' Kostler smiled down at James and Boody. 'And we shall savour what I'm sure will be a most powerful performance from our two young stars here. Third and fourth billing behind glamorous journalist Victoria Wo and the ambitious blackmailer, Stuart Sloman. The action will be improvised, but most convincing, I'm sure.'

'What do you mean?' asked James quietly.

'You can't do it.' Dr Leaver slumped down in his seat again. 'You can't film the slaughter of these innocents.'

James felt fear stab through him. 'Slaughter?'

'It's evil,' cried Leaver. 'It's wrong.'

'Wrong?' Kostler's voice was a whisper, but it riveted the room. Vasquez and Barron swapped apprehensive glances, like something big was about to break. 'There's no reason behind life and death. Was it right that my Zelda was taken from me?' He cast a clouded look at James and Boody. 'She died of renal failure. Did you read about that in the gossip rags, in the glossy magazines? Did you read about the way her body bloated, the confusion she felt, the crippling pain . . . And there was nothing I could do. Nothing.' He was trembling with outrage, eyes bulging and grotesque. 'I rose so far with her at my side. We were unstoppable. Irresistible. Then . . . a new ending to our story was passed down from on high. She was taken. The shot was called, only . . . I didn't call it.'

We all lose people close to us, James wanted to say. *Get over it.* But something in Kostler's unfocused gaze made him keep his silence.

'That's when I thought of the motto of the school, you see? The vision is loftier than the reality, but both must be sought.' Kostler crossed to a table facing the front row, and picked up the squat box of the movie camera. 'I've done that, you see? My little films take dreams and make them real. I *direct* reality – I am the one in control!' He clutched the camera to his belly as a child might a teddy bear. 'And each time I watch a man's last moments here in my little cathedral . . . as I watch and re-watch you, and the girl, and the dwarf and Sloman and that gutter-rag journalist and your poor, dear chaperone die . . . that's proof. Proof that I'm the one who gets to choose who lives . . . and who doesn't.'

Boody looked at James, her pale eyes wide and glistening. 'He's mad,' she whispered.

'Do you know, I almost wish I were, my dear.' Kostler reached down with a gloved hand and touched Boody gently under the chin, making her flinch. 'Perhaps then, I wouldn't hear and see my poor Zelda . . . wherever I go.'

Barron cleared his throat respectfully. 'Yours is the voice, boss. But you know, I think the boys will be ready by now. It's past five a.m. Safest to be through here before school starts.'

'Yes.' Kostler slowly withdrew his hand, looked at Boody and James with a reassuring smile. 'Please know, your deaths won't be in vain, children. They're going to ease a little of

245

the pain for my son and me. They're going to bring us such satisfaction . . . again and again.'

Boody screamed as Barron grabbed her and swung her over his broad shoulder. James tried to scrabble to his feet, but Vasquez knocked him to the ground, grabbed him by his collar and dragged him across the floor as he might a bag of rubbish. While Leaver held his head in his hands, James saw that Kostler had started filming, standing grey and solitary like a graveyard statue, the camera lens like a single eye. Like a weapon pointing after him.

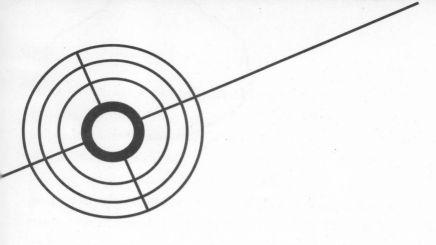

26
Shoot to Kill, Slowly

James had acquired a dozen more bruises by the time Vasquez had manhandled him through the shadowed corridors. Barron moved ahead, carrying Boody. Finally, he unlocked a large metal fire door, shoved it open and dumped her inside. James was thrown in after her, landing face down on a dirty floor, arms still tied behind his back and unable to break his fall.

There was a scraping metal clang as the door was slammed shut, and the heavy jangle of keys turning. The echoes kept them cold company for several seconds.

'Oh my God, James,' Boody hissed. 'What is this?'

James looked around at their spooky surroundings. The immediate impression was of a classic Western saloon, lit gloomily by lamps suspended from the distant ceiling. The set had been half destroyed, not by the staging of a boisterous bar-fight, but by old age. Mouldering crates stood here and there. Tables had been overturned. Broken glass littered the floor; James struggled to pick up a shard, hoping to saw through his ropes – but it was fake stuff that crumbled in his hand. Dark stains on the floor might have been red wine. Or blood.

Beyond the dilapidated saloon doors stood a gypsy caravan, some haystacks, and then open gloom; the saloon was only one set in a space as vast as a warehouse. The battered backdrop of a desert sunset stretched epic reds and golds across an expanse of rear wall, mottled with damp. Close by stood the remains of a city street, and beyond that, a rooftop fashioned from paint and plywood. Props from any number of productions stood in misshapen, cobwebbed heaps: a bundle of streetlights stacked against an ancient motor-car with all four wheels missing . . . a heap of scenery flats propped precariously against a truck, creating a strange, abstract sculpture . . .

It was a shadow-place of dreams rotting into nightmares.

'This must be where Allworld Studios used to make their films,' James murmured. 'Martyn said as much on the tour, remember?'

Boody nodded. 'So we're in that old building beside the mooring mast.'

James caught movement, something dragging itself towards him. Furiously he struggled against the ropes chewing at his raw wrists. 'Keep away!' he snarled. 'Get back—'

'James?' came the call from the dark. 'Jimmy-boy, is that you?'

'Tori?' Hope flared brighter than pain for a few moments. 'Tori, yes, it's me and my friend Boody. Are you OK?'

'Been better.'

As James's eyes adjusted to the low light, he saw Tori limping with the help of Stuart Sloman. She was barefoot, her black dress dusty and torn. Sloman was still in the dinner suit he'd worn to the party the night before, his features bruised and split. Beside him, holding his hand, was Dan, his head bowed. He stank of sick and looked pale and ill.

James's elation bled away. No help was coming. They were all trapped in this together.

Sloman extricated himself from Dan and Tori, crouched beside James and set about his ropes. 'We managed to untie each other . . . if you just hold tight—'

'Help Boody first,' James insisted.

'True English gent, aren't you, Jimmy-boy?' Tori crossed to Boody. 'Hey, honey, I'm Tori. Think you could get me a cold beer and a smoke? No?'

Boody couldn't muster a smile, let alone a response.

'This is all your fault.' James glared at Sloman. 'You thought you could blackmail Kostler, and you let Dan come out here with you! You must've known they'd try to use him against you to get that reel back!'

'It was you who stole it from Uncle's room and just gave it away,' Dan retorted. 'If you hadn't—'

'No, James is right,' said Sloman, picking at the final knot until finally it fell free. 'Sooner or later it would all have gone to the bad. I'm to blame.'

'It's Leaver's fault too,' said Boody coldly. 'What's happened to Hugo and Gillian?'

'I'm sure they'll be joining us shortly.' Dan wiped crossly at his nose and eyes. 'Oh, God, I don't want to die. I don't—'

'You know, troops,' Tori broke in, 'the sniping and the whining won't help us a whole lot right now.'

James knew she was right. He shook his hands to encourage the circulation, blew on his chafed-raw wrists. 'How'd they get you, Tori?'

'You know, I truly thought I'd made it. Got back to my apartment – and then they jumped me.' Tori grunted as she pulled loose Boody's bonds. 'Woke up and found your pals already here.'

'We've been looking all around for a way out,' said Sloman. 'Not a chance. The exits are boarded up, save for the door they used to put us inside – and that's plated with steel and bolted from the other side—'

'*You've got to know, Sloman, there's only one way out from here.*' Barron's voice barked out through a loud-hailer as a switch was thrown and more lights in the ceiling flared into life. The area around the saloon and the caravan was now floodlit, while in the wider studio the darkness had deepened.

James saw Barron standing perhaps thirty feet above them, leaning forward over the rail of a gantry – a system of high platforms spanning the length of the studio walls. Once, the gantry would have allowed access to lighting rigs, but now it led to blank wooden doors built high into the walls at regular intervals of perhaps forty feet.

What's behind those doors? James wondered. To the left of each, dark horizontal slits had been scored into the concrete in place of windows, like the holes in wartime dugouts through which soldiers could shoot while retaining their cover.

Barron raised the loud-hailer lazily to his lips. 'Here's the thing, people.' His voice distorted out into the cavernous space. 'I get a lot of guys wanting to join my private security firm, and with Mr Kostler's business expanding, we're always looking for reliable recruits. So, whenever we get a few people together who gotta be rubbed out, we hold . . . auditions.' He paused, letting the awful possibilities sink in. 'Pretty soon now, we're going to let some guys into this place who want to kill you. They're real keen, too, 'cos there's a cash bonus for whoever pulls off the fanciest kill. That's why some of our old hands are joining us, boosting numbers. And they all want a piece of you.'

'You can't be serious, Barron!' Sloman shouted up at him. 'Dan and Boody and James, they're just children!'

Barron shrugged. 'They're old enough for most things in this city.'

Boody looked to be in shock; she barely reacted. Dan had started weeping again. But James jerked his head round, taking in the ghostly studio in swift, decisive glances. At the same time he checked his pockets for anything useful; if only he'd taken time to sew one of his blades or penknives into the lining of his jacket . . . if only he hadn't lost his hard-won Queensmarsh.

'You can't just kill us, Barron!' Tori yelled. 'Don't you think we'll be missed? Looked for?'

'One thing about the old furnace here, it really does burn *everything*. And with half the cops in this city on our payroll, and the other half buying our story that you guys flew out to see another wonderful Kostler academy, who's going to come looking?' Barron opened the door behind him, which gave onto a softly lit space; James couldn't make out details. 'Oh, and guess what? My guys are already in there with you. Armed, of course. Mr Kostler has asked them to go after the ladies first. So you boys can either do the chivalrous thing and protect them, or you can run and try to save your own hides . . .'

As Sloman shouted and swore at Barron, James pictured Fedora Man, ready to stalk him through the studio, gun in hand, and shuddered. But he'd come up against people with guns before and lived. He wasn't ready to roll over and die just yet.

'We need to find good cover,' he said. 'Fast.'

'Good?' Tori banged her fist on a flimsy table and almost broke it. 'Everything's cheap props, unfinished, falling apart.'

A sudden buzz like an alarm came from inside the room off the gantry. Barron ducked inside, and came out holding a telephone receiver to his ear. James could imagine who'd just called. 'You got it, Mr Kostler. Cameras one and three . . . *action!*'

'Those scenery flats propped against the trunk near the far wall,' said Sloman. 'We can hide behind them.'

'Maybe there's an exit round there.' Tears were crowding Boody's eyes. 'There might be.'

'They'll shoot us down before we get halfway,' Tori muttered. 'They must be waiting there in the shadows.'

'We have to work together,' James insisted. 'Perhaps stand back to back and keep a lookout in all directions as we make our way over—'

Sloman shook his head. 'That'll just make us one big target!'

'Are you saying we should split up?' Tori snapped. 'Everyone for themselves?'

A gunshot cracked from the darkness, and an overturned table jerked as if kicked. James pushed Boody behind the saloon bar and jumped after her, quickly followed by Tori, Sloman and Dan. But another shot blasted out, and another, blowing splinters from the wood, peppering James's skin.

'They've got us already!' Dan whimpered.

James fell back against the bar, and it shifted under his weight. He turned, found a loose panel, clawed at it, wrestled it free; beneath the countertop, the body of the bar was hollow. Sloman grabbed the panel from him and held it up as cover while Dan, Boody, Tori and James crawled inside the gloomy space. The square of wood jumped twice in Sloman's grip as bullets slammed into it.

'That thing's holding when it should've been torn apart,' Tori noted. 'They're not coming at us with big guns.'

'Big enough.' Boody huddled closer to James as the bullets hailed on. 'You haven't got Queensmarsh?'

'No. But then, no ammo either . . .' He shook his head, took Boody's hand. 'Remember what you wrote to me? You said I could escape anything.'

She squeezed his fingers back. 'And you told me at Dartington, one day maybe all I'd have left was luck.'

James nodded, sought out her eyes in the half-light. 'Don't give up. Never. Not even when—'

A klaxon sounded a deep bass blare. The gunshots stopped.

'What was that?' hissed Sloman. 'End of act one?'

'The cameras can't see us in here,' Tori realized. 'I guess it won't make much of a movie if we buy it off screen, huh.'

'This can't be happening. Can't be.' Dan hugged his knees; the stench of sick was almost unbearable in the small, hot space. 'That scene I was going to star in, remember? The one that Martyn wrote . . .'

'*They went against the boss, so the boss has got to do this,*' Boody quoted.

'It's . . . execution,' Dan added.

James shivered. 'He was making them shoot a scene that could slot into *this* movie?'

'Then they'll record music for it,' Dan whispered, 'and cut the footage together and watch us dying—'

'Shut up. We need to think.' Tori had put her hands to her temples. 'Maybe they stopped 'cos they're trying to sneak up on us?'

James stared out through a crack in the claustrophobic space, and noticed the tattered gypsy caravan to their right. 'There's cover there. We should make a break for it.'

The klaxon blared again. At once, another bullet struck the wood close to Tori's arm. She took a shaky breath. 'Hunting season's here again.'

'No.' Sloman shook his head. In the thin light he looked suddenly steely and determined. 'I'm not doing this.' He raised his voice, bellowed, 'Barron, wait! I'm coming out. Don't shoot!'

'Uncle Stuart?' Dan watched, uncomprehending, as Sloman slowly crawled out, sweaty and dishevelled. 'No!'

'Are you crazy?' Tori hissed.

'Don't go out there!' Boody begged him.

James just held his breath, clenched his fists. Tense seconds burned. Boody pressed closer against him.

'All right, Barron . . . Kostler . . . All of you.' Arms raised, Sloman got carefully to his feet. Outside the shot-up saloon bar the old studio was silent save for the distant whirr of movie cameras. James saw movement in the gloom behind the old crates and boxes, maybe fifteen yards away. Figures stepped closer. There was Martyn Kostler, grim as any cowboy at high noon, gun-arm lowered. McGee showed his scarred face too, followed soon enough by men James didn't recognize; although Dürr, Fedora Man, was nowhere to be seen.

'I know I was wrong to do what I did,' Sloman went on. 'I was a fool. But for you to take it out on all of us in this barbaric way . . .'

The men ranged opposite stared at him in silence.

Sloman kept on, his voice hoarse, beginning to waver. 'You can't seriously contemplate the murder of a woman and three children. I can't believe—'

'Typical writer.' Martyn Kostler sighed and raised his gun. 'You talk too much.'

Too late, Sloman realized the depth of his misjudgement. He turned back towards the bar, panic-stricken. A shot boomed. Sloman blinked, and an almost serene look settled on his features. He twisted round through 180 degrees, facing Martyn again, and James saw a crimson stain on his back grow larger, deeper. Sloman held out his arms as if in a final, silent plea.

Then a storm of bullets broke around him.

Boody screamed, hid her eyes as Sloman jerked grotesquely, like he was on wires, blood blowing out of him in thick gouts.

'No!' Dan roared. 'No, no, no!'

As Tori clutched Boody to her and Dan dissolved in sobs, James shuffled round, turning his back on the scene. Stunned and sickened, he forced himself to think instead of feel. The scenery flats were too far away, but the gypsy caravan, whatever cover it afforded, had to be better than this tiny rat-trap. Under cover of the gunfire, he wrenched loose a plywood panel to create a rear exit, then turned to his companions. 'Hey. *Hey*,' he hissed. 'Caravan. Get ready.'

The shooting stopped at last. Who knew when it would start again? From an awkward crouch, James launched himself through the vacant space on the approach to the caravan. A volley of bullets tore through the saloon after him like this was the real Wild West. James hurled himself up the steps and through the heavy canvas into the caravan.

A man in a cheap suit and a ski mask was waiting inside.

He grabbed James by one arm, pulled him close and thrust a handgun into his mouth.

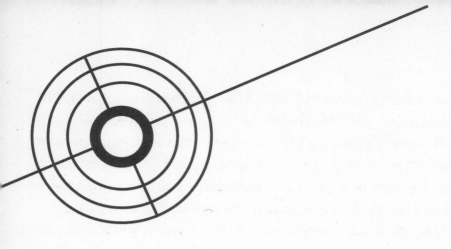

27
Divided We Stand

James guessed the gun was supposed to stop him warning the others. The muzzle almost broke his teeth. But the pain lent James strength. He swung his arm up and over the man's gun arm to break his hold, then stamped on the man's foot. His attacker dropped the pistol, and James punched him hard in the face, knocking him into the wall. James scrabbled for the gun – but someone else snatched it up first.

Tori.

As the masked man lunged for James again, she opened fire. The gunshot sounded deafening in the enclosed space. Blood sprayed from the man's thigh, and with a shrill cry he went down, groaning and gasping for breath.

Tori dropped the gun, staring in shock as Dan and Boody joined her inside, clinging together. James scooped up the gun, studied it – he'd read up on firearms these past months, having had so many pointed his way. This was a Colt 1908 hammerless semi-automatic.

'Look out!' Boody warned James as the wounded man grabbed for his leg. James jumped aside and brought down the gun butt on the man's forehead, putting him out cold. Then he locked the handgun's slide to the rear, cocked the release button in the base of the Colt and pulled out the single-stack magazine. Five .25 calibre rounds nestled inside.

'I . . . shot him. That man.' Tori turned away, and Boody put an arm around her. 'Should we do something about the bleeding?'

'He'll have help coming soon enough.' James pulled back the slide and reloaded. 'Besides, a gun this size doesn't deliver real knockdown power over distance. I . . . don't think Kostler wants us to die quickly.'

'Padding out the movie, huh,' said Tori.

'They killed my uncle quick enough.' Dan snatched the gun from James and pointed it outside, firing three times, the spent cartridges clattering to the floor. '*You killed him!*'

'No, Dan!' James yanked him back inside, snatched away the gun. 'You've let them know we're armed when we might have surprised them up close.'

Dan pulled free from James's grip and sank miserably to his knees. 'They . . . they killed him, James.'

'I know.' James put a hand on his shoulder. 'But they'll kill us too, unless we can think of a way out.' He fought to keep his cool. Now they had just two shots left.

Another klaxon sounded.

'Hold it, everybody,' Martyn's voice rang out. 'Be ready to move forward.'

'What *is* that siren for?' James muttered.

Dan wiped his nose on his sleeve. 'How can we ever get out of here?'

'It's hopeless,' Tori muttered.

'If only we could reach the gantry and get through one of those doors,' said James. 'They must lead back into the main building.'

He broke off as the klaxon started up again, making them jump.

'There's no way to get there.' Boody wiped her sweat-soaked hair from her face. 'But maybe we can make it to that old motor, and from there to the scenery flats.'

'Better cover and more places to hide,' James agreed. 'But they can turn up the lighting any time; we'll be easy to pick off as we run.'

'Oh, yes. Old hand at this, aren't you, Bond? Just as you were in Totnes.' Dan was breathing deeply. 'Give me the gun and I'll fire some covering shots. That's what they do in the movies, isn't it?'

James shook his head. 'You're coming with us.'

'Can't. Not up to it,' Dan said simply, peering out through the entrance. 'Enough's enough.'

Tori was testing the half-door at the back of the caravan; it twisted off on rotten hinges. 'If Dan distracts them by firing from the entrance, we can slip out the back here.'

But James couldn't let Dan just give up. 'While they come after us, Dan, maybe you can hide under the caravan? Get your strength back.'

'I'll try.' Dan held out his hand for the gun. 'Quick. I think they're coming.'

'Good luck.' James passed him the gun. 'I'll go first. I'm probably fastest.'

Tori nodded, brandishing the caravan door. 'Boody, you go after James. I'll go last and carry this.'

James licked his dry lips, prepared himself to sprint.

Dan screamed and fired the gun. James raced away. More gunfire. He heard Boody shriek behind him, but couldn't stop now; he kept his eyes on the sham city street across the gloomy studio space, and the wheelless Oldsmobile parked there.

He half expected a gunman to rise up from the car, pistols blazing. But no one was there. James skidded for cover behind the car. Tori joined him moments later, dropping her shield, then Boody, clutching her ankle.

'Shot,' she hissed through gritted teeth. James saw a blue-black dimple in the white flesh above her shoe strap. Blood welled there.

Tori swore. 'Can you walk?'

'I don't know.'

The lights grew brighter above them. More bullets zinged out. 'You'll have to run,' James said brusquely, helping her up. 'We need to keep as much distance as possible between us and them.'

'Listen to you.' Tori shook her head. 'They're just playing with us.'

'We need to keep moving,' James insisted, 'to buy Dan time to hide out in there. Come on, Boody. Lean on me. Here we go again . . .'

Tori ran off ahead of them, barefoot down the old, mouldering set. But halfway down the sham street a door was kicked open and McGee appeared, a gun in his hand. Tori yelped and ran behind a tree, which spat chunks of plaster as bullets bit into the trunk.

Boody gasped as James crouched, tore off her dangling shoe and threw it at McGee. The aim was true: the heel struck his cheek, jolted him against the doorframe.

Desperately, James pelted towards him. *If I can just get the gun in time—*

But he couldn't. McGee recovered in moments, had James in his sights for an easy kill.

Then the klaxon sounded, a baritone note wrenching at the air. McGee swore, aimed lower, at James's legs.

With a surge of desperate speed, James hurled himself at the big man. McGee dropped the gun as the impact carried them both through the open doorway in a tangle of limbs.

James landed on top of McGee, who hit the ground with a dull crunch of glass breaking and a sharp chemical reek. Then the big man bucked his body and, shaken loose, James tried to roll clear – but a punch to the jaw stunned him. McGee sat up, his shirtfront soaked where something had spilled or broken in their struggle. He tore off his jacket, began to pull at his shirt . . .

But Tori was standing over him, the Plaza matchbook in her hand. She struck a flame and flicked the lit match at McGee's chest.

He went up like a torch.

With a scream of panic, McGee staggered up and ran away, beating at the flames.

Boody shuddered as she helped James to stand. 'What happened?'

'Something broke over him when we landed,' James panted. 'Something flammable.'

'Most likely ethanol.' Tori was going through McGee's jacket pockets and pulled out a small bottle with cloth wadding crammed in the top. 'The son-of-a-bitch's stock-in-trade – a firebomb.'

James's stomach turned at the stench of burning hair and flesh. 'What happened to his gun?'

'Got it.' Boody showed him the small Colt. James checked the firearm, which still held three bullets, and slipped it in the pocket of his ruined dress suit.

'Quickly,' said Tori, 'while they're putting out McGee, let's make for those hunks of scenery and from there to the wall. Maybe we'll find an exit.'

James and Tori helped Boody stumble towards their goal. McGee's wails covered their footsteps.

'Good of you to put up a fight!' Martyn's voice echoed eerily through the gloom. 'You should have gone with me last night, Boody. Maybe I'd have spared you all this . . .'

'Keep quiet,' James whispered. 'He can't see us for the smoke, wants you to shout back so he can pinpoint our location.'

'He'll be able to follow Boody's trail unless we stop the bleeding,' Tori said. 'We need to make a tourniquet before you lose too much blood. You could pass out.'

'I wish,' Boody admitted. 'It hurts like hell.'

'But it proves you're alive.' James led them behind the towering stack of scenery flats propped up against the trunk. 'We're going to get out of this.'

No one answered. James set about tearing off his shirtsleeve to use as a bandage; Tori helped him. Smoke was still rising up towards the high ceiling, but McGee's screams stopped suddenly with the crack of a shot.

Tori shivered. 'They . . . they didn't just . . . ?'

'Put him out of his misery,' James concluded bleakly.

'Hold on! I think I know what the klaxon's for!' Boody's face was pale and waxy. 'Film Club!'

'She's delirious.' Tori started to wrap the torn shirtsleeve around Boody's foot. 'Stay with us, sweetie.'

'I mean, I know *because* of Film Club.' Boody pointed over to the nearest pillbox above them. 'There are cameras behind those slits in the wall, right? Several cameras dotted around, shooting from different angles so the action can be edited together. Well, like guns, cameras need reloading.'

'Go on,' said James.

'I don't know what exactly they're using, but—' She broke off, gritting her teeth as Tori applied the makeshift dressing. 'But a typical movie camera will hold either four hundred feet of film – that's about four minutes' worth – or a thousand feet, eleven minutes. Either way, it takes a couple of minutes to change magazines and reload in a dark bag.'

'And Kostler wants the gory bits on film,' Tori reasoned, 'so if his men kill us while he's not filming . . .'

'Kostler would make sure they regret it,' Boody agreed.

'So the gangsters stop firing till the klaxon sounds again to say the cameras are reloaded, and pick up where they left off.' James nodded. 'That's why McGee aimed for my leg when I ran at him and the horn went off. He couldn't kill me.'

'So we're safe whenever the first siren sounds,' Boody concluded.

'Safe? Don't think so.' Tori finished tying the bandage

and shook her head. 'They can still hunt us. Catch us. Get their close-up.'

'You're right,' James muttered. 'Knowing changes nothing. Except . . .' He eyed the precarious stack of scenery flats, huge backdrops and skyscapes. 'Look. If we can shift that truck so the flats topple over, they'll crash against the wall – and the tallest ones might reach the gantry.'

Boody looked at him. 'And then we can climb them like we're going the wrong way up a slide, and reach the door . . . ?'

'Right,' James agreed – as a shadowy figure in the smoke peered out from behind the façade of a town house across the way.

'Use the firebomb,' James hissed frantically.

Tori was already on it. With a whoosh, the wadding took light. She lobbed the firebomb high through the air . . .

It struck the wooden townhouse. James hid his eyes as incandescence exploded from the broken glass, and the flames took a fevered hold. A roiling mass of smoke mushroomed upwards amid shouts and cries.

'Wow.' Tori stared at the blaze. 'Guess I did it!'

The klaxon went off. It jolted James from the hypnotic rush of the flames. 'Quickly.' He beckoned Tori and Boody to follow him to the old truck. The handbrake was already off, and it wasn't in gear. As long as the wheels hadn't seized up . . .

'Push!' James hissed. 'Come on!'

Tori strained, her back against the bonnet. 'It's not budging.'

'Keep going!' James shut out the pain in his shoulder, the

ache in his head, strained to move the old truck. He tried to picture it moving in his mind, told himself over and over that the movement would happen if they only shoved hard enough. Beside him, Boody gritted her teeth and pushed, the shirtsleeve around her ankle already soaked crimson.

We can't fail, James thought, choking on lungfuls of black smoke, *we* have *to shift it*.

'What about Dan?' Boody panted.

'We can't go back for him now,' James said. 'Just hope he's held on.'

'Don't stop,' Tori urged them, her face screwed up with effort. 'I think it's going . . .'

Finally, with a complaining squeak, the wheels moved and the truck rolled slowly backwards. But James's laugh of relief was drowned by the creak and clatter of the towering flats beginning to collapse.

A bullet whistled into the front of the truck, barely missing Tori. She threw herself to the ground. Heart kicking, James helped Boody round to shelter at the back of the truck. But as more bullets struck the ground around Tori, she was forced to run off alone, the smoke swiftly stealing her from sight.

Boody made to follow, but James held her back as the stack of scenery gave way completely in an avalanche of plaster-board and timber. Some of the flats split apart upon striking the wall, sent debris smashing down below. Wiping his eyes free of smoke and tears, James looked up, hoping his handi-work had been enough. He'd created a kind of angled bank of broken scenery running steeply from the ground to high up against the wall. It stood between them and the assassins, forming a precarious path up to the gantry.

James looked at Boody. 'Like climbing the wrong way up a slide, you said . . .' More gunfire cracked through the smoke, like thunder through clouds. 'While being shot at.'

Boody bit her lip. 'You think Tori's all right?'

James didn't answer; gripping Boody's wrist, he helped her onto the lower slopes of the mountain of collapsed scenery. The old boards bowed and bent beneath their feet. Gunshots like firecrackers echoed out, as dark figures gathered, phantom-like in the gloom, getting closer. An explosion lit up the ruined soundstage, perhaps thirty yards away – the Oldsmobile must have had gas in the tank, and finally it had ignited. The air was fumy and hot, it made James's lungs crackle. Boody was choking, eyes streaming. The lights in the ceiling strobed and flickered in the mad dance of smoke and flame.

Up ahead, James glimpsed movement. The door in the wall had opened; someone was kicking at the scenery butting up to the gantry, trying to push it away so that the precarious slope collapsed completely.

Through the gusting smoke, James saw that it was Martyn's friend Brad.

'Move faster!' James told Boody, but she was choking too hard, and still hampered by her injured ankle.

'Go on,' she hissed. 'I'll follow.'

James clambered up the rise; the gantry was maybe ten feet away now. But the painted countryside shook as Brad kicked at it, and James lost his balance. He fell onto his belly as gangster bullets whizzed overhead. One ricocheted off the gantry, and Brad quickly ducked back inside the shelter.

Damn it, thought James. *If he comes back with help . . .* He glanced back to check on Boody.

'Keep going!' she shouted.

As he rose to his feet, James felt the wood crack and buckle. Bullets tore whorls through the smoke around him; he stepped as lightly as he could and as fast as he dared. At last he reached the gantry, vaulted over the safety rail, and saw that Brad had slammed the door shut behind him.

He was about to reach for the handle, when an awful, splintering rumble rose from behind him.

The scenery was giving way at last.

James whirled round, glimpsed men on the ground thirty feet below. He saw Boody struggling barefoot up the slope towards him like a pale apparition, closing the final distance. He reached out to her across the safety rail.

Then the bowed wood split at last. The gangsters beneath them scattered as the avalanche of rotten board and plywood began to fall. Boody threw out her arms as, silent in disbelief, she fell with it.

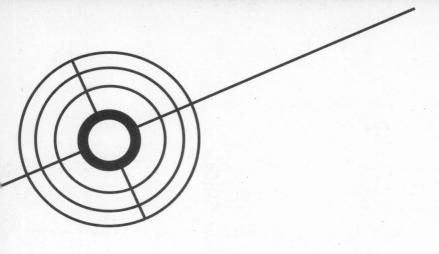

28

High Noon

James hurled himself forwards, bent himself double over the metal safety rail, hands reaching for hers. His fingers caught hold of her wrists; her own fingers gripped his in turn.

Got you!

But his elation died in a moment. He'd arrested her fall, but was leaning too far over the gantry; there was nothing to anchor him, and with horror he found that her weight was dragging him after her. His feet left the metal floor as he was tugged into the start of a fatal dive to the blackened, mouldering ground below . . .

His fall stopped as someone grabbed his legs before he could go all the way over. The counterbalance increased, crushing his guts against the safety rail, but giving him purchase to haul Boody back up. James didn't dare look back and see who or what held him now in case the miracle disappeared. Arms straining, grazed shoulder burning, James managed to lift Boody up through the smoke until she could swing herself over the rail. The two of them collapsed onto the gantry, coughing and panting for breath. Only then did James turn to his deliverer – and gape.

'I've lost my mind,' he panted. 'Thought I'd been touched by an angel . . .'

'Close! You were gripped by a Hugo.' His friend smiled and grasped his bloodstained hand. 'Next best thing, eh?'

'Next best thing,' James agreed, shaking hands warmly.

'Now, you selfish brute . . .' Hugo snatched back his hand to take hold of Boody's. 'Can we get this poor girl the hell inside, please?'

A bullet ricocheted off the safety rail. James dragged Boody to her feet. 'I can manage,' she said, limping across the gantry to the open door in the wall.

James followed her inside. There was the movie camera on its tripod, pressed up against the slit in the wall – and there was Brad, out cold on the floor. 'What happened?'

'You'd better ask the man responsible.' Hugo grimaced. 'He brought me along because I knew my way around the school a little . . .' He disappeared through the inner door. James followed him through, and came up against—

James froze. 'Dürr?'

'Do me a favour!' The German accent was gone, replaced by tones nearer to East London. 'Hugo says you've been calling me Fedora Man. Well, I've had one or two names for you, James Bond, believe me.'

'He found me and Gillian, told us we were in danger,' said Hugo excitedly, 'took us away to safety at his hotel, the Roosevelt, where Kostler couldn't find us.'

Fedora Man nodded. 'Once I saw how badly they wanted to get you, James, and since they already had Boudicca and Daniel, I figured I had to move fast.'

'Dan's still out there somewhere. Tori Wo too,' said James.

'We've got to find them,' Boody added.

'Impossible,' said Fedora Man. 'You must know we won't stand a chance going back in there. But if we can get hold of Martyn Kostler and hold him to ransom—'

'Who are you?' James demanded.

'Sit down. Get your breath back. We've a long way to go before we're out of this.' Fedora Man smiled grimly. 'My name is Adam Elmhirst. I work for the British Secret Intelligence Service.'

It was all James could do to stop his lower jaw hitting his chest. 'You're a spy.'

'That's what I said.' Elmhirst locked the door to the bunker. 'Alexander Roberts, the film producer, came to the government with this story of blackmail and extortion. That tied in with other whispers going around. So I was assigned to investigate Anton Kostler's attempts to gain political and cultural influence in Europe.' He stuffed the keys in his pocket. 'You know how much the cinema industry is worth to Great Britain? And as for the thought of Yanks compromising government policy . . .'

'So you know about Barron?'

'Hell, yes. And all his friends in Chicago.'

'Why pretend to be that German film-maker . . . ?'

'Because Dürr had a ticket to meet Kostler, and I needed to get in there and learn more about his plans.' Elmhirst peered out of the door, checking the way was clear. 'I had the real Dürr detained on faked charges. Kostler and Vasquez had never met him, so they didn't know I was a phoney. Can we get going now?' Revolver at the ready, he led the way out of the bunker and down a set of bare concrete steps. James chased after him while Hugo and Boody followed more slowly behind; her ankle was looking more swollen and bloody by the minute.

James was still bursting with questions. 'Why'd you chase me in the Alhambra the night before we left? Why try and shoot me?'

'I only fired to scare you, to try to stop you running.' Elmhirst paused at a half-open door leading onto a corridor, checking that the way was clear. 'I was on to Vasquez — knew he was after an incriminating reel of film. I followed him there, realized you had the film can, saw the damage, thought you must be involved.'

'I thought you were one of Kostler's men,' James admitted. 'Whenever stuff happened, you were around.'

'Makes sense. That's because I was *investigating* Kostler,' said Elmhirst reasonably. 'Listen, whose green Corvette was it saved your skin on your race from Kostler's party? That wasn't luck, you know.' He contemplated a junction they had come to and turned left. 'I was only chasing after you to find out what you'd learned — to tell you we were really on the same side. Come on, keep moving.'

'Where are we going?' asked Boody.

'I need to get you kids away from here and safe. The bad news is, the only way out is through Kostler's private cinema.' Elmhirst looked at James and Boody. 'Nice work with that fire, by the way. Kostler's goons are tackling the blaze themselves. With a highly flammable airship floating close by, you can kind of understand their urgency.'

James's heart skittered as he saw they were nearing Kostler's private cinema. 'You're really going to try and get Kostler?'

'Right.' Elmhirst smiled. 'I was going to say it won't be safe, but after what you've been through in there . . .'

'Stuart Sloman's been killed,' James said, looking at the floor. 'Tori and Dan too by now, for all we know. I want to see people pay for that.'

Now they were close to the door, Elmhirst silenced further conversation with a finger to his lips.

Kostler's voice was rising over his lieutenants'. 'Is no one at their posts? We should have more raw footage than this by now. Just how big can the fire *be* down there?'

'I've cut the school's switchboard.' That was Barron's voice, low and rasping. 'Staff and boarders might see the smoke, but they can't call for help . . .'

'Sounds like our cue,' Elmhirst muttered. Then he slammed open the double doors, revolver held ready, covering the room from the doorway.

Kostler, Barron and Vasquez turned in surprise. Dr Leaver barely looked up.

'Dürr?' Kostler snarled as Vasquez pulled a gun from his hip holster.

Elmhirst fired first. One shot hit Vasquez in the stomach, a second blew a hole in his head. Blood slopping over his face, Vasquez's dark little eyes shut and he collapsed onto the dusty carpet. Hugo and Boody recoiled in revulsion, and, lurking behind Elmhirst, James felt fresh sweat prickle his face

273

and back, bile rising in his throat.

Barron's only reaction was to slowly raise his hands. Kostler stared down at Vasquez, eyes wider than ever, points of colour searing his cheeks. One hand was groping unconsciously for the camera on the table as if his first instinct was to watch the stomach-turning scene through a lens.

'All right, now, listen. I'm Adam Elmhirst, British Secret Intelligence. Throw down the gun, Barron. Try *anything*, and I'll paint that silver screen seven shades of Kostler's skull.' He smiled tightly as Barron obeyed, then looked back at Boody and Hugo. 'All right, kids. Out you go. Get that foot looked at, Boudicca. And call the police.'

'Kostler's cut the telephone lines,' said Leaver suddenly. 'But my secretary will be in the office by now: she can drive them to the nearest ranger's office . . .'

Kostler and Barron stared at him like snakes might eye a mouse. Hugo supported Boody as best he could as they passed Kostler and Barron, making for the exit at the rear of the cinema. James watched them go, jubilant that they were getting out safely, longing for the moment when he too would be—

As Hugo reached for the fire door, it was kicked inward with savage force. He was thrown backwards against the wall. Boody shrieked as Martyn Kostler appeared, sooty, sweat-soaked and panting for breath, and grabbed her by the wrist.

Elmhirst automatically brought up his revolver to cover Martyn. But as he did so, Barron drew his gun and shot the agent in the chest from point-blank range. Elmhirst was blown backwards into the corridor, knocking into James, flooring him. The door swung shut on them, blocking the cinema from view.

'No!' James shouted. He scrambled for Elmhirst's revolver on the floor. The door cracked open, and James fired at the gap. The recoil kicked through his aching arms, the bullet smashing splinters from the heavy wood.

'Get over here, Barron!' Kostler snarled from the other side of the door. 'Leave Bond, he's not important now.'

Worming forward to the crack in the door, James saw that Martyn held Boody in a neck-lock, the pistol pressed against her temple. Hugo was nowhere in sight.

'The fire's almost out, Father,' Martyn reported.

'About time,' Kostler said, his precious camera now clutched under one arm. 'We'll take the girl with us to the *Zelda*, and on to Mines Field to board the *Allworld*.' He looked over at Leaver, who was sitting very still, staring at Vasquez's corpse. 'Come on, Tobias. We're going.'

'We're running away?' Martyn's face twisted as he gripped Boody even tighter. 'Father, you always said Kostlers never run—'

'The man Barron killed was a British agent. He may have been working with others. Until we determine the extent to which our operation is compromised, we retreat to the air — with a hostage for insurance. And on the way, Mr Barron, direct your men to kill anyone left alive in this building. Oh, and be sure I see close-ups.'

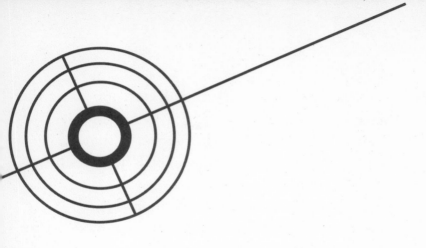

29

Ascent and Maelstrom

James stared at the gun in his hand, listening as Kostler and Martyn left the cinema with Boody, and Barron forced Leaver out after them. The door closed.

Suddenly, Hugo came crawling into view from the exit, his nose swollen and bleeding. 'If they hadn't had their hands full with Boody and Leaver, I'd be shot dead!' he groaned. 'I deserve it too. I let them take her . . .'

'We're going to get Boody back,' James vowed. He made to rise, then jerked back as a hand caught his ankle.

It was Elmhirst. Pale but still alive.

'It's OK.' Elmhurst smiled weakly, a little trickle of blood escaping his lips. 'I'm wearing a bullet-proof vest. Took some of the punch out of the slug.' He forced himself up onto his elbows. 'They're making for the airship? Makes sense. Getting out of reach. Kostler thinks he's untouchable . . .'

'Mr Elmhirst, Barron's telling his men to kill anyone they

find on sight,' James told him. 'Tori and Dan are still in the studio. You've got to help them.'

'I can't move too well.' Elmhirst struggled to stand.

James gave him his gun. 'Hugo, you'll have to be his crutch.'

'Marvellous,' groaned Hugo. 'Who'll be mine?'

'We must get away from here,' wheezed Elmhirst. 'Do as Leaver said, try to find that woman in the office. Bring help.'

Hugo looked worried. 'And what are *you* planning, James?'

'I only wish I knew.' James stooped to scoop up the gun lying beside Vasquez's gory corpse – then noticed a familiar gun handle peeping from the top of his jacket pocket.

'Queensmarsh,' he breathed, gingerly pulling it free; the customized pistol felt reassuringly solid in his hand. Vasquez had admired the gun from the beginning; after knocking James out, he must have found it and taken it for himself. James quickly searched the rest of the man's pockets. If he had found and taken James's intended ammo too . . .

Yes. There were four ball bearings in his trouser pocket.

James passed Vasquez's regular firearm to Hugo. Then he opened Queensmarsh's breech and loaded the little ball bearings inside.

Hugo stared at him in disbelief. 'You're going to get Boody back with a toy gun?'

'If I fire a real gun on an airship, the spark could ignite the helium and we'll all go up like fireworks.' James slipped the gun into his pocket. 'I think this is my best option.'

'At least you know you can rely on the workmanship.' Hugo looked at James. 'Be lucky.'

James nodded, took a deep breath and went racing through the exit after the Kostlers.

There were no signs pointing to the outer doors, and it was some time before James found the right way. He burst out of the old studio into acrid smoke and sunshine, and in the dazzling haze searched out the airship above the mooring mast. He heard German voices shouting urgently in the mid-distance – the ground crew unlashing the airship, set to send the *Zelda* skywards.

A noise behind made him turn. A dark blur streaked towards James. Someone was running – no, *jumping*, foot extended. *One of Barron's men,* James realized *– and he does judo too.* On instinct, James threw himself aside. His attacker sailed past. As the man landed, James grabbed his head and twisted hard. Breath coming out in retching coughs, James's attacker fell to the ground, gasping for air.

But to James's dismay, another figure stumbled out of the studio building; he recognized the ski mask with a thrill of fear. It was the man from the gypsy caravan who'd stuck the gun in his mouth, the one Tori had shot in the thigh. James pulled out Queensmarsh and cocked it, ready to fire, as the man removed his ski mask to reveal—

'Daniel?' James lowered the pistol, barely able to believe it.

'Well, I needed a change of clothes.' Dan took his hand and clutched it. 'Thank God you're all right, James.'

'And you,' James marvelled. 'A fine disguise, just lying there for the taking.'

'I put it to good use. In all the confusion, I bluffed my way out with a prisoner I found.' He beckoned through the open door – and a familiar female figure swaggered out, though one arm was badly cut and bleeding.

'Not bad, huh?' Tori Wo smiled weakly. 'Guess your friend here really *is* an actor.'

'Tori!' James grabbed her tight, until she cursed in his ear. 'You're all right.'

'Squeeze too hard, I'll come apart. Where's Boody? Kostler—'

'Up there.' Relief was lending James fresh resolve as he pointed towards the mast. 'Wait here. Hugo's on his way out with Rudolf Dürr, who's *not* one of Kostler's crew – we can trust him, he's . . . oh, you'll see.' He dashed away into the smoke. 'Just be careful. Barron's thugs are shooting to kill!'

Willing his body on, James broke into a sprint that carried him up the metal steps of the mooring mast, Queensmarsh gripped in one sweaty hand, he pushed himself harder, *faster*.

As he reached the top of the passenger platform, one of the Germans came at him with a crowbar.

The metal bar arced down towards James's head. Desperately, he ducked under the swing and fired his pistol. With a *phut* and a crack, the little metal bearing pinged into the German's skull, stunning him. But another man was rushing towards him. James fired twice – one of the shots caught the man's front teeth and he bellowed his pain, broke off his advance. James silenced his attacker with a punch to the neck that sent him sprawling onto the safety parapet.

A vast shadow swept over James as he panted for breath. He braced himself – but nothing was there.

The heavy canvas connecting-tunnel now flapped loose in the breeze, and the *Himmelstreppe* lay forgotten on the ground.

James swore. The airship had been set loose and was rising into the air. He recoiled as a huge sluice of water fell from on high, soaking him through – the ship was dumping ballast to rise faster.

But as he backed away through the smoke, he saw that one of the mooring ropes was still attached to the airship's underside, rapidly uncoiling from the passenger platform. Pocketing Queensmarsh, James grabbed hold of the rope without thinking – and gasped as he was snatched into the air. Suddenly, he was spinning through the smoke, retching for breath and trying to hold on. He knew he had to climb, and quickly. Muscles aching, gripping the rope with feet as well as his sore hands, James grimly scaled the distance.

Sooner than he'd dared hope, he found himself dangling alongside one of the airship's engine nacelles – an aluminium cage attached to the hull, containing one of those powerful Maybach engines. As the wind gusted harder, James tried to drag himself onto the heavy cotton cloth that protected the workings from the elements. Just as he managed this, the engine fired into life, tremors and exhaust catching him off-guard. Eyes shut, breath held, he clung on. A connecting ladder ran from a hatch in the top of the nacelle into the ship itself, and now James began to drag himself up again, rung after rung, panting and trying not to choke in the filthy air that blew around him.

Finally, he tore open the hatch in the canvas covering on the side of the airship and fell gratefully inside onto a small platform positioned between girders and crossframe.

Almost immediately, a young, wiry crewman in dark overalls appeared. James pulled out Queensmarsh and brought it

up as if to fire. The crewman mistook it for a real gun –
he looked terrified, shook his head, held up his hands.

The man was still shaking his head helplessly as James
advanced. Then a scream split the air. Boody's scream.

Galvanized, James darted closer and struck the man behind
the ear with his pistol's chunky wooden handle, knocking him
out cold. Then he crouched, listening.

Boody screamed again: '*Don't touch me!*'

The *Zelda* was like a smaller *Allworld*; James realized he was
somewhere above the control car in the gondola. Yes – there
was the open hatch up ahead that must lead straight down
into the nerve centre of the ship! The man he'd hit had probably just come up here for something . . .

Quickly, James unzipped the man's overalls, which were a
fair fit, and struggled into them.

'It's all over,' Dr Leaver was saying, the words rising
through the hatch. 'This time you're finished, Kostler.'

'Hardly.' Kostler sounded cool and distant as ever. 'Aren't you
forgetting my hunting party? With the fire extinguished, they
will soon reclaim my old studio and dispose of Mr Elmhirst.'

'But the British Government is investigating you!' said
Boody. 'They know what you've done. You think you can
blackmail everyone?'

'It's a long game I play. If I can't corrupt them, I will have
to dispose of them. A man like me has powerful friends, you
know . . .' Kostler studied his gloves, picking at flecks of dirt
fastidiously. 'In ten, fifteen years from now, I'll still be the King
of Hollywood, the man in control of every studio, every star,
every politician who has a say in how the Cinema should be
run. *I* will run it, for the world.'

'All world,' Martyn sniggered.

James pictured Martyn's arrogant smile and longed to rearrange it. But what could he do against so many enemies, alone, high in the sky over Beverly Hills?

Pulling up the zipper on his borrowed overalls, checking Queensmarsh was secure in a pocket, he ran lightly along the narrow girder that ran the length of the ship, his heart drumming faster with every step.

He was nearing the hatch when he heard a German voice say: 'What's happened to that airman?' It sounded like Captain Breithaupt from the *Allworld*. 'I could have fetched those tools myself in half the time . . .'

Tools? James ran back and checked. Sure enough, he saw a metal toolbox, in pride of place in a supply store. He hefted it; the thing weighed a ton.

'*Ich komme gleich!*' James called. Heart in his mouth, he crossed back to the hatchway and stepped down onto the first rung.

The second rung.

He shifted his weight, not wanting the toolbox to un-balance him . . .

'Hey!' Barron snarled. 'When he went up, that guy was wearing boots . . .'

Here goes. James slid the rest of the way down the ladder, twisted round in a tight circle and brought up the toolbox. The sharp metal corner tore into Kostler's cheek, sent him crashing into the rudder controls.

The whole airship lurched to starboard, everyone was thrown to the floor. Barron banged his head against a girder, Martyn fell on top of Boody and Leaver.

'It's Bond!' screamed Martyn.

Breithaupt struggled to his feet and tore wildly at the wheel. Barron stomped over to grab James, who emptied the toolbox in his path. Spanners, bolts and screwdrivers crashed onto the big man's feet, but he kept coming. James ducked a swiping blow – Barron's knuckles connected with the steel ladder instead and he shouted out. Dodging behind Barron, James swung the empty box into the back of his head, knocking him to his knees.

James turned, looking for Boody; she had crawled away from Martyn and Leaver, trying to reach him. Still at the wheel, Breithaupt brought his foot down on her bad ankle, making her wail.

James started towards her. 'No!' Boody shook her head, eyes wide. 'Behind you!'

While Leaver was struggling to rise, Martyn had jumped back to his feet. He kicked the toolbox out of James's grip, then knocked his feet from under him.

As he landed on his back, James came into range of Barron, who grabbed his hair and used it to haul him to his feet. James struggled to reach Queensmarsh in his pocket, then cried out as Barron punched him in the face. The second blow split his cheek. Boody screamed as Martyn joined in, punching James so hard in the stomach he doubled up, leaving torn-out hair in Barron's grip. James fell to the floor, groaning for breath, blood stringing from his lips.

Then Barron lifted James by his ears. The pain was so terrible, James thought he might be sick.

Boody sounded close to tears. 'Leave him alone!'

'Hold him tighter, Mr Barron. Hold him still.' Kostler was standing again; a livid, bloody bruise smeared his left cheek.

284

He was holding his Parvo movie camera, his gaze as hard and cold as the lens that lent him distance from the world. 'Now, how did Shakespeare put it, Doctor Leaver? "Cowards die many times before their deaths. The valiant never taste of death but once."' He smiled bleakly and raised his camera. 'I wonder how you'll care for death's bitter flavour, Bond? Because no one touches me. No one causes me pain. Not any more.' His lip curled in contempt. 'For all you've done today, I will watch you torn apart . . .'

'And so will she.' Martyn smiled at Boody, still on her knees, Breithaupt twisting one arm up behind her back. 'All right with that, my little jade?'

Boody tried to pull free, but couldn't. Dr Leaver stood watching the whole sordid scene, absolutely motionless. Like he'd already died.

James struggled feebly, his ears blazing in Barron's grip. His eyes were blurred with tears, but he made out Martyn coming closer, wielding a screwdriver, while Kostler watched from behind his camera and started recording for posterity.

'It's neat, don't you think, Martyn?' James could hear the smile in the mogul's voice. 'I shoot while you stab—'

'Please!' In the periphery of his vision, James saw Boody, still tightly in Breithaupt's grip. 'Don't let him do this!'

'Start with Bond's eyes, Martyn,' said Kostler quietly over the whir of the camera. 'The left one first, I think.'

'No!' James screwed both eyes shut. His head throbbed with pressure, fit to burst.

Then the gunshot came.

'Tobias!' Kostler screamed.

Martyn whirled round. 'He took my gun.'

The old man had edged round to the roof hatch that led up into the body of the ship, that labyrinth of gasbags and girders, pointing a Colt straight upward. 'You know your Shakespeare, Kostler,' he said calmly, firing a second shot into the zeppelin's heart. 'Past hope, past cure . . . past help.'

'Don't—!' Breithaupt let go of Boody just as Barron threw James to one side. Both men lunged for Dr Leaver, Barron reaching him first, shoving him aside.

But the third shot had already been fired.

The bullet must have struck the tiniest spark from one of countless girders up there in the dark.

It was enough.

Before James even hit the floor, a colossal explosion roared out. A column of flame burst down in a backdraught through the hatch, incinerating Barron where he stood. He collapsed beside the ladder, a charred, smoking heap. The force of the flames threw Leaver, Breithaupt and Kostler back against the controls, while Boody hurled herself towards James on the other side of the control cabin, rolling over and over as the airship lurched.

'Father!' Martyn shouted, trying to reach out to Kostler through the wall of fire. But the flames spread hungrily and Martyn shrieked and shook as his clothes caught light.

Horrified, James recoiled, hauling Boody away with him to the doorway. He glanced back to see a dark, misshapen figure burst out from the flames and grab hold of Martyn. James barely recognized Dr Leaver, holding the screaming boy in a deadly, blazing embrace, dragging him back into the firestorm.

'Oh, my God . . .' James choked as the smoke grew thicker. The whole airship began to drop with sickening speed as more explosions shook her disintegrating frame. With the hydrogen ablaze, there was nothing to sustain their weight.

'Come on!' Boody grabbed James by the hand and they staggered from the control car towards the lounge. The crewman James had KO'ed had recovered and was there already, wrestling with one of the windows. As the airship lurched he tumbled through, soundlessly. James raced over and saw that the airship must have circled round, for below them were the western fringes of the Academy grounds – and the crewman's body sprawled lifeless in the middle of a paved walkway.

'What can we do?' Boody shouted over the roar of flames and the scream of failing engines.

'Die!' shouted Kostler, flying like a demon from the inferno in the control car. Skin bubbling, half the hair scorched from his head, he'd found Martyn's gun and now fired it, aiming wildly. James shoved Boody down behind the cover of a table, desperately ducked through a doorway behind him.

It led to Kostler's private bedroom. The luxurious curtains were already ablaze, while artworks and film cans lay scattered over the circular bed. A bullet shot past his head, shattered a vase. James picked up a film can and hurled it at Kostler; it struck the mogul's face and he dropped to his knees. James picked up another, ready to hit him again – but then the airship dropped faster in a dizzying rush. James was thrown into Kostler and they tumbled back out into the lounge. The flames had taken hold. Burning canvas fell across

Kostler's back but he no longer seemed to feel pain. He gripped James's neck and squeezed.

Already choking on smoke, James found he couldn't breathe. He dug his nails into Kostler's blistered wrists, gasped and retched.

Then he remembered Queensmarsh. Desperately, he reached into the pocket of the overalls, pulled out the loaded pistol, fumbled with numb fingers for the belt-buckle trigger and fired into Kostler's left ear.

With a grunt Kostler recoiled, rolled over. James shoved him away as the floor bucked beneath him and started to split apart, metal rending with a hideous machine scream. They'd hit woodland; the windows went dark as spikes of foliage crashed through the exploding windows.

'Boody . . .?' James covered his face as the airship pitched backwards violently; he fell against the wall. But Kostler was thrown higher, further, faster. He had time for a brief, sickening scream.

James looked up to find the great director speared through the eye by a splintered branch.

For a few seconds Kostler's corpse dangled from its twisted wooden perch, before the branch snapped and the airship's frame contorted in the fierce heat; the body was lost from sight. Flames spread into the lounge with horrific speed. The whole room turned upside down . . . James saw his legs catch fire, threw back his head and shouted . . .

And then a thick, fast flood of freezing water broke over him. James was shocked alert, spluttering, choking in the deluge. Ballast tanks, he realized; they must have burst open. The section of wall he was pinned to broke apart. He glimpsed Boody as she fell across his chest. There were a few confused seconds of descent, light and darkness . . .

When James opened his eyes again, he was shivering on a hillside among the scrub, eyes full of tears. His whole body was wet and raw. Boody was cradling his swollen head in her arms. The airship was a mangled wreck behind them, belching black smoke into a blue sky that showed little sign of caring at all.

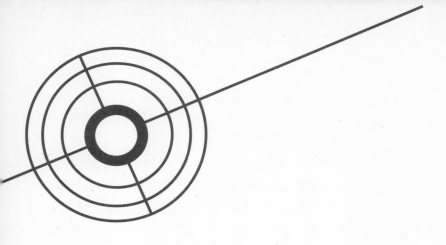

30

Hollywood Sunset, Roll Credits

There was no end of cleaning up to be done, but Adam Elmhirst made it clear — that was *his* department. He seemed anxious to spare James and his friends as many unpleasant details as he could.

A little late for that, James thought ruefully from his hospital bed. He knew he'd never forget the horrors. But nor would he forget how he'd lived through them.

Queensmarsh was tucked under his pillow, his good-luck charm. James sneaked it out to look at it. So ugly and lumpen when first he'd acquired it, it had been treated with kindness and reshaped into a thing of real use, if not quite beauty.

He studied the little letters Boody had carved there, named for the place he'd escaped from. 'Queensmarsh', as a name, spoke of both nobility and dirt. And though he'd never admit it out loud, James felt a certain kinship.

He tucked the pistol back under his pillow.

Hugo and Tori Wo had filled James in on their own ordeals as soon as visiting hours allowed. With Dan, they had helped Elmhirst reach the Academy's front office, just as Leaver had advised. The redoubtable secretary had summoned the ranger, who in turn had brought in the full array of emergency forces.

'It was just bad luck those wannabe gangsters split before the police could arrive,' said Hugo.

'At least Barron and Vasquez didn't destroy all my evidence,' said Tori, flexing her bandaged arm. 'And with access to all those film cans and files at Kostler's place and the Academy records here, the cops can pin all kinds of murders on those filthbags.' She smiled. 'I can print the biggest crime exposé ever seen in LA. And that's saying something.'

'Someone comes out a winner, then,' said James quietly.

'Someone always does, Jimmy-boy.' Tori patted his leg, and when he gasped with pain, stuffed a grape in his mouth. 'I'll see you around. Even if you see me first. Right? Stay lucky.'

'Lucky.' James closed his eyes. 'Right.'

Just nine days after Stuart Sloman had arrived in Los Angeles, his remains were buried in the Hollywood Forever Cemetery on Santa Monica Boulevard. The funeral was quiet; Los Angeles was too far distant for Sloman's family in England to reach in time by cruise liner, and they'd agreed he'd have wanted to stay on in Hollywood for always. Dan was there to represent them, though only he knew just how badly his uncle had wanted this job in the city of dreams, and all he'd done to get it.

It was set to stay that way too. Both Tori and Elmhirst had agreed to play down Sloman's involvement — here was just a talented writer on the Kostler payroll, tragically caught up in events.

James was discharged from hospital on the morning of the funeral, to find that Boody and Dan would be leaving with Gillian de Vries that same evening.

'Gillian doesn't want to stay here a moment longer than she has to,' Boody explained in the walled gardens of the hotel that afternoon. 'And since we have to take a ship back, it'll be weeks before we see home again.' She looked at James. 'You're staying on?'

'My aunt's cutting short her time in Mexico.' James shrugged. 'And Hugo's folks have said he can stay out here a little longer and join us.'

'Strange how Mother and Father aren't more keen to see me,' Hugo reflected. 'Perhaps they hope absence makes the dwarf grow longer?'

Dan shook his head. 'After all we've been through,' he said seriously, 'I can assure you you're bigger than just about any fellow I know.' He shook Hugo's hand. 'I'll see you next term. But you, James . . . ?'

'It's goodbye,' said James simply. They shook hands. James remembered their secret trip in the Hillman Minx — it felt like a hundred years ago. 'Be good to yourself.'

'You too,' said Dan. 'Good luck at Fettes, eh?'

'It's Fettes that'll need the luck,' said Hugo, grinning.

'Dan?' Gillian, looking pale and tired in her funeral attire, had appeared at the entrance to the garden. 'Would you finish packing, please? The car's coming in a couple of hours.'

'Come on, Hugo,' said Dan. 'If you give me a hand, I'll buy you a drink after.'

'A vodka martini?'

'A lime rickey.'

'I thought I was a big man, now . . . ?'

They all stood up and James watched as the boys left with Gillian. Then he turned to Boody. Around them, Los Angeles was darkening. He looked about; it seemed they were alone in the garden.

'Well,' Boody said. 'Not quite the Hollywood dream I'd imagined we'd find out here.'

He raised an eyebrow. 'You saw me as your leading man?'

'If I wanted leading astray, perhaps. But I'm on my own path, and you're on yours.'

'Yes.'

Put like that, it sounded pretty final, and James supposed that it was. Real life had little of the satisfaction found in Hollywood fare, where the action ended on a firm compass point: the hero and heroine, their labours ended, would surely go on to ride victorious through whatever fate could throw at them.

What a comfort, thought James, *to go through the motions of your life, knowing your destiny was all planned out and a happy outcome awaited you.* Instead, you stumbled on, your existence a long, difficult struggle against forces unknown. All you could hope to do was dress it up in a little luxury and find some friends along the way.

Friends, or maybe more . . . ?

294

He looked at Boody, who welcomed back his attention with a rueful smile.

'Thank you for all the magic you worked on Queensmarsh,' he said. 'She helped save my life.'

'And, therefore, mine too. A good investment of my time, I'd say.' Her eyes were large upon him. 'I was right about you, wasn't I? You can escape anything except yourself.'

He took a step closer to her. 'This is who I am. Wherever I end up in the future, I won't try to escape that any more.'

'The inescapable James Bond . . .' She snorted softly. 'I don't suppose you could ever truly have fallen for me, could you?'

He didn't answer.

'And a good job too,' Boody went on, filling the awkward silence. 'I don't want to addle my head with love. Tori's got the right idea: take on the world and make it treat you right.' She watched him, for some flicker of reaction, perhaps. 'This evening will be goodbye, then.'

'We could write.'

'Do you still think I'm so soft?' She smiled at him. 'We'll shake hands in front of Gillian. But while we're on our own, we'll kiss goodbye.'

'On the cheek, of course.'

'Of course.' Boody leaned in and kissed him softly on the mouth. 'Sorry. I missed.'

'So you did.' James placed his hands on the small of her back and edged her closer.

They kissed again, beneath the stars and the Hollywood moon. *Fade to black*, thought James. *Roll credits*.

★　★　★

They had a secret audience of one. A man who watched them from the shadow of a dust-choked palm.

Adam Elmhirst turned, walked quickly and quietly through the lobby and outside onto Hollywood Boulevard. He lit a cigarette, headed west. So, there it was: the girl was going home, while James Bond's plans for the summer were less certain.

The son of Andrew Bond had done well. He had got up to his neck in trouble, and climbed back out again. Danger ran in the family. Uncle a spy, and as for his father . . .

Yes. A real chip off the old block.

Elmhirst quickened his step along the neon-soaked Boulevard, losing himself in the drifting crowds. He had some people to call. He felt they would be very interested to learn the whereabouts of young James Bond.

Acknowledgments

Thanks to Brad Sears for sound auto advice, Alan Barnes for zeppelin research tools and Anthony Holbourn for good Latin . . . to Jill Cole, Sue Cowley and Paul Simpson for editorial assists . . . to Philippa Milnes-Smith, Ruth Knowles and Harriet Venn for doing their jobs so well . . . and, of course, to Charlie Higson.

My special thanks, too, go to everyone at Ian Fleming Publications Ltd for their faith and support, particularly Corinne Turner and Josephine Lane who have helped so much with my further understanding of the complex Bondian world.

Above all, I must thank the master – the extraordinary Ian Fleming. How many imaginations around the globe have been gripped by the exploits of his trail-blazing creation? His legacy goes on, and I feel privileged to play my small part in that continuation.

JAMES'S ACTION-PACKED ROUTE

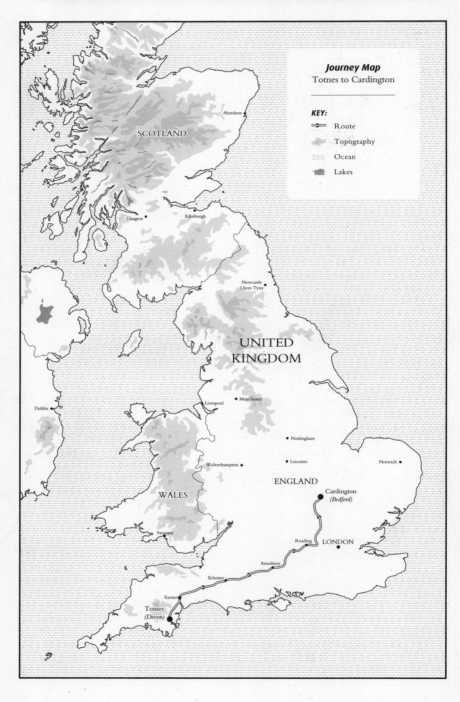

Journey Map
Totnes to Cardington

KEY:
⇒ Route
Topography
Ocean
Lakes

ACROSS THE WORLD . . .

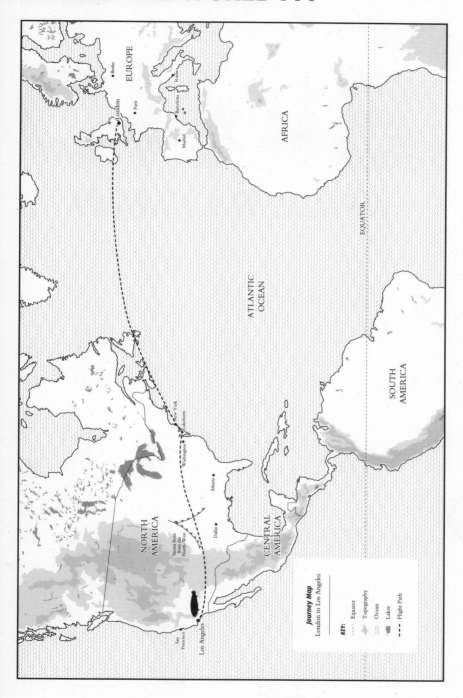

EUROPE

• Berlin

• Rome
• Paris

• London
• Barcelona

• Madrid

AFRICA

EQUATOR

ATLANTIC
OCEAN

SOUTH
AMERICA

• New York
• Nakahuret
• Washington

NORTH
AMERICA

• Atlanta

• Dallas

CENTRAL
AMERICA

Storm front
from the
North-West

• San
Francisco

Los Angeles •

Journey Map
London to Los Angeles

KEY:

... Equator
Topography
Ocean
Lakes
- - - Flight Path

WILL RETURN